# The Silent River

by

Christopher C. Curtis

ISBN: 978-1-916732-30-8

Copyright 2024

All rights reserved. No part of this publication may be reproduced, stored in a retrieval system, or transmitted in any form or by any means, electronic, mechanical, photocopy, recording or otherwise, without prior written consent of the copyright owner. Nor can it be circulated in any form of binding or cover other than that in which it is published and without similar condition including this condition being imposed on a subsequent purchaser. The right of Christpher C. Curtis to be identified as the author of this work has been asserted in accordance with the Copyright Designs and Patents Act 1988. A copy of this book is deposited with the British Library.

i2i Publishing. Manchester

www.i2ipublishing.co.uk

# Contents

Chapter One .................................................................... 5
Chapter Two ................................................................... 17
Chapter Three ................................................................ 29
Chapter Four .................................................................. 33
Chapter Five .................................................................. 37
Chapter Six .................................................................... 47
Chapter Seven ................................................................ 53
Chapter Eight ................................................................. 57
Chapter Nine .................................................................. 61
Chapter Ten ................................................................... 65
Chapter Eleven ............................................................... 67
Chapter Twelve ............................................................... 77
Chapter Thirteen ............................................................. 83
Chapter Fourteen ............................................................ 89
Chapter Fifteen ............................................................. 101
Chapter Sixteen ............................................................. 113
Chapter Seventeen ......................................................... 129
Chapter Eighteen ........................................................... 151
Chapter Nineteen ........................................................... 161
Chapter Twenty ............................................................. 175
Chapter Twenty-one ....................................................... 187
Chapter Twenty-two ....................................................... 197

Chapter Twenty-three ............................................................ 209
Chapter Twenty-four ............................................................ 215
Chapter Twenty-five ............................................................. 227
Chapter Twenty-six ............................................................... 233
Chapter Twenty-seven .......................................................... 239
Chapter Twenty-eight ........................................................... 249
Chapter Twenty-nine ............................................................ 267
Chapter Thirty ...................................................................... 275

## Chapter One

*Vauxhall – South London.*

Before the meeting there was time for a brisk dusk run along the river towards Battersea Park. Dexter exercised not only for pleasure and health, but also for work. You needed stamina in this game, and a lot of it. The run was measured. First a light jog, before slowly evolving into a manageable sprint.

On the return, he was looking over his left shoulder at the murky river when he nearly collided with a girl running the other way. He managed to swerve at the last second.

'Hi,' she said. The smile was dazzling, the poise East African.

Dexter regained his footwork. 'Evening,' he uttered, somehow continuing to jog. He couldn't help but glance back over his shoulder. The girl had done the same. She smiled and waved. Dexter was left puzzled, wondering who this tall, lean, and athletic stranger was. He half-heartedly returned the wave, as she ran off into the distance. He noted her running sharp and precise – no novice, that was for sure.

Back at the flat Dexter made a mint tea and went on the balcony. He sat down at a table, taking a few minutes to recollect if he had met - or seen - the woman on the run before. He hadn't, and with that, he picked up his tea and headed to the lounger.

Everyone enjoys a good sunset, including Dexter, and in all fairness, he had seen a few. From the glow of the Antiguan sun in the Caribbean to the warm orange blur lighting up Bagamoyo Beach in Tanzania, East Africa, he had enjoyed the company of many. It was a personal, choice of course, and he respected that, but sitting on the balcony of his apartment in Vauxhall he was adamant about one thing: nothing quite did it for him as watching the sun setting over the river Thames on a warm August evening in London.

The tea was on the table to his side. He leant over, giving the fresh leaves and sugar one last stir before taking a sip. He paused a few seconds to savour the taste as well as feel the nourishing air against his face. The aroma reminded him of his last job and the wonders of Marrakesh. *Ah, Marrakesh!* He hadn't been back in the smoke long, so memories of the Red City were still vivid.

Sitting back, he remembered taking a coach from Taroudant to Marrakesh through the Atlas Mountains at 6 am. As the rising sun illuminated the mountains around and underneath its sphere, it was as if you could reach out and touch it. It was that close, or so it seemed. The erratic driving added to the experience. He'd watched the few tourists grip the seats as the driver navigated hairpin bends at breakneck speed. Dexter had taken it in his stride, knowing he would arrive safely at the destination. He knew the driving game and could spot a bad driver a mile away. This one he'd known he could trust.

Chelsea Bridge looked splendid in the distance. Counting the lights hanging from the main cable on the bridge, Dexter realised how good it was to be back in the comfort of his own home, enjoying a much-deserved break. As he pondered a holiday destination – Turkey, or Greece this time – his phone rang. It was a private number. Curiosity made him take the call.

'Heard you were back,' came a familiar voice. 'Been a couple of days now, Jasper.'

'Let's cut to the chase... Fancy another job?'
'Was just thinking just how pleasant it was to be back and deciding on where to take a–'
'No rest for the wicked, I'm afraid. Not in this game, anyway, should know that by now.' There was a pause. '9 pm Ronnie Scott's.'
'What about–'
The phone went dead.
'Jasper... Hello... Jasper?' Dexter looked at his phone. The call had been terminated. He waited a few seconds to see if Jasper would call back. As expected, he didn't.

Dexter threw the phone on the table, a little angry with himself about the call. He picked up the mint tea then put it down again. The chill out mode had gone, replaced by a concoction of excitement and anticipation and the main ingredient of the industry: adrenaline. He couldn't be bothered to continue counting the brightly lit bulbs on the bridge, which had become irrelevant and out of focus. The distraction was too much. Dexter looked up. The sky was changing. Clouds were becoming a hue of burnt orange with smoky outlines, contrasting with the soulless slate grey of the murky river Thames, the mysterious piece of water that continuously ebbed and flowed as it divided the capital. Some things never changed. Finishing the tea, he stood up and stretched. It was 7 pm, time for a quick bite to eat and shower. So much for the planned break and rest period he'd promised himself

Then again, the last assignment wasn't that bad. A week in Morocco followed by a couple of days in Paris. It wasn't something one could complain about. But even though it went relatively smoothly, it was still work. Whatever you did for a living, be it acting in Hollywood or working on the buses, everybody needed a break. In

Dexter's profession you definitely needed one. Travelling to exotic locations around the globe, staying at five-star hotels and mixing with international folk may have sounded like the stuff of dreams but, at the end of the day, it was still work.

There was never a plan for Dexter to become a private detective; things just sort of… evolved. He was happy and content with the chauffeur and driver gig when Jasper, then a regular customer, offered him a job for some extra cash. A friend of Jasper's had decided his wife was probably cheating on him and asked Jasper to investigate, who put it to Dexter one evening after driving him from Shepherd Market to the Clermont Casino in Berkeley Square. It appeared relatively straightforward: all he had to do was follow her after work a few times to see where she went. It was hard to say no, Jasper was a regular client, the money was good, so he'd agreed. It went well, the man's suspicions were valid: the wife was meeting another man. Dexter had watched as she met him after work and tailed them to various restaurants in and around the West End before they headed off to either the opera or theatre.

Though the downside was being the bearer of bad news, the upside was learning how to use a camera. An appreciation of photography followed, and now, wherever he was in the world, whatever country, or city he was in, he made sure to check out the local photography galleries as well as dabbling a bit himself. As for the new line of work, he quickly learned that proof is always needed. He also grasped the concept that the camera never lied and that a good photograph could seal the job. He still had the print of the first photo he took. The location was Wyndham's Theatre in Leicester Square. It was raining as they the lovebirds hailed a cab from under the canopy. Dexter captured the moment beautifully as they ran arm in arm to the waiting car. Even the cuckolded husband had commented on its artistic content.

Dexter pondered over his L.P. collection before his shower. Music was a must for him, and it took only a few seconds before having to make a choice. The ambience for the shower had to be exact and mostly boiled down to either some Miles Davis or The Who. Not for the first time, *Quadrophenia* had the honour of being the soundtrack to his grooming routine. He stood under the water through the silence of *I Am the Sea* before adding vocals to *The Real Me*. The citrus and lemon shower gel from Jermyn Street was fresh and invigorating.

The grey cashmere polo-neck and matching Italian linen trousers were complemented by some finest English handcrafted leather accessories Aspinal leather belt and Loake shoes. As always, he checked the doors and windows before taking the lift down to the ground floor.

■■■■■■■■■■■■■■■■■■■■■■■■■■■■■■■■■■■■■■■■■■■■■■■■ι

'Where to, Guv?' the driver asked, after pulling up on the south side of Vauxhall Bridge.

'Frith Street,' Dexter said.

The driver turned off the orange light and Dexter got in. After the bridge it was the first right then down Millbank towards Trafalgar Square. On the left was Thames House, home to M15. As the cab passed by, Dexter paid particular attention to the doors of the ornate entrance, thinking about the spies, agents and other government officials who had passed through them. Not for the first time, wishing he was one of them.

Some of the jobs Dexter took on would have been better suited to them. He had a good record – it spoke for itself – but there were many times when being on your own, without government back up, wasn't easy, especially when you were up against it. He had come to understand that MI5 was an old boys' network. He'd crossed paths with a few of them along the way and, though he wasn't one of them, they were pleasant enough. They were well connected and, regardless of nationality, pretty much of the same ilk. Education at Oxford or Cambridge seemed to be the common denominator. It was a pass that clearly held a bit of clout in awkward situations. Dexter also came to realise that it also was a game, and one that some didn't like some upstart from a state school to be playing, let alone getting results.

He was soon reminded of why he had missed London, even after just over two weeks, as they drove up Whitehall, around Trafalgar Square then into Soho. The last three days spent in Paris had been cool; the jazz clubs were great and he had a good time there. But passing the cinemas and theatres on the Haymarket going to Ronnie Scott's was something else entirely. It was approaching 9 pm and the city was in transition. The theatre and restaurant goers were soon to be replaced by the clubbers and night owls.

Once they arrived, he leaned forward, passing a note over the driver's shoulders. 'Keep the change.'

The driver reached to put the orange light back on. 'Thanks Guv. Have a good evening.'

From the pavement, Dexter watched the cab make a u-turn then turn left into Old Compton Street. Sometimes he missed the driving game. There was no stress to it. If the passenger wanted to talk, you listened, if they didn't, you just drove… either way you were getting paid. He went inside.

'Good evening, Mr Spencer. Mr Carrington is expecting you. Come.' Dexter followed the receptionist who pointed out Jasper discreetly. 'Over there, seated at the bar.'

Dexter nodded. 'Thank you.'

'Looking good, Dex,' Jasper's Etonian accent was still as clipped as ever. He fetched a stool for Dexter. 'Must be that Parisian air.'

Dexter sat down. 'Was only there two days.'

'Drink?'

'Please.'

'Usual?'

'Please.'

Jasper beckoned the bartender over. 'Gin and Tonic for my friend and for myself…'

'The Bullshot?' prompted the bartender.

Jasper pondered for a few seconds. 'Go on then, why not?'

'Don't know how you can drink that,' Dexter said in reference to the vodka and Worcester sauce cocktail.

'Need a little reviving. Anyway, how was it?'

'Mission accomplished. Client satisfied?'

'Very.' That was all that counted in this game. The logic was simple: if successful you get more work.

The bartender returned with the drinks. 'For you, sir.' He placed the chilled G&T in front of Dexter. 'And, this is for you, Mr Carrington.' He delivered the Bullshot.

'Was Noel Coward's favourite,' said Jasper. 'Good for hangovers, so I'm told.' There was silence as he took a sip of the blood-red beverage. After wincing, he asked where they were in the conversation?

'Something about Parisian air?'

'Ah, yes… Tell me, how was Morocco and France?'

'Good. No problems.' Dexter played with the slice of lime underneath the bed of ice with the stirrer. He took a deep breath 'Never seen so much hash as when I went to that farm in the mountains.'

Jasper took another sip of the Bullshot. 'Thought they were being clever by using Paris as the transit route instead of the Netherlands.'

'Was surprised it was being laundered through a jazz club. Bit upsetting for me, personally. Still, being paid to listen to jazz was a bonus.'

Jasper gave Dexter a knowing look.

Dexter smiled. 'Cheers!' He held up his glass.

There was applause as a band took to the stage. The style was a fusion of modern and traditional jazz, sounding good and befitting. When it came to jazz, Dexter was somewhat of a connoisseur. Like many others, he couldn't be fooled. Just like in the private detective game, you had to be both talented and prepared to graft the scene to become successful. There were no shortcuts; the jazz punters wouldn't have it. They expected nothing less than hardship and despair. The more messed up you were, the more you were appreciated. A happy jazz musician who didn't have a drink, drug or women problem wasn't playing the part and wouldn't get very far. 'Thanks, see you soon,' the lead vocalist said at the end of the band's set. They hadn't played the part. The tepid applause at the end said it all.

Jasper ordered more drinks. A dry Martini replaced The Bullshot. Dexter stuck with his trusted Gin and Tonic. 'So?' Dexter turned back to face Jasper, before cutting to the chase. 'Why do want to meet?'

The bartender was wiping the bar, and Jasper waited for him to leave before leaning over. 'Got a big one, Dex if you're interested of course. If not, we can hand it over to the M15 boys.'

Dexter knew that Jasper didn't want to do that. There was history between him and the British Security Service. Besides, he was playing a guilt game, knowing that Dexter would take it on because of this. There were a few seconds of silence as they both took sips of their drinks. 'What does it involve?'

'Diamonds... Russia... Sphinxes... Egypt and'

'That's enough,' Dexter held up his hands.

'There is more, but I don't want to put you off – especially as you've just come off a shift.'

'Sounds a tall order.'

'I know you can pull it off. Come to my office tomorrow and I'll tell you more.'

Dexter knew that Jasper rated him, and that he wouldn't give him anything that he couldn't handle. He nodded and held up his glass. 'Cheers!' He already looked forward to the details. Dexter's namesake, the great Jazz Saxophonist Dexter Gordon, was playing in the background. From tailing some wife having an affair to diamonds, Sphinxes, Egypt, and Russia. It didn't get much better than this, he thought, as his tumbler connected with Jaspers.

Another band took to the stage shortly after. The vocalist reminded Dexter a little of the singer playing at the club he went to for surveillance in Paris. She tried her best to sound decadent and heartbroken but didn't have the conviction of... Alina. That was it... *Alina.* How could he forget the name of the half-French, half-Guadeloupe singer from just a few days before? He had met many beautiful women on his jaunts, but Alina was special; not conventionally beautiful, but a beautiful person with that

Parisian swagger money or looks couldn't buy. They had hit it off straight away, sharing an interest in photography. She'd taken him to the opening of an exhibition of some chic Parisian photographer who was a friend of hers the evening before he left.

'Dexter?' Jasper prodded him in the ribs. 'Seem a million miles away. Can't switch off? Thinking about the last job?'

Taking a sip of his G&T, Dexter smiled. 'You know it.'

Dexter could have stayed in Ronnie Scott's all night, but he was tired and needed to hit the gym in the morning to keep up the health routine. He'd had a couple of days' rest. It had done him good and was better than nothing. The holiday had to be put on hold as he prepared for this job. He asked Jasper what time tomorrow?

'Twelve?'

'Perfect.'

They finished their drinks and said farewell to the bartender. Dexter looked at the singer for the last time. Caught up in her angst, she continued to sing about being cheated on by her man. He had to return to Paris to see Alina. he had promised her after all.

The Soho air was refreshing and the activity on the street made Dexter wake up a little. Jasper hailed a taxi. 'Don't forget… twelve' he said before jumping in and closing the door.

Dexter walked down Shaftesbury Avenue to Piccadilly. The little amble did him good. Anteros, the god of requited love and avenger of unrequited love formed a silhouette against the dark sky. Love… he wondered when he would find such a thing or if it existed. He was an unapologetic bachelor boy, loved the single life. How would he cope without the company of the exotic female?

His close friend Mike had been in love once and though it was a long time ago, never stopped going on about it. The way it still consumed him was frightening.

Dexter flagged a taxi and chose the route: Piccadilly to Hyde Park Corner then down Grosvenor Place to Buckingham Palace. The Royal residence looked quiet, only a few lights were on. Mike was a former bodyguard to the Royal family. You couldn't get any gossip out of him no matter what. Journalists and diplomats used to ply him with drinks, trying to extract anything for a story, but not a word was uttered. A true professional. Dexter respected that. Some of the lackeys he'd come across were anything but, would tell you what you wanted to hear, if the price was right. The professionals, though, always stood out; there was something about them.

Dexter indicated to the side of the road as they crossed the bridge. 'This is fine,' he said. It was only around the corner from his apartment, but the fewer people who knew the exact location the better. Dexter entered the reception area.

'Evening, Dex.'

'Evening Terry,' said Dexter. 'Didn't see you on the way out.'

'Probably in the car park.'

Terry was the friendly Concierge. Had been there since the apartment block had been built a little over five years ago.

'Good evening?' he asked.

'Bit of jazz. Nothing too heavy…' The phone rang on Terry's desk and Dexter was a little relieved; he needed to sleep. Terry held up an apologetic hand as he picked up the receiver. Dexter nodded and made for the elevator. On the way up he looked at his watch, a Patek Philippe: it was 11:55 pm.

Once back on his balcony, Dexter turned the chair eastwards towards Big Ben. The detail of the famous clock seemed so close, almost within touching distance. The chimes rang at exactly midnight. He looked at his watch; they were synchronised. Dexter closed his eyes. The bells sent shivers down his spine. Nowhere in the world was there anything like the sound of Big Ben, he thought after the twelfth chime had echoed for a few seconds. Closing the balcony door, he went to the lounge and kicked off his shoes. After putting on *Quadrophenia* he slumped on the charcoal grey Italian sofa. *Love, Reign o'er Me* brought the day to a satisfactory conclusion.

## Chapter Two

Dexter wondered what Jasper had in store for him as he ran along the river in the morning. It didn't really matter what the job was or what it entailed; that fear had long gone. Fear could cripple you; people sensed and exploited it. And as Mike once eloquently put it, 'never let the opponent know your weakness.' Sure, there was some initial apprehension – that was natural – but Dexter had built up enough experience now to handle most situations.

After a shower, Dexter enjoyed a light breakfast of coffee and croissants before deciding to leave. It was 11 am and the weather was a little cooler than the previous day, so he threw a sweater over his shoulders and tied the arms in front. A little cologne was added to complement the casual but smart look. Terry was at the door, looking out. 'British weather!' he sighed. 'So unpredictable.'

Dexter agreed. 'Not a bad thing though,' he said.

Jasper's office was in Shepherd Market, Mayfair. It was a good twenty to thirty minutes by foot. Dexter always tried to walk there if he could. The philosophy was to try to walk everywhere at first and, if that was not possible, take a train or bus. The last resort was down to the garage for the Jag. This was to be avoided if possible; much as he loved his sleek car, he had to keep fit.

He enjoyed the stroll anyway. There were different routes to take, each one interesting, making sure it never got boring. Today's choice was to cross Vauxhall Bridge then go up Vauxhall Bridge Road and through Victoria and Green Park. He loved taking the side streets, but he wouldn't today; there wasn't time and there was an exhibition at the Royal Academy to see after, so had to ration his energy.

'Door's open,' Jasper said through the intercom when Dexter arrived.

Dexter climbed the old, worn wooden stairs to the first-floor office. Jasper was waiting, holding the door open from inside.

'Good morning,' he said.

'Good morning,' Dexter said.

Before closing the door, Jasper poked his head out and looked from side to side. 'Can never be too sure,' he said. 'Please… take a seat.'

Dexter went and sat down as Jasper settled into a chair behind his pride and joy: a polished Captain's office table dating from the 1950s. On the wall behind were various framed pictures of him during his time with the Royal Air Force. Jasper loved the military; said he never regretted the day he joined. One lament though – something he still felt to that day – was not being chosen to become an esteemed Red Arrow. He went for an interview, got as far as doing a flying trial, but narrowly missed out. He often cited the reasons as high standards, but Dexter had been told that MI5 got one of their boys in there. It was political. Whatever the reason, the pain of rejection was there for all to see. After the Air Force, it was on to the Civil Service, where roughly twenty-five years were spent travelling the world on various assignments. He met all ranks of government officials during this time, building up contacts and getting a taste for his present business: a bespoke agency, providing agents and PIs for clients who needed something investigated.

Jasper peered over his glasses as he inspected various documents and shuffled a few papers around his desk. 'Nearly there,' he said. He opened one of the drawers in the desk and took out a brown folder. After selecting a sheet of paper, he typed something into the computer. Dexter watched painfully as Jasper used one finger on the keyboard. A few seconds later, the antiquated printer in the corner began to roll out a couple of printouts noisily. 'I can manage.' Jasper took off his glasses, put them on the desk and then got up to retrieve the paper from the machine. 'Right, here we go... ready?'

Dexter nodded.

Jasper sat on the side of the desk, papers in hand. 'A good friend of mine, chairman of a bank here...' He pointed behind Dexter's shoulder 'Has a suspicion that money is going missing. Needs to find out if there is and who is responsible.' He got up, walked around the desk, and sat down.

'That it?' said Dexter.

'He suspects a lot is going missing.'

Dexter straightened up. 'Why come to you? Why not speak to the accounts department – or call in an auditor?'

'The bank is concerned about its reputation. Doesn't want the publicity. You know what it's like.'

Dexter nodded. 'Thinks there is some sort of embezzlement going on.'

'Also has a suspicion the money may be being used for other activities.'

'Typical. Thought there was more to it. Hence Russia?'

'Hence Russia.'

'Where do diamonds and Egypt come into it?'

Jasper got up, leant over the desk, and handed Dexter one of the printouts. 'Intelligence has suggested that the money is being used to buy diamonds and then invested in Egyptian antiques amongst other things.'

Dexter looked at the paper. Images of gold lacquered vases and figurines of Egyptian cats were next to the Sphinxes. 'Not hash or arms, but Egyptian artefacts now?'

'Must be the new way to launder. Seen the prices?'

Dexter looked at the column beside the images. He took a deep breath and whistled. 'Wow.'

'Exactly. Millions.'

'Where does it stop?'

Jasper picked up his glasses. 'That's what you have to find out.'

Dexter knew it didn't stop there. As per the norm with diamonds, it would inevitably end up in arms and propping up some dictatorship or fuelling a civil war. 'The link to Russia?'

'The cash from here goes there,' said Jasper. 'Then to Amsterdam to buy diamonds then, we think, to Egypt – but we're not too sure.'

Dexter perked up when he heard Amsterdam. He liked it there – some great jazz clubs. 'Amsterdam?'

'Yes Dexter, Amsterdam. But we have someone going there for surveillance. It'll be Moscow for you.'

Dexter didn't mind. He liked Moscow too. He'd been there once and, though you had to be on your guard, he'd never had any problems. 'The suspects are Russian?'

'One has started to work in the accounts.'

'Surprise, surprise,' Dexter said.

'You may need to go to Egypt if there's a link…which there probably will be.'

Dexter had never been to Egypt. It was one of the few places left he wanted to travel to. He tried his best to conceal any indication of excitement; he didn't want to appear too keen. It wasn't professional. Money being siphoned off

from a bank wasn't a joke. Nobody liked to lose money.
'Cairo?' he asked.
    'We don't know yet. That's something for you to work on.' Jasper looked at Dexter. 'You in?'
    Dexter knew there would be no shortage of takers for a job like this. It was already sounding like serious stuff. A challenge. He felt honoured even to be considered. He handed the printout back. 'In,' he said. He sat back, already thinking about the Pyramids. His imagination wandered as he visualised the sun setting behind them, he could feel the arid dry heat when Jasper interrupted his reverie.
    'Now I know you like to do it solo… But it will be different this time.'
    'I've got company?' Dexter asked.
    'A superagent. Lives in Sweden. Been trying for ages to get her. A true professional.'
Dexter was surprised. 'Her?'
    'It'll be better to be seen as a couple. Won't look as suspicious.' Jasper put the file back in the draw. 'A single man may raise suspicion. Also, you'll need someone to speak Arabic.'
    The window was slightly open. There were murmurs from the lunchtime crowd milling around below. Dexter thought of the hustle and bustle of the souks in Cairo. 'Who is she?'
    'Jasper stood up. I'll let you know soon.' He held his hand out. 'I'll draw up the contract for you to come and sign.'
    Dexter shook Jasper's hand. 'Thanks.'
    The mood changed from business to pleasure. 'Anything planned for this afternoon?'
    'Royal Academy.'
    'What's on? Not that I'll know anything about it.'

'Anish Kapoor.'

Jasper frowned. 'Never heard of the chap, I'm afraid.'

'A sculptor.'

Jasper sat back down and started to prod the keyboard again. The frown was still visible. 'Hmmm… no kidding. I'll be in touch soon, Dexter.' He got up and walked to the door.

Dexter tried one more time. 'Who is this person. Do I know them?'

Jasper didn't look up as he answered the question. 'I believe you've already met her.'

'Have I?'

'Recently. Very recently, in fact. You'll be meeting her again very soon Dexter, don't worry.' Jasper looked at his watch. 'That's all for now. Have to be at The Royal Air Force Club for a meeting at 1 pm.'

\*\*\*

It was less than ten minutes' walk from Shepherd Market to The Royal Academy of Arts in Piccadilly. Dexter went the back way, cutting through Berkeley Square and Old Bond Street. On the way he tried to picture who Jasper meant. Was it the singer at Ronnie Scott's? The girl on the checkout at the supermarket? He was still none the wiser to the identity when arriving at Burlington House.

The exhibition had been good. Kapoor, as always, delivered. The aesthetics of the clashing mirrors and colours took Dexter by surprise. The vivid reds and yellows were intentionally there to be marvelled at. Though years apart, Kapoor was in the same creative mode as the Academy's founders: Blake, Reynolds and Turner. As always, Dexter felt better after. When it came to the arts, be it music or photography, he understood the benefits. A major part of the enjoyment of his work, whether in Beijing, New York, Helsinki or Rome, was indulging in the local creative vibe.

The downside of this appreciation was the other side of the art world: the dark side, a realm of fakes, forgery, and corruption. It made him sceptical sometimes, wary of some galleries and exhibitions. Were the exhibits genuine? Kapoor's sculpture at the V&A seemed legit, though. It couldn't be faked anyway; unlike for Egyptian artefacts, there wasn't the market.

Exhibitions and shows drained Dexter. It was now mid-afternoon, and he needed refuelling. In the café, he ordered tomato soup, a crusty roll and a side salad. A strong filtered coffee followed. Sitting back, he opened the latest edition of *GQ* bought on the way. There was an article about the latest watches on the market that had caught his eye.

'Dexter?'

He looked up to see the woman from the run 'Yes?'

She pulled a chair out from underneath the table. 'May I?'

'Please.' The woman sat down at smiled at him. Dexter closed the magazine. 'Mind telling me who you are?'

She squeezed her legs under the table. 'We need to talk.'

'Tea, coffee?'

'Water. Still, please.'

Dexter went and got a bottle of water and two glasses. He sat down and poured. 'Saw you earlier.'

'Yes, was a good run.'

'Who are you and how do you know my name?'

'Oh, sorry. I'm Uba, by the way.'

'Dexter. Now… Uba… who *exactly* are you?'

Uba took a sip of the water. 'You need to say *darling* now.'

Dexter was becoming impatient. 'Really? And why's that?'

'Because you are going to be my husband.'

'Look… Ub–'

'In Cairo. Relax.' The smile persisted.

Dexter had just taken a sip of his coffee and spluttered. 'Jasper?'

Uba smiled and nodded. 'How did you recognise…He realised why Jasper had asked what he had planned for the afternoon. 'Somalian?'

'Impressed. How did you know?'

'I live in London. He said someone Swedish.'

'I was born in Somalia, grew up in Sweden, then college in the U.S.'

'Let's talk about work.'

'When in Cairo, we are a couple, okay?'

'So, I've been told.'

'We will attract attention. There will be jealousy and a lot of comments. Ignore them, you need to be strong.'

'Jealousy?'

'Everybody wants a Somali girlfriend.'

'If you say so.'

'You know David Bowie, right?'

'Heard of him.'

'His wife.'

'What about her?'

'Iman. Somalian.'

'And?'

'Beautiful, right?'

Dexter held his hands up. 'Can't deny that.'

Uba finished her water, put her glass down and leant over the table. The smile disappeared. 'Now you listen... I'm here for work, okay? Let's keep this professional.' She sat back; the smile returned. 'So, what are you doing for the rest of the day... darling?'

'Nothing planned... darling.'

'Very good. Relax. Save your energy.' Uba got up. 'Thank you for the water.' She stretched across the table, holding out her hand. 'Until next time.' She walked away. As well as being tall, slim, athletic, she certainly had swagger. Dexter could see she took care of herself, probably did a martial art. He had enjoyed the brief interaction. He liked passionate, temperamental women. In this game people had to be straight to the point; it was the only way. Any other approach could be costly and dangerous. He took a sip of the water, sat back, and opened the magazine again.

Deciding on a slow walk home, he cut through St James Park. As always, there was a brief pause in the middle of the bridge. The day was bright and clear, so the view towards Whitehall was picturesque. The greenery of the trees and shrubs provided much needed shade for the ducks and various birds. A crane stood along the bank. Apart from the odd movement of the head it stayed still, motionless. It made him think of his Tai Chi training in the evening. Despite having a black belt in Shotokan Karate, Dexter loved his Tai Chi. He'd been studying and practising it for a few years now and it had become an important part of his life. It was a skill that could be practised anywhere and anytime. There were many sunsets around the world that had witnessed the relaxing flow of his movements, one of which was called *The White Crane Spreads its Wings*. He watched to see if the movement in the Tai Chi form had any resemblance to the real thing. The crane then tilted its head to one side, balancing on one leg. The Chinese were clever, he decided, as he took out his phone to make a call.

'Good afternoon…The Royal Air Force Club… Richard speaking. How may I help?'

'Richard, it's Dexter.'

'Dex! How's it going?'

'Good. Is Jasper there?'

'He is. Saw him earlier. Hold on, I'll go and get him.'

Jasper came to the phone a couple of minutes later. 'Dexter?

'Thought I'd let you know, I just met Uba.'

'Terrific, isn't she? Good C.V. From distinguished, diplomatic stock. Bit temperamental but gets the job done. Stick with her.'

'When do you think it's going to start?'

'Have to speak with the client. Tie a few things up… come to an arrangement. A week, max.'

'Suits me. Enjoy the club.'

Leaving the park, Dexter found a spot under some trees and practised a Qi Gong set he'd learnt from a Tai Chi master in China. It always helped to put him in a positive frame of mind. On the way home he thought about his new work colleague. A part of him was excited; a part unsure. He'd met a few Uba's on assignments. They weren't that great and were only there because of work or family connections. They didn't last long either. After the novelty wore off, they often moved upstairs – admin work, out of danger and where it was more lucrative.

Dexter accepted that he would never climb that ladder. He wasn't brought up around diplomats and government. Wasn't part of the Oxbridge gang. He learnt his craft the hard way: a sequence of trial and error.

Terry came and opened the door for him. 'Turned out to be a nice day, Dex.'

Dexter smiled. 'Didn't it just.'

Dexter never disclosed his exact line of work with anyone, including Terry. All he said was he was in the security game – which was true, more or less.

Once upstairs with some John Coltrane as background, Dexter fixed a strong G&T and went onto the balcony. As expected, he couldn't settle. There was an urge to celebrate a new job: go out, hit a jazz club or maybe call an ex-girlfriend to come and spend the evening. He knew it was the excitement of the new job kicking in. After a few seconds he realised they were not great ideas. He gazed towards Chelsea Bridge with a feeling that this job was going to be a little more eventful than it appeared and for that he needed his energy.

28

## Chapter Three

*One week later:*

The venue was the Pizza Express Jazz Club in Dean Street, Soho. The reply was as decisive as they come. 'Yes,' Dexter said.

Jasper took a slug of the Bullshot. 'Just making sure.' He handed over the contract. 'Have a read.'

Dexter trusted Jasper so glanced briefly over the words before coming to the important part: the finance.

'Not bad, eh?'

Dexter decided to celebrate by ordering pizza. Having spent the last week running, pushing weights and on other stamina training, he deserved a night off. He handed the contract back 'When is Moscow?'

'I'll arrange that tomorrow when you come and sign it but be prepared to leave at any given time.'

Dexter was excited. He loved the packing the suitcase, travelling to the airport and arriving in another city; he thrill of checking into a hotel or a rented apartment, going to his room, throwing down his suitcase, closing the curtains and diving on the bed. He knew a couple of jazz clubs in Moscow. The nightlife was good. Jasper mentioned that Cairo was a strong probability due to more intelligence coming through. Dexter couldn't wait for that one. His heart raced, but he couldn't show the excitement – not for now, anyway. 'How's Uba getting on?' he asked.

'Spoke briefly with her yesterday. In good spirits. I'll confirm with her tomorrow. Get her to sign the contract. Hopefully she's still up for it. Fickle business, this.' Jasper held up his glass, bracing himself for another blast of Bullshot. 'Cheers!'

'Cheers!' Dexter hoped she was still on board. From their brief interaction at the R.A., he liked her.

'Very choosy what she takes on. Speaks nine languages, you know.'

'Nine? Impressive. What attracts her to this assignment?'

'She's a bit… let's say, political. Into human rights.'

There wasn't really a lot more to say. The deal was signed. The buzz for Jasper was securing the deal. Now that was done, it was the logistics, itineraries, expenses and all the admin stuff. For Dexter it was signing the deal. The money was good and the buzz was the excitement and adrenaline he would feel until a few days after the job was completed, whenever that would be.

'Damn rain,' Jasper said, as they left the club. A taxi was hailed and pulled up. Dexter opened the door for him. 'Remember Dexter, you're working as from now.'

Dexter understood. 'I know,' he said. After closing the door, he headed towards Soho Square. The rain looked cool as it passed the lights on the lampposts. It suited Soho, made it more how it should be: dark, moody, ambiguous and wet. He dawdled, knowing he wasn't ready for home. He was on a jazz vibe. Remembering what Jasper said about working as from now, he decided not to go to a club. Instead, there would be a short pilgrimage to the bottom of Wardour Street where one of the shrines of London's jazz scene once stood: the legendary Flamingo Club. He turned and walked down Dean Street, crossing Shaftesbury Avenue into Gerrard Street. Standing opposite the venue he thought of the greats who had walked through the doors in front of him: Dizzy Gillespie…Ella Fitzgerald. Then there was the infamous fight between Aloysius 'Lucky' Gordon and Johnny Edgecombe that led to one of the biggest scandals in British history: the Profumo Affair. He stayed a few minutes to absorb the history before walking the couple of hundred yards down to Coventry Street to where the Flamingo had originally started. Again, Dexter marvelled, finding it incredible that the likes of Billie Holiday and Ella Fitzgerald were among the many esteemed singers to perform there. He wondered if the punters at the time realised how lucky they were to witness these American jazz greats.

Once back home, Dexter poured himself a gin and tonic. The liberal amount of gin tasted good. It had been a near perfect day. Work had been secured and he was to visit Egypt. Relaxing on the sofa with some Chet Baker, he reflected on his life. It wasn't difficult to remember the driving. He loved that job, had some good regular clients, including Jasper. Driving around London in the twilight hours listening to jazz, coming home, crashing on the sofa, sometimes with a girl he'd met brought back fond memories. He gulped the last of the drink, smiled to himself then went to bed.

\*\*\*

Dexter hadn't experienced the pleasure of a hangover for a while. As soon as he opened his eyes and tried to sit up, he realised he hadn't missed it. Holding the head as he staggered to the shower was an ordeal, but worthwhile, as he felt a little better after. Next was a cooked breakfast and a strong cup of coffee. As the mushrooms and sausages were frying, he put some freshly ground coffee in the mocha pot he'd bought in Rome a couple of years before. The combination of aromas livened him up a little more. As he waited, he saw a message on his phone from Jasper: *Sent an e mail.* it said. Dexter fired up his laptop and found the email in his inbox.

<u>Suspect Name</u>:
LEONID ANDREYEV
<u>Nationality</u>:
RUSSIAN
<u>Place</u>:
GLOBALINK INTERNATIONAL
<u>Occupation</u>:
SENIOR ACCOUNTANT

*Leonid Andreyev.* A fine Russian name. Dexter took a sip of the coffee. Though not doubting Globalink's credibility, he'd never heard of it. It may not have been one of the big boys of banking, but he knew that some of these lesser-known independent ones had more than a handful of wealthy, loyal customers that didn't want or need the attention of a Coutts or a big-name bank.

A little research unearthed that Globalink was a UK-regulated bank with assets of 1.3 billion. Dexter sat back, whistled, and took some more coffee. Globalink's speciality was in investment banking, wealth management and real estate. It had a total of twenty-five employees with branches in London, Amsterdam and Moscow. One of the directors and a major shareholder were Egyptian. This was all Dexter needed to know for now. He stared at the screen for a few seconds, knowing there was a lot of money involved. When he got the green light from Jasper, he'd move into action, starting with the obligatory surveillance work.

## Chapter Four

As expected, the call came sooner than later. 'The client is happy with the arrangements, just need to sign the contract and we're ready to go,' Jasper said, the following morning. Dexter understood the terseness of the call. The relationship always changed after contracts were signed. It became more professional. There was to be no more frequenting jazz clubs and niceties together until the job was completed. The wining and dining were like any other form of employment. The courting was part of it. 'Be at the office for midday,' Jasper added.

■■■■■■■■■■■■■■■■■■■■■■■■■■■■■■■■■■■■■■■■■■■■■■■■■■■■■

Dexter felt different when leaving the office. He paused on the stairs, wondering if he made the correct decision. It took less than two seconds to realise he had, but was nice to ponder, nevertheless. Work mode had now started. This time there was no leisurely walk to Piccadilly; he opted for a taxi straight back to the apartment. The first thing was to go through his photographic equipment. He enjoyed this part, selecting the lenses was always fun. First into the bag was the zoom lens. This was a must; many a job had been proved with this trusty accessory.

Later Jasper forwarded a photo of Leonid, a good-looking blond boy with chiselled features that wouldn't look out of place on the catwalk. The additional info was brief: thirty-two years old and living in Barnet, North London. Dexter had exchanged the gin and tonics on the balcony for coffee in front of the laptop. The preparation for research had begun. Leonid was merely a suspect at this stage, nothing more.

Globalink International had a couple of branches in London. One was in the City, the other –the headquarters – based in Mayfair. Coincidentally, the latter wasn't too far from Jasper's office. Dexter hadn't asked how Jasper knew the owner but had assumed it would have been from some local dining room or gentleman's club, of which Mayfair has more than its fair share. The bank's opening hours were as per usual: 9 am – 5 pm, Monday to Friday. The branch in the City was smaller, probably some offshoot. For now, Dexter would concentrate on surveillance at the HQ in Mayfair. The five-storey townhouse on Curzon Street had been painted a kind of metallic grey-blue, the sash window frames a brilliant white gloss. Dexter knew the area well from his driving days and given the number of Arab and other international businesses and banks in the area, he knew also how suspicious they were and how seriously they took security. The last thing he wanted was to be rumbled or put under any scrutiny. Hanging around waiting wasn't an option. He had to be patient. Even to catch sight of Andreyev might take a couple of days.

Dexter's hunch was that the staff would arrive around 8:30 – 8:45 am, depending on how keen they were, of course. The timing had to be such that he'd walk down Curzon Street just like any other commuter going to work around that time. The first morning he passed at 8:30 am. He saw a couple of staff, but not Andreyev. On the second day he strode by at 8:40 am and, again, no Andreyev. One member of staff who caught his eye was an attractive lady scanning her pass at the side entrance. She didn't look like your average bank worker, more of a creative type. His attention was discreet and from what he could see was unnoticed by the lady. The third day was more successful: passing at 8:45 am on the corner of South Audley Street, he finally caught sight of Andreyev, who walked straight past him.

On the fourth day, Dexter drove and parked where he could get a good sighting of Andreyev without being seen. He succeeded in reeling off a few quick shots unnoticed. In another location, this may not have been too impressive, but considering the environs and how early in the assignment he was, it was a major achievement.

As an advocate of change and evolution, Dexter was a fan of all things digital, but as far as he was concerned you couldn't beat the dynamics, mechanics, and quality of a good SLR. He loved the process: loading the roll of the film, setting the light, shutter, and aperture controls and hearing the noise as he pressed the release button.

The darkroom built into his apartment was where he was able to lose himself and escape from the outside world. The sight of an image slowly coming to life after soaking in the chemicals was immensely satisfying evidence of his own skill and talent gradually revealing itself. There was a sense of pride and achievement in hanging them up to dry.

Soon after, sitting at the table with a coffee, he studied the five prints closely. As always, he liked most of them and, as always, he selected one for his personal collection. This was always the most striking one, something arty and chic, which was never given to the client. His selection was Andreyev approaching the side entrance to the bank, cigarette in mouth and looking sideways. It could be a cover for an album or a magazine editorial. Dexter was traditional when it came to his assignments; he would scan and download them later, but for now it was the trusted brown folder. *Night Boat to Cairo* he etched with a marker pen on the front. This was then carefully placed into the secret safe behind a framed copy of a Jean-Michel Basquiat piece in the hallway. For his few selected visitors, this was the picture they always seemed to be drawn to. At first, he was afraid that the attention might jeopardise the secrecy of the safe. Later, though, he found it amusing. If they only knew what was lurking behind the copy of a painting that had sold for a cool 110.5 million at Sotheby's.

He sent scanned images of Andreyev to Jasper as an attachment to double-check that he had the right man before proceeding. The reply was instant: he had his man. Dexter knew his next move, having done it so many times. He felt a surge of adrenaline… it was now game on.

## Chapter Five

Dexter's sleep was peaceful and without interruption. Unlike the night before, there had been no gin and tonic. It was work time. His run was intense. He thought about Uba as he pounded the pavement, hoping she was on board. Some agents he'd met could talk a good game but went missing at the eleventh hour. They couldn't handle the heat.

After a quick shower and breakfast, he chose a light blue short-sleeved summer shirt, faded jeans and brown moccasins. The Ray Bans and baseball cap were in the rucksack, ready for when he exited Green Park underground station. It was another day for surveillance, but it would be less satisfying than the previous day. Observing and taking note of when and where members of staff took their lunch break could be tiresome, as well as a little intrusive. Dexter had lost count of the times he'd been watching a suspect for one thing only to witness some unrelated misdemeanour such as an unexpected liaison. If it didn't interfere with the case, it was fine. Such was life. Human beings were by nature sociable. Of course, there would be attraction. If he wasn't being paid to expose it then why bother? It didn't pay the bills and no one really gave a damn anyway.

'Anyone sitting here?' he asked a young lady who was reading a book on a bench in Mount Street Gardens. It was the same young lady he had seen scanning her ID at the bank earlier.

'No.' She moved her bag close to her side, as if erecting a barricade.

'May I?'

The lady shrugged her shoulders.

Dexter sat down and unwrapped a hot mozzarella panini he'd just bought from an Italian deli. He took a bite. 'Nice day.'

'Very nice.' She continued reading her book. The cover was hidden.

'You seem captivated. What's the book?'

'*The Power of Now.*'

'Eckhart Tolle?'

She closed her book and turned to him. 'What is it you want?'

'Just making conversation.'

'Is that why you followed me here from Curzon Street?'

'Curzon Street? Did I? Mere coincidence.'

She closed the book. 'Taking unauthorised photographs of members of staff? *Mere coincidence?*'

There were not many times Dexter could recall being rumbled and when he did, he always had an answer. This time, though, he was speechless. He quickly took another bite of the panini to muster up some sort of explanation, but still found himself wanting. Part of him was angry, annoyed that he'd been outed so early on; the rest was sheer embarrassment. What would he say to Jasper? How was he going to explain this one? What about his reputation? Gossip spread quickly in these circles, he'd be a laughingstock.

'Sure, it was me?'

'Denying it?'

'Just not admitting it.'

'There's a difference?'

'I think so.'

'Answer my question.'

Dexter felt trapped and didn't want to embarrass himself further by persisting with the denial. The worst thing to do was try to make out she'd mistaken him for another person. There was no way out. Sometimes you just have to hold your hands up. He looked at his watch: it was 1:40 pm. 'Have you time to talk?'

'You know I don't – being as how you knew what time I left and know what time I have to be back. Watched you three days in a row using different techniques around the bank to see who comes and goes.'

'You don't miss much, do you?' Dexter pointed to the closed book clasped between her hands. 'Enjoying it?'

'So far.'

'Good book. About enjoying life in the moment.'

'What do you want?'

'There is a reason why I was observing your place of work. It's a long story. I'll explain in more detail if you'd like to meet. I'm Dexter, by the way. Some people call me Dex.'

'Perdita. Some people call me Perdi. When?'

'As soon as possible. What time you finish?'

'I'd have thought you'd know that.'

'5:30. Marble Arch station?'

Perdita put the book in her bag and stood up. 'Still haven't answered my question.'

'Later. I promise.'

'Okay.' Perdita walked off towards the South Audley Street entrance.

The reality of what had just happened hit Dexter. He'd been rumbled. *How did that happen? How did she know?* Trawling over his movements of the last three days, he knew that he'd been careful. So, where and how had she sussed him?

He finished the panini and threw the wrapper the short distance towards the bin. Hole in one! Normally this childish pastime would bring on a wry smile but not this time; he had other things on his mind: like what was he going to say to Perdita?

He didn't want to go home and come back, so he stayed up west a while, mooching around Carnaby Street, going to Ray's Jazz in Shaftesbury Avenue, then to Hyde Park to top up the fading North African tan.

He took his shirt off and sat in one of the idiosyncratic green and white deck chairs. The attendant was from Kenya. Dexter said he liked Nairobi.

'What were you doing there?' the attendant asked.

It wasn't appropriate to mention the ivory smuggling trail he'd been on. 'Business,' he said.

Looking out onto the shimmering Serpentine, he couldn't shake off what had happened. If she saw him, who else did? How and where had he made a fundamental mistake? He had to learn from this. Maybe complacency had set in. Perhaps this was meant to happen – to shock him out of laxity or complacency and keep him on his toes. Thinking about Perdita and her book, he closed his eyes and focused on the moment. He concentrated on the call of the different birds. 'Right here, right now, everything is okay,' he said to himself quietly. The feeling of the sun against his skin made everything okay… in the moment.

There was still an hour left before meeting Perdi, so he strolled down to the Serpentine Gallery. Some architectural exhibition was on. It wasn't bad, if you liked that sort of minimal, cubist style. Dexter did, as an aesthetic, but he couldn't live like that. White rooms with a pristine sofa and table and chairs looked great, but the practicalities were a little different. Things got dirty. Nothing stayed perfect. The concept of living was fascinating – how we aspired to different lifestyles as individuals. He loved his penthouse apartment on the Thames, it was his bolthole: a real bona fide bachelor pad. He wouldn't change it for anything.

Walking from the Serpentine to Marble Arch, something occurred to him: why had Perdi agreed to meet him? Had she mentioned it to anyone at work? Had anyone told her she was being followed? Was she setting a trap? All these possibilities were out of his control. There was nothing he could do about it – other than keep walking to his rendezvous.

He was waiting across the road when Perdi arrived at the Oxford Street entrance. He looked at his watch: exactly 5:30 pm. After a few minutes of making sure she was alone and hadn't been followed, Dexter crossed the road. 'Hi,' he said.

Perdi had just taken out her book. 'Hi.' She looked up. 'Coffee?'

She closed the book then put it carefully in her bag. 'Why not.'

'I know a place on the Edgware Road.' He looked at his watch. 'Have to be quick, though.'

'Why?'

'I don't drink coffee after 6 pm.'

'You've only got twenty minutes.'

Dexter detected a hint of sarcasm – and confidence. She knew she had him at a disadvantage. He would have to comply with whatever she wanted. Jasper couldn't find out about this blunder. And Uba? What would she think? 'I know somewhere near,' he said. His sense of gloom continued for the short walk to the Arabian restaurant.

'Everything okay?' Perdi asked.

He tried to look unbothered. 'Why wouldn't it be?'

'I don't know. You tell me.'

He opted to change the subject. 'You enjoy reading?'

'Love anything self-help. Finished *A Road Less Travelled* not long ago.'

'Haven't read that one.'

'Same as this in a way.'

'Spiritual?'

'Guess so.'

Having travelled to China, Malaysia and Singapore, Dexter knew a little Buddhism. 'It's down to individual experience and interpretation?'

'Yes, I suppose so.'

He opened the door for her when they arrived. 'And your interpretation may be different to mine. Even though we've read the same words.' He sensed Perdi becoming a little more relaxed and comfortable. 'The same sentence, same paragraph, same chapter. Only our take on them may not be the same.'

'Exactly.'

He knew the proprietor, Ali. It was a time just before it would get busy, so coffee and cake would be okay. Ali said it was good to see him again and led them to a table at the side. There was an awkward silence for a while before Dexter decided to get straight down to the point. 'So, how did you notice me?'

'Which time? Observing certain members of staff or when you took photos of our accountant?'

Trying not to appear too taken back, he nodded his head.

'I noticed you from the first day.'

The coffee arrived in two glass cups. Ali placed some milk and sugar on the table next to them. 'Milk?'

'No thank you,' Dexter replied. He put two sugar cubes in the thick, hot coffee. 'How?' he asked, once Ali made his way towards another table.

'You need to answer my question from earlier.'

'What do I want?'

Perdi nodded.

He thought for a moment of how best to phrase it and chose simplicity. 'I need some help.'

'With what?'

'Information.'

'Do you work in the security industry?'

'Sort off. Out of curiosity, what made me catch your attention?'

Perdi took a sip of coffee. 'When you walked past. If you work in security, you should know that staff have some security training, especially around Mayfair.'

'Was it that obvious?'

'To me it was. So, what information do you need?' She put her cup down. 'This is exciting. Like a Bond movie.'

He sighed. 'You know Perdita, I'm going to be truthful with you. Maybe I shouldn't, but I'm going to put my cards on the table. That way, I have nothing to hide.'

'Sounds very philosophical and all that. Now, tell me what sort of information you want from me?'

Dexter grimaced. Again, the straightforwardness unsettled him. 'I've been given a little job regarding the bank you work for.'

'Which is?'

'Which is…' He leaned over the table. 'Someone in your organisation is maybe taking money out…without permission.'

'It happens. Quite common. Was that why you took pictures of Leonid?'

'Is that his name? Was told he works in accounts.'

'He's only been there six months. Is it him? Anyone else under suspicion?'

'Everyone is at the moment. Some more than others.'

'Including me?'

Dexter wanted to say yes, turn the tables on her so she didn't have the upper hand. But she wasn't, and he wanted to stay truthful for as long as he could. Things worked out better that way. 'Like I said, everyone.' He called Ali. 'Cake?' he asked. Perdi nodded. 'Two slices of Sfouf, please, Ali.'

'Are you a Private Detective?'

'Sort of.'

'Wow! Bet your job is exciting and glamorous. Is it?'

'Not really.' Dexter replied.

'Do you work for M15?'

'No,' he said, abruptly.

'Government?'

Ali returned with the sweet Lebanese delicacy.

'Can you help me or not?'

'What information do you want?'

Dexter divided the Sfouf and passed some to Perdi. 'You said he's only been there six months. Do you know where he was working before?'

'No, I don't.'

'Could you find out?'

'If someone at work finds out I'm talking to some Private Investigator regarding confidential matters I could be fired. It's in our contracts.'

'Not if it's helping to catch a criminal.'

'And if Leonid is innocent?'

'Speaking from experience, I'd say he's…'

'Not?'

'Didn't say that.'

'You were about to.'

'How did you see me photograph Leonid?'

'My office is on the first floor. Saw you in the car.'

He knew she would play clever with the next question but had to ask it. 'Did anyone else see me?'

She finished the Sfouf and coffee. 'Maybe,' she smiled.

Dexter understood the game. She had edged ahead again. 'Did they?'

Perdita ignored the question. 'Tell me more about what you do, and I'll find out where Leonid worked before. Deal?'

Perdi was certainly full of surprises. 'Okay... a friend has hired me. Thinks money is going missing.'

'You've already told me that. Look, let's put it like this...' She stood up. I may have some other things to say. Have a think about it. I need to go.' She started to walk towards the door.

Dexter left the money on the table and followed her. 'Wait, where do you live?'

'Bayswater.'

'Are you getting the tube or bus?'

'Bus.'

'I'll go to Marble Arch with you.'

Dexter thanked Ali as Perdi waited by the door. 'Thank you for the coffee,' she said, as he opened the door for her.

Walking down the Edgeware Road, Dexter explained a little more. 'The missing money is being used to buy other assets.'

'Being laundered?'

Dexter had to be professional. 'That's what I need to find out.'

Perdi stopped outside a jewellers. 'Do you like diamonds?' she said.

'There is something about them.'

'A girl's best friend.'

'So I'm told.'

'But they cause problems.' She turned to him. 'Do you know what a "blood diamond" is?'

Dexter did a job in South Africa where diamonds were being used to fund an uprising in Namibia. What an assignment that was! He kept this to himself for the time being. 'Rough uncut diamonds being used to finance an insurgency or a warlord.' he said.

'Clever.'

They approached the bus stop on Oxford Street. He asked how he could get in touch with her.

'Do you have a card?'

'Take my number,' he said. 'Give me a missed call.' Perdi tapped in the digits and pressed the call button. Dexter's phone vibrated. 'Got it.' The 94 bus was approaching. 'Why are you so keen to help?' he asked.

'Give me a call and I'll tell you. Goodnight, Dexter.'

He watched the bus turn left into the Marble Arch one-way system. He took a deep breath. The new job was barely three days old and already the drama had started.

## Chapter Six

Even down the phone line, it was obvious that Jasper couldn't contain his disbelief. 'Say that again.'

'She saw me photographing Andreyev?' Dexter mumbled.

There was an uncomfortable silence before Jasper said, 'So, what did you tell her.'

'Not a lot. I had to hold my hands up, Jasper. She saw me. I couldn't deny it, could I?'

'You're normally on top of these things. Careful.'

'I promise you, Jasper I *was* careful. She must be one smart cookie, that's for sure. Anyway, something good come out of it.'

'Which is?'

'Says she has something to tell me.'

'Can you trust her?'

'We'll see.'

'Where does she work in the bank? Which department?'

'She didn't say.'

'Did you find out her name?'

'Perdita. Nice name. Unusual, don't you think?' Dexter waited a few seconds. The silence was deafening. 'Jasper... You still there?'

The response when it came was terse. 'She is the niece of my client.'

If there was ever a time for the ground to open and swallow him up, this was it. 'What!'

'It's my client's niece,' Jasper repeated, in a calm matter-of-fact way. Then his tone became sober and serious. 'Careful, Dexter. This is an important one. I don't want this coming out. It would seriously damage my reputation.'

There were no excuses. 'I understand.' It was all he could say. He was glad he had explained the situation. It took away the worry Jasper might find out from another source. He was expecting worse; folk had been taken off cases for far less. With his mind clear, he could move forward. The reason for not saying he would continue speaking with Perdi was deliberate. He couldn't proceed with Andreyev until he had spoken with her. He knew Jasper wouldn't want him to have any more contact so, for now, until he got the relevant information, it was best to keep quiet. Charles Mingus played as Dexter got ready for his karate class, something he was looking forward to, as Mike would be there. Dexter was in work mode, so had to build up a few contacts for the case, and they didn't come in more useful than an ex-M16 government official.

\*\*\*

Mike was a former agent who had been stationed in nearly every South American country you could wish to mention. His favourite was Venezuela. 'For some reason, they love the Scots there,' he used to say, adding that he used to tell locals he was from a fictitious clan. He was in Caracas for three years to monitor unlicensed mercenaries stationed or passing through. Venezuela had a lot of resources and foreign interests, so corruption was rife. Contracts taken out on politicians, government officials and businessmen were common. Life was good for Mike there; a government-paid apartment in a plush suburban district and a car were the perks of the job. He even married a local beauty queen who later divorced him. Mike never stopped going on about Roseli. 'Love of my life,' he would say. There was always sadness in his eyes whenever he mentioned her, which was quite often.

Dexter always used Mike as a sparring partner, knowing he could take a whack or two. The training was always tough, but tonight's was particularly strict. Press ups, sit ups – you name it – were ordered by Sensei Tibbs, both before and after the lesson. Sensei Tibbs was old school, and notorious in the world of Shotokan karate. Being one of the first to be trained by the Japanese when they came to teach in the UK in the sixties, he was something of a pioneer. The tough disciplined regime stayed with him and was passed on. Dexter loved it, though. It had to be strict, otherwise he couldn't learn and wouldn't have obtained his current grading: 2nd Dan black belt. Mike was a little higher: 3rd Dan black belt. The lesson was spent practising the blocking and striking of kicks with emphasis on focus on the latter.

Almost inevitably, the conversation turned to Roseli in the changing rooms. 'Loved that girl,' Mike lamented, placing his folded-up karate suit neatly into his sports bag.

Aware that Roseli had re-married and had children, Dexter never really knew quite what to say. The fact that she left him for some American Secret Service agent also didn't help. Dexter had never been in love so intensely, so couldn't really understand why someone would go on so much about a marriage that ended twenty years before. Not for the first time, Dexter had to offer some empathy. 'You'll find someone,' he said.

'In this business?'

'Now that, I do understand.' Being in this line of work made relationships difficult. First there was the security side; that alone made any form of intimacy difficult in the first place. Then there was the travelling and being away from home a lot, which caused a strain. Dexter had met some beautiful women around the world – Alina in Paris was one – and had a few relationships, but nothing had been permanent. Sometimes he just wanted to meet a girl, fall in love, get married and start a family like the next man, but the relationships never seemed to last. Then there was the other side: did he really want to change and settle down? The truth was Dexter loved different women.

Mike continued to lament the past as they walked slowly to his car. 'She was something else. Should never have let her go.'

Dexter had to put it into context: 'You mean you never should have left.'

Mike stopped in front of his car. He shrugged his shoulders. 'True.'

'What's it like being in love, Mike?'

Mike put his keys in the car door. 'Good question.' He opened the door and slumped into the seat. 'You can't explain until it happens to you is all I can say. Anyway, enough of that. Any jobs coming up?'

Dexter had got to know Mike over the past few years and had become a trusted friend. As much as it was vital to be cautious and trust no one, it was just as important to have one person you could talk to, a confidant you could trust. Problem was, such people were very few and far between. Mike was one of them, though. Dexter knew all about his life, where he'd been, the assignments he'd undertaken, both privately and within M16, but he would never reveal them to a third party at any price and Mike knew this. Mike was a true friend and an asset, whose experience had helped Dexter out a few times. 'Got one the other day.'

'Already? Haven't you just come back from…'

'Marrakesh?'

'That's it. Love that place. How did it go by the way?'

'Was successful.'

Mike managed a smile. 'Any girls?'

There was a temptation to mention Alina, but Dexter wanted to keep it private. 'After what you just told me, I don't think I'll bother,' he joked.

Mike looked all serious again. 'It's a nice feeling, though.' He seemed to snap of it. 'Anyway, the new job… any good?'

'Similar to Morocco. Except the currency is diamonds instead of hashish.'

Mike sighed. 'Diamonds…'

'I know.'

'Could be dangerous.'

'I know. Diamonds via Russia, in fact – though not yet proven.'

'Tip of the iceberg, Dex.' Dexter knew this. It happened a lot, as most cases lead to the same source. The fun of it for him though was not so much the destination but the journey. 'Then onto the Netherlands?'

'You got it. Probably involves some diamond mine in Angola or somewhere.'

'Anywhere else?'

Dexter was cautious with his reply. 'Not at the moment.' He had deliberately omitted Egypt. Even though Mike was a trusted friend, he still had to be careful.

'Sounds like a big job, Dex. Congratulations.'

'Thanks,' Dexter said.

'Coming Thursday?'

'Of course,' Dexter replied, still basking in the feeling that only a good full on karate session could give you.

After Mike drove off, Dexter sat in his car for a moment. He thought of the conversation earlier with Jasper. He had ridden the wave, and learnt something, which was to be more careful and not take your eye off the ball. He could have been fired… taken off the job. Maybe it was better to get the mistakes out of the way at the beginning, I mean, who knew what would have happened in a similar situation in Russia, Holland or even… Cairo.

He started the car and drove slowly out of the car park into the monochromatic London evening. The karate club was just off Sloane Square, not too far away, but Dexter wasn't in the mood to go straight home. Even after the meditation at the end of the lesson he was psyched up and in the driving zone, so decided to take the longer route. The dashboard looked exciting: greens, oranges and dials were illuminated and moving around. After a slow cruise down the Kings Road, he put his foot down when hitting the Chelsea Embankment; it was made for it. He thought about the next move, and he couldn't wait.

## Chapter Seven

'Perdita?'
    'Who's this?'
    'Dexter. From yesterday?'
    'Dexter, of course...'Bit early isn't it. Everything okay?'
    'Thought I'd try and get you before you go to work.'
    'You have good timing, just about to leave.'
    'I've had a think and I'm interested in what you want to say. Possible to meet?'
    'When?'
    'Today?'
    'When today? And where?'
    Dexter changed the time and location. 'Hyde Park Corner. 5:45 pm?'
    'Where exactly? Lots of entrances.'
    'The Rose Garden.'
    'That's fine with me. See you then.'

\* \* \*

The run had been invigorating. Dexter was pleased with his fitness, the build-up of stamina in particular. *Quadrophenia* sounded relevant again, as he sang along in the shower. The beige chinos and a light grey merino wool sweater drew a comment from Terry on the way out. 'Good choice, Dex. Autumn's kicking in.'
    Dexter felt the cooler air as he walked for a haircut and shave. He had to give the usual Geo F. Trumper a miss this time, as the Curzon Street location was a little too close to Globalink. Jermyn Street Barbers was a suitable alternative, though. What a difference a trim and some

pampering with hot towels could make, Dexter thought as the air braced his skin after. The little spare time left before meeting Perdita was spent looking at maps and atlases in Waterstones. Since childhood, Dexter loved maps. He could get lost in them. It played a part in him doing the London cabbie knowledge before the chauffeuring game. Many hours were spent looking at the map on his moped. Even then he would look at different cities and towns in other countries – wishing that one day he would get the chance to visit some of them. Now here he was, ticking some of them off. He went to the African continent section and paid particular attention to one city and country in particular: Cairo in Egypt.

'Sure no one is following you?' Dexter asked, as Perdita sat next to him on a bench in the Rose Garden.

'Who? I haven't told anyone.'

'You can never tell.'

'This is so cool,' Perdita gushed.

Dexter frowned. 'What?'

'The situation. It's like a movie – meeting in secret places, being tailed. It's exciting. Cool.'

Dexter just agreed. 'I guess it is.' He was still aware that she had seen him and could tell anyone at any time. Another factor was that her uncle was indirectly his employer. He couldn't get too familiar and complacent. 'Let's go and sit by the Serpentine,' he suggested. After settling into a couple of deckchairs overlooking the Serpentine Perdita asked Dexter the reason for wanting to meet her. Dexter looked at her. 'Because I feel as though you need to tell me something.'

'What makes you think that?'

'Am I right?'

'Maybe.'

He got up and adjusted the chair so that he could lie back and look at the sky. 'I'm listening.'

'Leonid and another man were both hired the same day. I thought it was a little strange. The atmosphere changed immediately.'

'In what way?'

'Used to be a fun place to work. That was what Sebastian wanted – a happy workplace for all. Now, it seems more serious.'

Dexter had to acknowledge the Sebastian bit. 'Who's Sebastian?'

'My uncle. The founder and present owner of Globalink International.'

Dexter was glad that one was out of the way. 'Besides Andreyev, who else started that day?'

'A new manager for the Accounts Department.'

'You know who?'

'He introduced himself as Nasser.'

'Which company did he come from; do you know?'

'He didn't say. But I heard it was from a bank in Amsterdam.' Perdita looked him in the eye. 'Dexter, I think it's true.'

'What is?'

'About money going missing.'

'How do you know?'

'Something is definitely not right there. Do you think Leonid Andreyev is taking it?'

He sat upright in the deckchair. 'That's what I'm going to try and find out. Can I ask a question?'

Perdita nodded.

'Why are you telling me about Andreyev and Nasser?'

'Because my uncle is a good man. He has done many good things charity, et cetera. He places trust in his staff and wants a happy workplace. I don't want to see him taken advantage of and hurt.'

He understood her sentiment, but also knew that these assignments could be hazardous – even life-threatening. 'Let me take care of everything. If they suspect anything that you are onto them, they can be dangerous. Be careful.' He stood up. 'Ready? I'll walk you to the bus stop.'

'It's a nice evening,' said Perdita. 'Think I'll walk.'

'Only one thing I want you to do,' Dexter said. 'Nasser… find out his full name.' Perdita agreed before walking west towards the Notting Hill area.

'And remember…' Dexter said. 'Be careful.'

Dexter had the feeling he should expect a call very soon. He walked towards Knightsbridge for a meal at one of his favourite restaurants: Mr Chow. As always, the food was excellent. Sticking to his fitness routine, he decided to walk it off. He cut through the back way until reaching Sloane Square, where there was a temptation to jump on the No 19 bus, but he kept going. Chelsea Bridge Road soon became Churchill Gardens, where he grew up. It still hadn't changed. He remembered Dolphin House as a youngster. He would look at the apartments, see the professionals and politicians coming and going, dream that one day he would have a similar place to call home. Here he was, twenty years later, living the dream. The temperature was beginning to drop. Autumn was kicking in. He upped his pace. Across the water he could see his apartment block. He thought of Perdita, happy that he no longer felt as though she had something on him. Things were beginning to move, he thought, as he finally arrived at Vauxhall Bridge.

## Chapter Eight

The following afternoon, Dexter's phone rang. 'Amare Nasser,' Perdita said.

'Wait... I'll write that down.' He went to get a pen from the drawer. After writing it down on a piece of paper he sensed that she had more news.

'He worked for a bank in Amsterdam before.'

'Any idea what they specialised in?' He waited for the inevitable answer.

'Diamonds.'

'The name of the bank?'

'I'll find out.'

Now was the time to assert himself. 'You've done enough. It's greatly appreciated, but you must leave it to me now. We can't mess it up for your uncle.'

'Mess it up?' Dexter knew what was coming next. 'It could have been anyone that saw you. You're only lucky that it was me.'

It was also time for him to come clean. 'Listen... I messed up. I admit that. Was a stupid mistake. In the years I've been in this business that has rarely happened. I should have been more careful. Now we need to move. In my experience, this assignment will become dangerous. That's why I'm saying you have to leave it to the professionals.'

'Cool. Perdita was animated. Assignments... danger...'

'Listen, Perdi... This isn't a movie. You've done great, and I understand you wanting to help your uncle but–'

'Okay,' she snapped, 'I won't get involved anymore!'

He didn't want to mention what people like Nasser and Andreyev – if they were up to something – could do if they suspected their livelihood or freedom was threatened. 'Much appreciated.'

'Please help my uncle. He's a good man. He doesn't need this sort of scandal.'

'Don't worry. We'll sort this out. But don't say anything to Nasser, Andreyev or anyone else. It could jeopardise the investigation. I'll call you with any updates or if I need any help.'

'Thank you, Dexter.' Perdita sounded mollified.

He put the phone down and went to his home gym. It was 2 pm: time for some free weights and bench presses before making his way up to Mayfair.

\*\*\*

The clothing was nondescript; it had to be. He had learned his lesson from Perdita and had made an extra effort not to stand out. The baseball cap was plain, as were the jacket and trousers – no designer logos or brand names on show. The time was exactly 4:45 pm when he arrived at the betting shop opposite the bank. After placing a bet on a race on the 3.15 St Leger at Doncaster, he positioned himself by the door so he could see the staff entrance to the bank. He wasn't a betting man, but this was an exception. Typically, the horse came in first. Going to collect his winnings, he noticed Andreyev pass the door. 'Many thanks,' Dexter said to the cashier, handing her a twenty-pound note.

He quickly stuffed the rest of the winnings in his pocket he went to the door. Andreyev was walking in the direction of Park Lane before turning right into South Audley Street. Before opening the betting shop door, Dexter looked over at the bank. Sensing it was clear, he opened the door gently and began to walk casually to South Audley Street. When he reached the corner, Andreyev was walking past the Embassy of Qatar. He stopped to take a call on his phone. After speaking for a few seconds, he turned around and started to walk back towards Curzon Street. Dexter had to continue walking, it might have caused suspicion if he hadn't. Andreyev walked past, not even giving Dexter a second look. After about fifty yards, Dexter risked turning around in a shop front and set off cautiously after Andreyev.

Andreyev turned right, heading towards Park Lane. Dexter knew Park Lane would be busy at this time and he didn't want to lose sight of Andreyev. So, he upped the pace, keeping a safe distance as Andreyev walked past the Hilton, down Old Park Lane before arriving at the renowned Playboy Club.

Dexter had a choice: call it a day and go home or wait a while to see what happened. These establishments closed in the early hours, so it could be a long wait. *Why not?* He was here anyway. Who could tell what might happen? The problem was, there wasn't anywhere to wait. No benches or bus stops were near and this wasn't the sort of area to loiter.

He had decided to call it a day and was walking down Old Park Lane towards Piccadilly when Andreyev came out. He stood at the entrance and lit a cigarette. Dexter was on the other side of the road as a car pulled up outside the club. The doorman opened the back door and a man got out who went and shook hands with Andreyev, who lit a cigar for him. Dexter couldn't miss this opportunity; he got his camera out of his rucksack and quickly took a few shots of the two men. Andreyev flicked his cigarette to the kerb before the doorman opened the door as they walked into the club, laughing and patting each other on the back. Dexter called Perdita to ask what Nasser looked like? He was looking at the images on the camera as she gave a brief description.

    'Fond of cigars?' he asked.

    'How did you know?'

    'Tell you later.'

\*\*\*

The Tai Chi lesson in the evening was about meditation. Dexter loved meditation. When he had to get into shape for a job, there had to be something spiritual to complement the physical. Meditation provided that. When working on a job in China, he took time out after, training with a renowned Tai Chi master in the Wudang Mountains. 5 am to 7 am and 5 pm to 7 pm were spent sitting in silence overlooking the mountains. That was when the energy was at its best, the master used to say. The lush aroma of the morning earth and rolling mist would stay with him forever. Like many experiences it was one to which he vowed to repeat; like many experiences, he never did. For wellbeing, Dexter had to make a choice: Tai Chi or yoga. He had given yoga a go, but preferred Tai Chi. It was similar, except in Tai Chi you moved instead of being stationary. The other benefit was that as a martial art, it could get you out of trouble.

    Later, Dexter developed the images in the darkroom. There was always a buzz in the darkroom late at night. A kind of eerie, city feeling enthused him as he hung up the photo paper. He was pleased with the results. There was his man: Amare Nasser, someone who needed further investigation. He held up the photo. The one he liked had a side view of Andreyev exhaling. The smoke was captured in the air. Nasser had his arm around him. This was the one for the personal collection.

# Chapter Nine

'Nasser?' Mike asked. 'Amare Nasser... works where?'
'Globalink International.'
Mike said he was familiar with the bank. 'How long has he been there?'
'About a year. Before that worked for a bank in–'
'Amsterdam.'
'How did you know?'
'No wonder he went off the radar,' said Mike.
'Is he wanted?'
'Not as such. Suspected in a bit of laundering involving–'
'Diamonds?' Dexter offered.
'How did you know?'
'Training tomorrow?'
'Of course.'
'I'll get some more info. See you then.'

Dexter went to his collection, put some Wes Montgomery on the turntable then returned to the darkroom to look at some more shots. Sometimes you could see something unintentional in the background, be it a car or a person, something accidental that could prove a case. He was pleased he had called Mike and told him about his new assignment. Mike had worked on jobs tracking down fraud and embezzlement, especially government money, so had contacts. Some of the big boys owed Mike; he could help on this one.

The stories of recovering assets and cash from offshore accounts, as well as helping to convict people and getting them thrown in jail, excited Dexter when Mike recalled them in detail. Dexter went to the window. In between Vauxhall and Westminster Bridge was Lambeth

Bridge. Nearly three years before on a cold January morning, a banker was found underneath the bridge. Cause of death: suicide. It didn't make the local news. Rumour had it that he was syphoning money from his employer: the Vatican. Mike had been hired privately by the bank to recover what had been taken. He managed to track down some of the cash that had been shifted to some offshore account in the Virgin Islands before being laundered into the art game.

Thinking they were clever by avoiding the usual cocaine route, the cash was invested into the Metropolitan New York art scene. Problem was that, not only did Mike know the scene, he knew how they thought and what their next step would be. *Once you know that, you're halfway there, Dex,* he would say. *It's a psychological game.* Dexter looked at the bridge a while, wondering what *did* happen. Nothing was ever mentioned regarding the motive and the victim was virtually forgotten. Mike never spoke about either; it was all about how to get the money back.

Big Ben chimed the bells at midnight. *Time for a nightcap,* Dexter thought, going back inside. After putting a glass in the ice box to frost he went to the drinks cabinet to choose a bottle of gin. The choice was either London or Plymouth, Dexter chose the latter. He took the bottle to the kitchen, took out the glass and poured a little. After adding some Mexican tonic water and a slice of lime Dexter went to the lounge to catch up on some e-mails.

There was one from Jasper: "your holiday companion would like to meet with you, wants your number." it said.

Dexter replied. "Ready when you are sir."

Five minutes the phone rang. Even though not recognising the number, he had an idea who it would be. 'Dexter Spencer speaking.'

'Hi.'

'Uba?'

'Yes. How are you?'

'Good. Yourself?'

'Fine. Can you talk?'

'Yes.'

'We need to meet soon, you know, have a chat, see how we're going to play it.'

'Sounds good to me.'

'Maybe go for something to eat?'

'Anywhere in mind?'

'Have you tried Somali food?'

Dexter hadn't. 'Can't say I have. Any good?'

'Of course.'

Dexter was a little sarcastic. 'The best right?'

Uba's tone changed. 'Dexter?'

'Yes?'

'Can we keep this professional. We must work together, right? So please, let's get on.'

'Friday good?' Dexter asked.

'Time, place?'

'Where are you based?'

'Not too far from you.'

'7 pm. Southbank?'

'Done,' Dexter announced. After saying goodbye, he got up, taking his drink onto the balcony. Watching Mother Thames ebb and flow below he wondered how Mike knew Amare. He looked over towards Lambeth Bridge. The surface of the water was slightly lit as it moved under the bridge and washed up against the silted banks. The banker who had met his fate there crossed his mind. For good measure he had been weighed down with bricks, probably just to make sure the job got done. Mike never did mention the reason why he took the money - if indeed he did – or who else was involved. This is a numbers game though, and as long as you get the job solved, everyone's happy. The reason doesn't really matter, it's irrelevant. Rationale, compassion and reasoning just isn't part of the vocabulary. As Mike said, it's just a game. *Can be an enjoyable game though,* Dexter thought, taking another sip of his beloved gin and tonic. His thoughts then turned to Friday and Uba; he couldn't wait for that one.

# Chapter Ten

The sparring was intense. It gets like that sometimes. Mike was going for it so Dexter had to be prepared, otherwise he would be on the floor with an injury, such was the intent. Experience had shown that some assignments can be dangerous, and the rule of thumb is that knowing how to look after yourself is a must: if you want to increase your chances of survival. Once in Cape Town, South Africa, he had to fend off two alleged muggers - who turned out they were working for the Israeli Special Forces. They wanted him to stop meddling or be taken out. Dexter didn't back down: it got physical. With Table Mountain as a backdrop, he managed to overcome them. Dexter was left with a bruised face and a broken rib: the other two were left unconscious. Some agents are more highly trained than others. With Moscow on the horizon - and the reputation they have – Dexter had to push himself. Even Sensi Tibbs picked up on the vibe, putting both Dexter and Mike on the floor a couple of times. Thanks to his superior blend of control, technique, and experience, neither was hurt.

In the changing rooms after Mike said he had something to tell Dexter. 'Did some research,' he said.

Dexter was still catching his breath from the press-ups and sit-ups that came at the end of a lesson. 'I'll tell you after,' he added.

After changing they both threw their holdalls over their shoulders and walked to the carpark.

'Did a little research,' Mike said. 'Found out Nasser was working for a bank in Amsterdam called AIB, short for Amsterdam International Bank. Was there for three years. Now, the interesting thing is they have a sister branch in........'

'Russia?'

Mike put some classical music on. 'Called the RIB – Russian International Bank.'

'Must be the same company.'

'Some of the shareholders and directors are the same. Another thing is that the RIB once had someone work for them by the name of……...'

'Leonid Andreyev?'

Mike nodded. 'And the RIB main investments are……'

'Diamonds.' Mike nodded. 'Where?' Dexter asked. 'Angola.'

Dexter sighed. 'So, what's Cairo got to do with all this?'

'Where Nasser's from.' Mike was tapping his fingers on the steering wheel to the tune of Chopin's *"24 Preludes, Op. 28: No 15 in D-Flat Major, "Raindrop."* 'Making sense?' he asked.

'Sort of, bit confused about why I have to go to Egypt, why not Angola where the mines are?'

Mike looked at Dexter. 'Sure, they have a reason,' he said logically.

'I'm sure they do,' he said, as he opened the door. 'Thanks for that Mike,' he added.

'Anything else, I'll let you know,' Mike said.

Dexter slammed the door closed and walked to his car. Thinking about what Mike had said he knew he'd be on the way to Russia soon. *Perks of the job,* he thought, as he started the engine. He'd been to Moscow a couple of times but Cairo…. never. The Pyramids were always on the bucket list, as were the bustling streets of Cairo he had heard so much about.

## Chapter Eleven

'Bakerloo line to Oxford Circus five stops to Finsbury Park,' Uba said.
'Thought we said the Southbank?'
'We did. Change of plan. Now Finsbury Park. Outside the Arsenal shop.'
'Do you like Jazz?'
'Depends.'
'On what?'
'What type? Don't like trad.'
Dexter didn't either. He preferred modern. 'There's a live gig tonight at The Jazz Café, Camden Town, not too far from Finsbury Park.'
'And?'
'Want to join me?'
'For a while.'
Dexter liked the no-nonsense approach. 'Brilliant, see you then,' he said.

Dexter loved The Jazz Café; it was one of his favourite venues. He couldn't wait. After a quick workout and shower, Dexter made his way to the wardrobe. With the company of a beautiful Somalian and some Jazz on the cards, the dress code had to be right. The decision was to go with a grey cashmere polo neck sweater and black linen trousers. A generous splash of cologne was then applied. Taking a step back he looked into the mirror. *Who would have thought?* he said to himself, referring to the fact that just over five years ago he'd be chauffeuring around some Diplomat or foreign attaché around London.

Dexter was waiting outside Finsbury Park underground when he heard someone shout his name.

'Dexter!' Uba was waving from a cab. 'Come,' she yelled. Dexter got in and closed the door. 'Sorry I'm late,' she said.

'Hope it's not like this on our honeymoon,' he joked.

'Very good. Getting into the character already, I like it.'

'Where are we going?' Dexter asked, as the cab passed under two rundown bridges.

'One minute, Uba said, as she leant forward to talk to the driver. 'This is fine,' she said. The taxi pulled up beside the old Rainbow Theatre. After getting out Uba pointed across the road. 'Over there,' she said.

The proprietor was expecting them. 'Fiid wanaagsan,' *(Good Evening)* he smiled when they reached the door.

'Fiid wanaagsan,' *(Good Evening)* Uba replied.

He turned to Dexter. 'Good evening, sir, Ahmed.'

'Good evening Ahmed, Dexter,' Dexter said.

'Please, this way,' Ahmed said, before continuing the conversation with Uba. 'Waad ku mahadsan tahay imaatinkaaga.' *(Thank you for coming)*

'Waa codsigeyga. (*It is my request*)

'Miyaan kuu heli karaa cabitaan?' *(Can I get you a drink?)*

'Laba koob oo shaah ah fadlan.' *(Two cups of tea, please)*

Ahmed pulled back a curtain and showed them a table. 'Please,' he said. Dexter sat opposite Uba, to the right was a window giving a view of the busy Seven Sisters Road. Ahmed left, returning after a couple of minutes with a tray. Two glasses of tea and a bowl of sugar were placed on the table.

The curtain was closed again. 'Been here before?' Dexter asked.

'Never,' Uba replied.

'Seems to know you,' Dexter said, taking a sip of the tea. He grimaced. It was sweet, a little too sweet for his liking.
'I take it you like your tea strong?'
'Afraid so,' Dexter admitted. He turned his chair a little to an angle so he could get a better view of the old Rainbow Theatre. The curtain opened again. It was a different man who asked if they were ready to order. Dexter left this to Uba, who ordered a selection of different dishes. 'Thank you,' the man said. After the curtain closed Uba asked Dexter if he was looking forward to the assignment?
'Very much,' he replied.
'Enthusiasm, that's what I like.'
'What about you?'
'Looking forward to it? Yes, I am.'
'You do this as a profession?'
Uba took a sip of the tea before answering. She looked Dexter in the eye. 'Yes, I do.'
'You went to university; you have a choice.'
'How do you know I went to university?'
'From the same place you knew I would be at The Royal Academy.' He looked at The Rainbow Theatre, knowing Miles Davis had played there.
'What did you study?' he asked, expecting either politics or law.
'Politics.'
'Where?'
'Stockholm. Where did you go to?'
'I didn't.'
'Funny. Really, which one?' Dexter didn't say anything. 'You can't get a job like this without going to Oxford, Cambridge or...what's the other one, beginning with B?'

'Bristol?'

'That's it.' Dexter continued to look at The Rainbow. Ella Fitzgerald, Oscar Peterson……

'Well, which one?'

'None. I am what you call self-taught.'

Uba laughed. 'Love the British sense of humour. I understand your being guarded.'

'How do you know Jasper?'

'He contacted a friend, passed on his number for me to call him which I did. Liked what he had to say, flew to London to see him where he explained a little more. Returned yesterday to sign the contract.'

'Will you be staying here until Cairo?'

'Leaving tomorrow.'

'Stockholm?'

'Amsterdam.'

The curtain swiftly opened. Two men carrying trays began to distribute the plates onto the table. Ahmed then came with another bottle of water and a plate of sliced banana.

'Mahadsanid,' *(Thank you)* Uba said.

'Mahadsanid,' Ahmed said, before closing the curtain again.

Uba was explaining the plates of food. As well as listening Dexter noted she was very attractive, had that Iman look: tall, thin, a good bone structure. 'This is Bariis iskukaris,' she said, pointing to the main dish of rice, fried potatoes, onions, peppers, and peas. 'The meat is lamb, and these are assortments of meats,' she added, indicating the side dishes. Dexter opened the bottle of water and poured some into the two glasses. The food tasted good, especially the fried potatoes and onions. The dessert was xalwo – a sweet confectionary – and a glass of milk - spiced with cardamon. Uba remarked it was good for sleeping.

After the plates had been cleared Dexter mentioned The Jazz Club again. 'Fancy it?' he asked.
'It's my last evening here, why not,' Uba replied.
'What will you be doing in Amsterdam?'
'Surveillance. Nothing too heavy.'
'Do you know when Cairo will be?'
'Jasper didn't know when exactly, only said to be prepared at short notice.'
The milk was warm and nourishing. Dexter looked out onto the Seven Sisters Road. *Herbie Hancock, The Dave Brubeck Quartet.......'* Why did you sign the contract?'
Uba looked at him. 'Why did you?'
Dexter was about to say money, an excuse to travel and kick ass, but after meeting Perdi a bit of morality had crept in. Her uncle seemed a good man and was getting turned over. 'Someone is taking money illegally, investing it in something that has a bigger profit.'
'Is that it? What about the money?'
Dexter sat back. 'Has an influence, obviously, I have bills to pay, but it's not the entire reason. Yours?'
Before Uba could answer, the curtain swished back. It was Ahmed. Everything okay?' he asked.
'Thank you,' Dexter answered.
He turned to Uba. 'Aad baad ugu mahadsantahay imaatinkaaga.' *(Thank you very much for coming).*
'Waadna ku mahadsan tahay haysashadaada.' *(And thank you for having it it)*
'Sidee cuntada ahayd?' *(How was the food?)*
'Cunnadu aad bay u fiicnayd. Saaxiibkay waa ka helay.Waxay ahayd dhadhankiisii ugu horreeyay ee cunnada Soomaalida.' *(The food was very good. My friend liked it. It was his first taste of Somali food).*

'Let's go,' Uba said. They both got up as the two men rushed in to clear the table. Inside the restaurant a small group had gathered. They were looking at Uba in an intrigued way.

'Thank you for choosing my restaurant. Say hello to your mother and father.' Ahmed said, opening the door onto the Seven Sisters Road.

'Was enjoyable. Will do. thank you,' Uba said. After saying goodbye, they began walking to the station when Dexter spotted a taxi going in the opposite direction. 'Where to now?' Uba asked, as Dexter somehow managed to flag it down.

'Camden Town,' he replied, crossing the road with Uba in tow.

'Where to guv?' the driver asked.

'Camden Parkway,' Dexter replied. He opened the door for Uba then closed it after getting in. The taxi was now in the shadow of the Rainbow, Dexter looked up: *Duke Ellington, Art Blakey…...*

The journey wasn't long, taking less than ten minutes. After paying the driver they both entered the venue. 'Nice place,' Uba remarked.

'Drink?'

'Water,' she replied.

Not only was Dexter on a health trip he also didn't want to look unprofessional. Nobody trusts a drinker. 'Think I'll join you,' he said.

A live band came on. A jazz funk combo. The music was low enough to strike up an informal conversation. 'Must be some cool jazz places in Stockholm.'

'I'm sure there are, I don't really go out much to be honest.'

'Never?'

'Sometimes to the cinema, occasionally eat out, that's about it really.'

Uba's terse answers meant she wasn't giving much away. Dexter liked this. Pleasure not to be mixed with business. Showed professionalism, but he had to know her a little personally, especially if they were to be a couple. He asked about the people at the restaurant. 'Seemed to hold you in high regard,' he asked, trying a different angle to make some sort of leeway.

'They have heard of my father.' Dexter frowned. 'Was a Diplomat, before we moved to Sweden.'

'I see, held in high regard.'

Uba turned to Dexter. 'Look, I appreciate the casual talk, but this is – and will be – a working relationship, okay?'

'No problem... darling,' Dexter uttered quietly, taking a sip of the water.

The band finished and a D.J. continued the theme, playing acid jazz and other funky beats. Dexter felt a little more relaxed. Hoping Uba was as well, he had another go. 'Where have you been staying in London, hotel?'

Uba smiled. 'Rented apartment.'

'What's funny?'

The smile evolved to a giggle. 'You make me laugh.'

'Do I?'

'Yes, you do.'

'That's nice to know. You didn't answer the question.'

'Which was?'

'Where's the apartment?'

'Vauxhall.'

'Nice area.'

'I like it,' Uba said.

'Near where you nearly collided into me?'

'Not far.' Uba moved a little closer, 'tell me, Dexter, you said this assignment wasn't entirely about the money?'

'And you never told me your reason for taking it on?' Uba moved away. 'You seem a little different from the rest.'

'Because I am a little different from the rest.' Asking what he meant, Dexter explained he hadn't trained at any military schools, or been in the British Civil Service or any other agencies. 'Self-taught, a big difference,' he smiled.

'What's funny?'

'Your curiosity.'

'Well, we do have to know each other…. a little,' Uba said.

'Reason for taking this?'

'Long story, basically, after the civil war we had to flee. Sweden has links with Somalia, so we applied for diplomatic immunity there.'

'Not Italy?'

'Was an option, but we decided on Sweden. There were a few other government officials and diplomats who made the same choice and came with us. Being around them, I listened to many stories of injustices not only in Somalia, but Africa in general. There are lots of resources that are exploited, as are the people. It started to affect me, and I wanted to help. When I went to college in the U.S I had an opportunity to train in security. I did a bodyguard course, took it from there.'

'Do you remember your first job?'

'Was for the Saudi Royal family when they visited Washington. Loved it. I was thrown in the deep end as close protection, but straight away knew it's what I wanted to do. I also enjoy the research and surveillance.'

'Never done close protection, more investigative.'

'What was yours?'

'First job?' Uba nodded. 'Not as glamorous I'm afraid. Just seeing if a wife was cheating on her husband.'

'Was she?'

'She was. Really enjoyed it, told I did a good job, was offered another and it sort of evolved into a profession.'

The next couple of hours were spent discussing politics around the world, especially in Africa. Jasper was right, Uba was political. Dexter sensed that there was more to this job than the money. There was some injustice and exploitation thrown in that she wanted to correct. Dexter was interested in the security aspect and how it differed compared to the U.S., Russia and Europe. Uba admitted it was a sensitive topic. 'Corruption,' she summarised. At 11 pm she had to leave. 'Early the flight, need to pack,' she said.

Dexter decided to stay. He wouldn't have minded staying with her a little longer but remained professional. Walking to the cloakroom he was aware that heads were turning, it's not every day you get a slim six-foot Somalian walking through a club. He told the doorman he was going to hail a cab outside and would be back. 'Well, hopefully see you soon,' he said, as they approached the entrance.

'I'm up for this one,' Uba stated.

Dexter asked the doorman if he minded finding a cab for his lady friend 'No problem, sir,' came the polite reply.

After a cab pulled up, Dexter opened the door. 'Have a good flight,' he said.

'You're a good man Dexter. Have a good evening.' Dexter closed the door and watched the cab head down the Parkway towards Regents Park.

'Wow, who was that?' the doorman asked.

'Work colleague,' Dexter answered with a wry smile. He then walked to the bar. 'Gin and Tonic,' he said to the bartender.

Finding a seat, he pondered the evening. The food, music, and of course Uba. It was something else. One thing was for sure: he was looking forward to Cairo. He noticed a lady on another table looking at him: *and the night hasn't even finished*, he thought, smiling back.

## Chapter Twelve

'You got acquainted, am glad.'

Dexter was on the opposite side of the desk facing him. He had just disclosed the previous evening with Uba. 'Said her father was a Diplomat.'

'Well known in East Africa.' Jasper gathered a pile of papers, before leaning to one side to put them in a draw. 'That's why he had to leave. Wouldn't play the game, tried to help the people, tried to stop the war.' After closing the draw, he looked up. 'Dexter, get yourself ready, you're going to Russia in a few days' time.'

Dexter knew this was the reason for the early morning call. He was ready. 'I'm ready,' he stated with confidence.

'Good. We need to get this one sorted asap. The money is going into the wrong hands, it's causing problems.'

Dexter knew that Sebastian had been onto Jasper and that there was a good chance that Perdi had been onto Sebastian. 'Do you know his niece?' he asked.

'Didn't know he had one, why?'

'Nothing.'

'Passport up to date?'

'Was the last time I looked.'

Jasper got up and sat on the side of the desk. 'I'll transfer some funds into your account for expenses and I'll book an apartment.' He looked at Dexter. 'This is a big one, be smart.'

'Will do.' Dexter got up and walked to the door and turned around. 'Question?'

'Quick Dexter, I have a lunch appointment at the Army and Navy club at 2 pm.'

'Why not just sack Andreyev and Nasser?'

'That would be letting them off. My hunch is that it doesn't stop at taking the money.'

'Dexter agreed. 'Definitely,' he said.

'My client would prefer them to be caught legally and face justice through the courts. Besides, it's a job, we're getting paid.'

Dexter thought about Nasser, the NIB, and the RIB. Maybe they've been embezzled as well. He kept this quiet from Jasper though, you never give away your source or contacts, Jasper probably didn't want to know anyway. His job was deciding whether to take on a client, negotiate a price, find the personnel for the job, and deal with the logistics.

Dexter opened the door. 'I'll be ready,' he said. Jasper didn't even look up, let alone say goodbye. Dexter had come to learn that this was his way of dealing with an assignment, and that's the way it was going to be until the job is completed. The contract had been signed: the deal had been done.

The early morning call from Jasper put Dexter in a different mode, a driving mode. After a little waxing and polishing earlier the Jaguar F-Type Convertible looked the part. The day was a little cooler, but still warm enough for the roof to be down. There is something about driving and the West End of London. They seemed to go together. Dexter made a little detour to drive around Berkeley Square. Being as he was there; he went around twice. *Why not*, he thought, *get it in while you can, may not get another chance, had to savour the moment.*

Navigating Piccadilly Circus was always special. Dexter loved opening up when he had the opportunity. Bystanders turned to watch this titanium beauty as it purred down the

Haymarket towards Trafalgar Square. As he swept down Millbank and over Vauxhall Bridge, he remembered that he had left Maria, the lady from the Jazz Club in his apartment.

Michael was at the desk as he rushed through reception to the lift. After a yawn he greeted Dexter.

'Morning Dex.'

'Morning Mike, tired?'

'Had to get up early, drive someone to the airport.'

'Bit of private work?'

'No, from here. A lady that had rented for a couple of days.'

'Nice, where was she going too, anyway exotic?'

'Sweden,' Terence replied. 'If you call that exotic,' he added.

Dexter stopped just before the lift. 'Name?'

'Come on Dex, it's confidential, you know that.'

Dexter gave one of those looks. 'Go on,' he said. Michael sighed before looking through a pile of papers on his desk. 'Let me see, got it written down somewhere. Here we are, Ahmed.'

'Uba Ahmed?'

'That's it.'

'Tall, pretty, short hair?'

'That's the one. Quite striking. Was a little surprised.'

'About?'

'She kept singing "*Won't get fooled again,*" by The Who. Showed me a CD she'd bought.'

'Which was?'

'"Quadrophenia"'

Dexter smiled. 'Good album......he remembered Maria. The lift doors opened. 'Have to dash,' he said, jumping inside.

The walk down the corridor was sprightly. *Second mistake*, he said aloud, angry with himself. The key was inserted quietly. Dexter paused before slowly opening the door. After squeezing in through the narrow gap he tip-toed to the lounge area. 'Maria?' After a few seconds he entered the lounge. 'Maria…… Maria, you here?' There was a note on the table:

> *Thanks for the evening. Really enjoyed your company. Made some coffee, hope you don't mind. Would like to see you again.*
> *07908909912*
> *M*
> *Xxx*

Dexter looked around before a deep sigh of relief. He went to the kitchen; you couldn't even tell someone had been in there. The bedroom was as he left it. He went back to the lounge, closed the curtains, kicked off his shoes and crashed on the sofa. *Must be more careful from now on*, he thought. Maria could have been anyone, a plant, an agent, *what was he doing leaving a stranger in his home?*

He put on the TV and flicked through the channels. Nothing was on, and what was, was of little interest. It was time to delve into his trusted vinyl collection. John Coltrane "A Love Supreme," was the choice. He placed it on the turntable and turned the power on. Giving the stylus a little blow, he placed the needle carefully onto the edge of the rotating record. After closing the curtains, the phone rang. 'Dexter?'
    'Yes Mike?'
    'Some news.'
Dexter turned the music down. 'I'm listening.'

'It's Nasser. Found out he's also involved with a bank in Egypt. An investor and shareholder there. Been told they have been receiving a lot of money as of late.'

'From a good source I hope?'

'Very good, but that's all they know. Where it's coming from or who's depositing it is a secret. No one's talking.'

'Best to go in person. Have a mooch?'

'Not on your own though. Too suspicious, also make out you're interested in investing in something.'

'What would be a good commodity?'

I think…I'll tell you in person.'

Dexter told Mike that he was on standby. 'Ready to leave for Russia at any moment,' he said, though through experience it would be at least a couple of days. Dexter thanked him for the information. It was helpful: he now knew the reason for Cairo. He suspected Jasper knew as well. He turned the music back up; game on, he thought, wondering if Uba knew as well?

On cue there was an e-mail shortly after:

*Russia, two days' time,*

*Jasper.*

## Chapter Thirteen

Dexter woke up the next morning in work mode. There was a good, pounding run followed by some weights on the bench. After a shower it was some rest. This was an important component. Like an athlete or an elite sportsperson, rest plays a vital part. There were two days to get into shape, not only physically, but mentally. It was time for some leisure, a hobby. He took his camera and walked to St. George Wharf where he bought a ticket to travel on the Thames Clippers boat to The Tower of London. Though he'd been many times, Tower Bridge never failed to fascinate him.

There were seven stops and seven bridges to go as the boat headed eastwards. Passing under Lambeth Bridge Dexter's thoughts turned to Sonetti. He wondered – not for the first time - who really was behind it. Sonetti was obviously shut up not because of embezzling the cash, but to stop him talking. He knew too much. Rumours were one thing, facts another. Mike had done a decent job but could only go so far. They obviously let him carry out a little token investigation just for a little transparency, but it came to a sudden halt. Mike hadn't really been the same since he called time on the assignment. He had that constant worried look on his face, as if he knew he was on borrowed time. Just by association, Dexter knew he had to be careful; no one was to be trusted in this game.

He sat at the front, taking in the bow waves. Tourists around him were excitedly snapping the sights. He couldn't blame them, The London Eye, Big Ben, the Houses of Parliament, were looking spectacular under the bright blue sky.

The South Bank and The Heyward Gallery were on the other side. Dexter had seen some good exhibitions at both. As for the Tate Modern and the Millennium Bridge – a little further up – he wasn't a fan. They were relics of the late nineties early two thousand era. As a driver he saw London change around that time. The established hotels and restaurants were taken over by the Cool Britannia brigade, losing some of the traditions in the process.

It wasn't long before the Tower Bridge stop was announced. Such was the relaxation a brief contemplation of maybe staying on to Greenwich was entertained, but a courier was delivering his visa and travel documents later in the afternoon, or early evening, so he had to be home.

A couple of hours was spent idly taking photographs in and around the Tower. He enjoyed the spot where Michael Caine and Murray Melvin were scamming the tourists with photographs in the movie Alfie. The location looked the same as in *1966*. He looked around, wondering if the same would be possible today. He doubted it. The tourists were still here but armed with mobile phones. Sitting for a coffee in Trinity Square, he thought about the itinerary Jasper would provide. which city he was going to, and for how long. Walking back to the Clipper he got that quick rush of adrenaline last experienced just before Marrakesh.

Back home Dexter selected appropriate clothes for the job. He had a special wardrobe for what he called the *"tourist clothes."* These were basically plain and dowdy, no designer labels to draw attention. Purpose was to be like any other run-of-the-mill tourist. After packing a suitcase, the intercom buzzed. It was Terry. 'Delivery for you Dexter,' he said.

'Send him up Terry. Thanks.' Dexter stood and waited. A few minutes later there was a knock on the door. He looked through the keyhole. The courier had his helmet on. Dexter couldn't see any documents; his hand was also in his jacket pocket. Might have the wrong address, but I doubt it, Dexter said to himself as he went onto the balcony and took to the fire exit.

The action was swift. One arm across his throat, the other pushing his arm slowly up his back. 'Who are you?' Dexter asked.

'De…li…very,' the man gasped.

'Company?'

'Bullitt.'

'Manager?'

'Steve.'

'First letter of surname?'

'M.'

'Keep your hands up,' Dexter ordered. As he slowly turned him around, he patted his pockets, satisfied there was no weapon, he released his grip.

'Blimey,' the courier said as he loosened the helmet strap around his neck. 'Only my second day, wasn't expecting this.'

'Learning process.' Dexter then asked for his documents.

'Mr Spencer?'

'Yes.'

The courier took out a bag hidden under his clothes 'For you sir,' he said, handing over a sealed package.

'Thank you, and… apologies for any misunderstanding.'

'Have a good day sir,' the courier said, before a making a hasty walk back to the lift.

Dexter closed the door and went to view the CCTV. He smiled as he observed the courier walking through reception before disappearing out of shot. He sat down, analysing the forearm speed and technique he'd just applied. The conclusion was it wasn't that bad. Training is one thing – the opponent knows what's coming and in general will be compliant – but real-life situations are a different ball game. Russia has some of the best-trained agents and you have to be up there - on their level - to stand any chance. A man he had met in South Africa once said; there may not be a second chance.

He got up to pour a gin and tonic before sitting down to open the package. Departure was tomorrow at 5:40 pm from Heathrow and was a direct flight to Domodedovo, taking roughly six and a half hours. The visa stamp was for tourism, valid for thirty days. His name, date of birth and birthplace were all correct. Inside were two envelopes, one containing Russian rubles, the other sterling. He threw the cash, tickets and passports on the coffee table and sat back. He knew what he had to do. Locating the RIB would be easy enough but taking some shots for evidence would be a little trickier. Russians can be funny towards cameras, especially outside banks. You only get one shot, if they rumble you, you must get out, quickly, there are no second chances, it's as simple as that.

\*\*\*

He put on Quadrophenia before stepping out onto the balcony. Drink in hand, he gazed at Chelsea Bridge for a while "Won't Get Fooled Again," played in the background. The night was quiet, and he wondered whether the empty apartment below was being rented out.

Then it made sense. Uba must have rented it, hence how she knew the lyrics.

He had to call Mike to let him know that he wouldn't be at training due to travelling. Apologies for missing training on Thursday Mike, let Sensei know.'

'Will do. Where you staying?' Mike asked.

'Khamovniki.'

'I always stay in Presnya.'

'Have to be on the river,' Dexter joked, explaining his preferred district of the Russian capital.

'Shouldn't take that long though should it Dex, a few days, week at the most?'

'In theory, but you know what can happen in this game Mike.'

'I know, anything can happen. Where you staying again?'

'Khamovniki district. It's in the centre.'

'Apartment or hotel?'

'Apartment.'

'Nice. Anyway, have fun, and be careful.'

'Thanks Mike, will do.' Dexter put the phone down and finished his drink. As he turned the glass slowly between his palms, he wondered why Mike was so keen to know where he was staying. Probably showing an interest, nothing more, he thought. He put the glass down and waited for the chimes of Big Ben at midnight. Once done, he locked the balcony door and went to bed.

## Chapter Fourteen

Dexter was on the Heathrow Express when he took a call from Perdi. 'Guess who I walked to Green Park station with yesterday?' she asked.

Dexter knew. 'Andreyev?'

'Well done. Impressed.'

'You didn't mention anything about meeting me, did you?'

'Don't be silly, just made light conversation.' There was a pause before she continued. 'Said he worked at a bank in Russia before being transferred to Holland. Seems to have a lot of experience in the banking sector. His older brother still works there.'

'Did he say the name of the bank?'

'He did, but I can't remember. I can ask tomorrow.'

Dexter didn't think that was a good idea. He knew how quickly they became suspicious. One wrong word and that's it. 'Don't say anything more.' he said.

Perdi agreed. 'Okay,' she said. 'Sounds like you're on a train.'

'Taking a little break for a few days.'

'Nice, anyway, just thought I'd call to tell you about Andreyev.'

Dexter couldn't mince his words. 'Just be careful. Don't make him suspicious. Any other information, call me,' he said.

***

Dexter got off at Terminal 4. Heathrow felt familiar. Walking through the ticket barrier he became aware of how relaxed and assured he was. Airports can have a nervousness to them, it's easy to get caught up in the anxiety of people thinking they will miss a flight for some reason or another, but Dexter remained calm, instead, liking the transient and anonymity feeling they can give.

First port of call was the duty-free shop where a couple of bottles of London Gin and a carton of cigarettes were purchased. Apart from being worthy currency - especially in places like Russia - they also make good gifts. You never know who you will meet, and when you would need a favour. There was a little time to be enjoyed in the exclusive members-only departure lounge before boarding. British Airways were the best, a little on the expensive side maybe, but the best. The supple leather seating made the flight bearable, and the six and a half hours passed quickly.

\*\*\*

Domodedovo airport was roughly about 26 miles southeast of Moscow. Like Heathrow it was always busy - which was a good thing - as not much attention was paid to the passengers arriving.

Dexter was impressed by the glass and its stainless-steel interiors. Lots of curves and tubes gave it a soft feeling. Even though travellers were arriving and departing, hustling and bustling, waiting and collecting luggage, it wasn't harsh.

After collecting his bags from the carousel, Dexter made his way to the adjacent rail station to catch the Aero Express into central Moscow. On the way he was approached: 'Вы хотите машину, сэр?' *(Do you want a car Sir?)* a man asked.

'Нет, спасибо, *(No thanks)*' Dexter replied.

As a rule – and it was a personal one – Dexter never took a taxi from an airport when first arriving. He didn't trust it, hence the decision of not having someone meeting him from the airport, the driver could be anyone. He'd heard many stories about agents and detectives being duped by someone pretending to be a driver, so it was always a coach or train. In this instance Dexter preferred to take the latter.

He went to the booking office and bought a single ticket. 'Paveletsky пожалуйста, *(Paveletsky please)*' he said.

The clerk handed over the ticket. 'Спасибо, *('Thank you)*' he said.

'Спасибо,' Dexter said.

In keeping with the Soviet theme, the train was a brilliant red. Dexter took a seat next to a window and kept his one suitcase and holdall where he could keep an eye on them. A Russian man returning to Moscow from London sat opposite. He said what a coincidence it was that they were on the same flight, Dexter agreed. Yes,' he smiled. Dexter was also prepared for the next question. 'So, what brings you to Russia?'

'Business,' came the terse reply.

Apart from the brief conversation - and a guard asking for a ticket - most of the duration of the twenty-six-mile journey was spent looking out the window onto the flat landscape.

Paveletsky station was less busy than the last time Dexter was there. Like the airport, this thing was huge, a massive monolithic of Russian dexterity. It had reopened in 1987 and was six times the size of the smaller and original station, which – unlike some of the refurbished buildings - had been respectfully incorporated in the more modern structure.

Dexter was feeling tired so wasted no time in venturing out of the station to find a car. Another precaution was not to take the first in line at the taxi rank. His favourite number was three, so he approached the third car. Much to the annoyance of the first two drivers he opened the boot, threw his case inside then quickly jumped in the back. 'Presnya пожалуйста, *(Presnya please)*' he said. 'Где на пресне?' *(whereabouts exactly?)*'

Dexter took out the itinerary. 'Ulitsa Lenivka.*(Lenivka Street)*'

'Нет проблем. *(No problem)*'

'Спасибо, *(Thank you)*' Dexter said, as the driver proceeded to do a sharp U-turn amongst the chorus of horns being pressed.

Dexter wanted to see one of the world's most famous landmarks - The Kremlin. He asked the driver to pass it, even if it meant a slight detour. Of course, the driver agreed, the fare would be more. Dexter sat back, put his arm over his holdall and relaxed during the short ride along the Moskva River, which was like the Thames, only a little cleaner.

'Rain,' the driver announced in broken English, as he put the windscreen wipers on. Dexter didn't mind, it added to the setting. 'Soon,' the driver added, pointing to his left.

Dexter sat up and after wiping the window, marvelled at the illuminated Kremlin as the driver slowly passed.

Not far away the car pulled up alongside a row of houses. Dexter gave the driver a note. 'Сдачи не надо, *(Keep the change)*' he said.

'Спасибо, *(Thank you)*' The driver inserted the ruble, neatly into his leather wallet. 'Nikolay,' he said, pointing to himself then holding out his hand.

'Dexter, pleased to meet you.'

Nikolay got out and opened the boot, taking out Dexter's suitcase. He took out his card. 'In case you... ride back, airport.'

Dexter took the card. 'Спасибо,' he said, as he was handed his suitcase.

The entrance was a large white wooden door on ground level. Dexter pressed the intercom. As he waited for an answer the door opened. 'Mr Spencer?'

'Yes,' Dexter confirmed.

'May I take your bag?'

'It's no problem,' Dexter replied, as he followed the man to a desk in the corner of the reception area.

The man took some keys from a cabinet behind him. 'Maxim, I'm the concierge,' he said. Dexter had to fill in and sign a form before he was handed the keys. 'Apartment, second floor, turn right when you leave the lift.'

Dexter put the keys in his pocket. 'Thank you, Maxim,' he said, before making his way to a lift that wouldn't look out of place in Marylebone or Mayfair. It was one of those beautiful iron-gated ones After closing the gate Dexter pressed the number two button and a few seconds later the lift slowly - but surely - made its way to the second floor.

The apartment was spacious, ornate, a mixture of pastel blue and white with high ceilings. The first thing was to open the curtains. The Moskva was in the distance, lit up by reflections of its surrounding buildings, looking calm. There was a slight temptation to go out, hit a jazz club or some late-night eatery but Dexter closed the curtains instead, knowing it wasn't such a great idea. The reason was straightforward; he knew he was being watched. He went to the bedroom, throwing the suitcase and holdall on the bed. Grabbing his toiletry bag, he headed for the shower. The provided towels were freshly starched, as was the bathrobe. It started to rain when he went back into the bedroom. Deciding to unpack later in the morning, he got into bed. The linen felt cool as he looked up at the ceiling and listened to the rain beat on the windows. One thing was certain: Dexter was looking forward to his time in Moscow. He woke up. It was 7 am. Dexter looked at his travel alarm clock. *Six hours, uninterrupted, not bad*, he thought. He went straight to the living room and opened the curtains. The Moskva looked different in the morning light, more active. After a quick shower and a recap of some karate moves it was time for work. He set up his laptop at the window, not only for some natural light but also the view.

The RIB was in central Moscow, on the other side of the Moskva. He'd find somewhere to take some breakfast and coffee first then make his way there. Maxim suggested a cheap but good place to eat. 'You are a photographer?' he asked, referring to Dexter's camera slung around his neck

'Trying to be,' Dexter joked.

'Anything specific?'

'Not really, anything that catches the eye.'

Maxim abruptly changed the subject. 'Enjoy your food Mr Spencer,' he said.

A quick thank you was all Dexter could muster up as he walked towards the entrance.

The omelette, bread and strong coffee certainly hit the spot. Dexter felt re-energised as he walked to the bank. Being the tail end of August there were still plenty of tourists around, it helped Dexter blend in with his SLR and rucksack. As expected, The RIB bank was some drab nondescript building on the Kadashevskaya Naberezhnaya (*Kadashevskaya Embankment*). He walked past to begin with, deliberately not paying much attention to it. He remembered Perdita seeing him, so had to be careful about when to take a photograph. There would only be one chance and he had to get it right. Nobody – especially in Russia – takes kindly to unauthorised media intrusion. He would struggle to answer why he was taking pictures of a dreary-looking building. He crossed the road and turned around. This time he looked across, nobody was entering or leaving the building. The camera's settings had been set in the morning; all Dexter had to do was focus and press the button. A few snaps rolled off in quick succession before he continued walking the way he came. There was no drama as he reached The Moskva. *Job done!* he thought, casually walking back to the apartment on the Ulitsa Lenivka.

Dexter walked through the reception area. 'That was quick,' Maxim remarked. 'Catch anything special?'

'Beautiful city, so much to see,' Dexter replied.

'Very beautiful,' Maxim said, sitting back, observing Dexter.

Dexter sat down in his apartment and transferred the images onto his laptop. He sat back and looked at them, now, he thought, was the next step: finding out how to get to Leonid Andreyev's brother.

Dexter emailed Mike, asking if he could come up with some info on RIB. Mike replied, saying he'll find out and give details later. Still aware there was a good chance of him being under surveillance, looking for any devices wasn't such a good idea for the moment, instead deciding to go for a walk and buy some groceries.

There was a small supermarket on the Ulitsa Volkhonka - a street just off the Ulitsa Lenivka – suggested by Maxim.

Dexter bought some cold meats, cheese, bread, milk – and some tea of course.

After lunch he sat at the dining table facing the Moskva. Gazing out onto the river, plans were made for the evening. If he was under surveillance at the apartment, he had to act as a visitor would. Tonight, he would visit a jazz club. Moscow and jazz went well together. He remembered one from last time; Igor Butman. Before that though he had to rest, sleep off some jet jetlag. He had a feeling he was going to need as much energy as possible.

Jasper was clever, he knew what Dexter liked, and how he worked better if his demands were met. One was a rented apartment in the centre of a city or a town, preferably by a river. Jasper found the latter a little strange at first, saw no logic, but accepted it. Most of the major cities in the world have a river running through it, and Moscow was no exception.

\*\*\*

Dexter put on a black polo-neck cashmere sweater and grey Italian linen trousers. A grey Jaeger suit jacket was taken for the cool evening.

Maxim said he looked different. 'Mr Spencer, you do not look like a photographer, more James Bond,' he joked.

Dexter joined in the fun. 'If only,' he said.

The Igor Butman was in the Tangansky district, on the eastern side of the city. As the evening was drawing in, Dexter decided to walk. From The Kremlin Embankment the Moscow Kremlin was lit up. Such a building is open to interpretations, but for Dexter, it was a beautiful building, a worthy piece of architecture to be appreciated, not some reminder of Russia's past and the Cold War era.

The club nestled between a restaurant and a theatre. Access was via some stairs which separated the two. Dexter went straight up, paid, then proceeded to the bar. 'Yes Sir,' the bartender asked, in near-perfect English.

'Gin and... no...' Dexter hesitated. Time to mix it up a bit, he thought. 'Moscow mule,' he said.

'Of course, sir,' came the confirmation.

He sat on a stool, taking in the surroundings, absorbing the vibes. Jazz clubs and bars seem pretty much the same wherever you go, with one exception: Paris. They tended to be a little different there, more cultured and glamorous. He thought of Alina, she wouldn't fit into this, too formal, maybe too clean and modern. Dexter looked around, he liked it. The bartender placed the cocktail on the bar. 'Спасибо, *(Thank you)*', he said.

It wasn't as packed as last time, maybe because it's the middle of the week. He pulled up his sleeve and looked at his Tag Heuer, *still early though,* he thought, as he took his drink and sat down to order something to eat. As he was waiting for the food a band came on. It was a simple but effective set-up. In the jazz game all you needed was a double bass, drums and an alto sax. Vocals – and guitar - were optional. He noticed a lady on the next table. She seemed engrossed in the music, tapping her feet and totally oblivious to her surroundings – including Dexter. There was something about her that caught his attention. Her friend noted the interest, subtly whispering something to her. After a few seconds, she glanced over. On cue, Dexter held up his Moscow mule and smiled.

Dexter's philosophy was *not* to be too professional, that could attract just as much attention as *not* being professional. The secret of this business was to be normal, but, in a professional way - if that makes sense. He never used alias, always travelled under his own name – Dexter Spencer – and never used a false identity, He'd met a few who did, they seemed to be confused, not really knowing who they were, or which identity to use. Dexter wanted to keep it simple and as uncomplicated as he could. Now, if this slim attractive brunette was part of the case, then he would behave differently, but she wasn't - not now anyway.

She smiled back, nervously, but that was all Dexter needed. He knew that was enough for the time being. Contact had been made. He finished his meal then moved to a seat closer to the stage to watch the rest of the show. After a few songs he decided to call it a day. Moscow was two hours ahead of London, so Mike would have replied by now with some information. He used the bathroom and on the way to the entrance looked over at the lady. She looked over and a mutual smile was exchanged. He noticed how radiant and healthy she looked.

The taxi ride back to the apartment was brief. Maxim asked how the evening went. 'Good, very good,' Dexter replied.

'You enjoy Moscow?'

Dexter nodded. 'Always,' he said.

Dexter showered, changed into a comfortable tracksuit then switched on the laptop. Mike had replied. The RIB had twelve employees – including Andreyev's brother. He sent names for a couple of directors who had shares in both RIB and AIB. Dexter replied saying thank you, much appreciated. Needing to listen to some music he called Maxim, asking if any portable speakers around. Maxim said there was, he'd bring them up. He walked to the window and opened the curtains. The apartment looked over the Bolshoy Kamenny Bridge. What looked like light rain started to hit the glass. He opened the large sash window and felt the gentle breeze brace against his face. It felt good, refreshing. "From Russia with Love," he said aloud, with a smile, closing the window. A few minutes later there was a knock at the door. Dexter opened the door. 'Here Mr Spencer,' Maxim said, in that adorable broken English.

'Maxim, thank you, much appreciated.'

'You are welcome, Mr Spencer.'

'Oh, by the way. A good Russian classical composer – any suggestions?'

Maxim didn't hesitate with the answer. 'Tchaikovsky, of course.'

'Any particular piece?'

'The Seasons.'

Dexter nodded in acknowledgment. 'Thank you. 'I'll have a listen,' he said.

'That's great Mr Spencer,' Maxim said, before saying goodnight and turning around to go back downstairs.

Dexter closed the door and waited for a few seconds before returning to the drawing room where he sat at a table facing the large ornate marble fireplace. There were twelve pieces in The Seasons. Dexter chose one at random: "*September: The Hunt, in G Major.*"

Above the mantelpiece was a framed Ilya Repin print. It was a self-portrait of him and his wife when they were living in Kuokkala. Dexter fell into some sort of Russian mode. The detail and theme of the painting accompanied by the music was a potent blend. Both were powerful and passionate, that had a sadness at its core.

Looking at the couple, he wondered how comforting it must be to have a wife, somebody there, with you. He then questioned this notion. What if it doesn't work out, must be horrible and would you deal with the emotional aftermath? He'd always been alone, he liked it that way. Attachment wasn't his thing. He enjoyed the company of different women and would find that very difficult to give up. Then again, coming home to a wife…He thought of Mike, and how he's never been the same since Andrana left him. How would he deal with that?

He turned the music off and sat back. The painting was different without the music, not as sad, in fact, was the opposite, Repin and his wife looked happy, content, loyal and supportive. Did Dexter envy him now? Again, yes and no really. It was 1 am. That was it, the late nights would have to be put on hold for a while, there was work to do. The light filtered through the top of the drapes as he lay in bed. It kept him awake a while. Knowing he was being observed, he turned over and thought of the girl in the jazz club and how he would like to see her again.

# Chapter Fifteen

The clerk got up and went to a door behind the desk. After knocking on the door and waiting a few seconds she went inside. Dexter took a seat.

The clerk returned to the desk, accompanied by a tall blonde woman, who came and approached Dexter.

'Доброе утро, чем я могу помочь? (*Good morning, how can I help)*'.

Dexter stood up. 'Good morning. Speak English?'

'Good morning, sir.' The switch impressed Dexter. 'My name is Irina.' She smiled. 'How can I help you?'

'Dexter. Dexter Spencer.'

'Nice to meet you Mr Spencer.' Irina paused. 'And how can I help you today?'

'Here on a business trip.'

Irina beckoned Dexter to the side. She asked the same question, this time lowering her voice. 'And how can we help Mr Spencer?'

'Well, I'm a promotor, sports promoter. My company would like to stage a major sporting event here in this wonderful city of Moscow.'

Irina continued to smile. 'And what would you like us to do?'

'I'd like to make an investment somewhere, you know, with a reputable bank.'

'One second Mr Spencer, please.' Irina went to a door in the corner. Dexter sat back down, watching as she knocked gently on a door before entering. A few minutes later she returned. 'Can you wait for…' she looked at her watch. 'Five minutes?' she asked.

Dexter did the same, deliberately showing the Patek Philippe. 'No problem,' he said.

Irina returned to the room she came from as Dexter waited.

'Mr Spencer?'

'Yes.'

A man approached him; hand extended. 'My name is Viktor Lebedev, pleased to meet you.'

Dexter shook Viktor's hand. 'Pleasure,' he said.

Victor lowered his head towards Dexter's. 'My colleague mentioned something about investing… in sports?' he whispered.

'Yes.'

Viktor straightened up. 'Then please, follow me.'

Dexter walked behind as Viktor opened the door to his office. After closing the door behind he dragged a chair to the desk. 'Please,' he said. 'Drink?'

'No thanks.' Dexter sat down and looked around the office as Viktor fixed himself a drink in the corner. It was very bland and non-descript, probably built in the early nineties, when Russia was in the midst of another resurgence of capital. Apart from a dated computer on a desk and the two chairs, there was little else in the way of furnishings.

Viktor put the glass on the table. 'Sure?'

'No thank you,' Dexter said.

'No problem.' Viktor went and sat on the other side of the desk. 'So, tell me, what do you have to offer Mr Spencer?'

'I'm a company director of a sports consultancy agency. We look after sports stars, you know, boxers, football players, snooker, that sort of thing. We're looking to expand overseas, expand our horizon. Need to find somewhere to put on and promote major sporting events outside the UK, somewhere with sporting pedigree.'

Viktor pulled his chair closer to the desk. 'The name of your company?'

Dexter took out a business card. He handed it to Viktor, knowing the next step.

'May I?'

'Please.' Dexter said.

Viktor took a sip of his drink before looking at the card then typing in the company name on the outdated P.C. 'Impressive clientele,' he said.

'Only the best.'

Viktor sat back. 'Why us? I mean, there are many more commercial banking options, bigger than we are with more capital. I'm sure you have the contacts?'

'Many.' This time Dexter leant forward. 'But we need a good, personal relationship with a bank, if you see what I mean. He sat back. Besides, heard through the grapevine that you have a good reputation.'

'You are kind Mr Spencer.'

'In sport there are lots of sponsors, endorsements, multi-million-pound contracts, big TV money. We must be very selective who we choose. Then there's the matter of trust...To cut a long story short, we need to use a bank to deposit money as we negotiate sporting events in Russia.'

Viktor nodded. 'Of course,' he said. 'Can you give me a brief outline of the....' He frowned as he struggled to find the right words in English.'

'Proposal? Business plan?'

'Business plan. That's it.' He laughed, tapping the top of the desk with his pen. 'Business plan,' he repeated, happy to have learnt a new phrase.

Dexter took some paper documents from his bag. 'Sometimes better than e mail,' he said, handing them over.

Viktor put on his glasses and looked carefully at the two sheets for a few minutes before taking them off again and placing them on the desk. He looked at Dexter. 'What exactly would you be investing Mr Spencer?'

Dexter was waiting for this one, he knew it would be coming. He uttered the magic word that opens many doors. 'Cash,' he stated. Though Viktor tried to remain calm, his demeanour said otherwise. His eyes lit up, causing him to shuffle the papers around the desk a little. Dexter sensed he was onto a winner here. 'Who doesn't want to be around sporting superstars?' he added, knowing that boxing and football had clout here: everyone in this country wants to be the next Roman Abramovich.

'The figures you quote, this how much you want to invest?' Dexter nodded his head. Viktor gathered the papers and stood up. 'Let me talk to my manager, see what we can up with.' He asked Dexter where he was staying and for how long?

'By the Kremlin. Three days.'

'How can we contact you?' Dexter gave his business card. 'Will be in touch,' Viktor said.

Dexter stood up. 'Thank you,' he said. As they walked to the door, he commented on how professional it looked.

'We try,' Viktor said, holding the door open for him. As he walked to the entrance, he saw Irina. 'Прощай, *(Goodbye)*' he said.

'Прощай,' Irina replied.

A man was about to enter. Dexter held the door for him. He rushed past. 'Спасибо *(Thank you)*,' he said.

'Прощай,' Dexter caught sight of his face. *Andreyev's brother for sure* he thought.

Dexter knew that it would be sooner than later he would receive a phone call from the RIB. He also knew that he was now definitely under surveillance. He didn't take it personally; he would be more surprised if he wasn't.

Halfway over the Bol'shoy Kemenny, he stopped, deciding to enjoy the vista of the new Russia and its fast-emerging skyline. The small cluster of skyscrapers was different to New York, Kuala Lumpur, or L.A. Though impressive, it seemed strangely surreal. The ambience was one of secrecy, a lack of invitation, not a place where you feel welcome to come to do business or invest - unless – of course - you were a sports promoter.

He looked at one of the business cards. He'd done a good job on a fictitious business, the paperwork had passed Viktor's scrutiny. He then noticed a man hovering around the beginning of the bridge. He smiled, wondering why they make it so obvious. The man lit a cigarette, leant on the bridge, looked around, then backtracked the way he came. Dexter couldn't be bothered with the cat and mouse game so proceeded straight to his apartment 'Good day Mr Spencer?' Maxim asked.

'Such a beautiful place.' Dexter replied. 'Where is Spartak's stadium?'

'The Otkrytie Arena is in the northwest of the city. Take the metro and get off at Tushinskaya. You a football fan Mr Spencer?'

'Yes. I am. You?'

'I like Chelsea,' Maxim said, predictably.

Dexter went up to his apartment and drew the curtain. As expected, the man was not too far away, he noticed Dexter, who pretended not to notice him, as he opened the window. He plugged in and switched on the laptop. He had to look at his business card to remember his company's website.

After typing in the name, it came up. It did look impressive and professional. Jasper had done a good job. He sent an e-mail to him, saying that he'd pitched the idea and so far, so good. He didn't mention Andreyev's brother, that was between himself and Mike.

Jasper replied straight away, saying well done, and was he being followed? Dexter smiled as he replied. *Of course*, he said.

Dexter had a little rest before getting ready for a jazz club. It was important to act normal and be seen about, the first thing to draw suspicion was to close the curtains and hide away. The shower was cool and refreshing. Dexter hooked up his speakers to the laptop in the hallway. "Quadrophenia," accompanied him as he got ready. He called Maxim to order a taxi. 'Leaving in half an hour,' he said.

'Looking good, Mr Spencer,' Maxim commented, as Dexter came down.

'I try,' he said. Jumping in the taxi he took a quick glance in the rear-view mirror and noticed a car parked not too far behind. The driver was the same man who had followed him earlier.

The Kozlov Club was a ten-minute drive if that. They passed The Bolshoi Theatre on the way. The neo-classical building looked stunning bathed in a golden light. *Have to get to see something there one day,* Dexter thought, thinking that three days was not enough to savour a cultured city like Moscow.

The Kozlov was more like it. It had a Ronnie Scott's feel to it, was housed in an old building in a quaint urban street. It had red interiors and felt rich and velvety. This time Dexter felt a cold beer. He went and sat down and ordered a burger and some fries. It tasted good, especially with the beer. Sitting back, Dexter felt satisfied, the only thing missing was some company. As he went to watch the band, he noticed the girl from last night sitting at the bar, this time she was on her own. Dexter didn't waste time; he may never get this opportunity again. You have to go for it, grab the chance whilst there. Past experience had proven that women prefer a decisive, confident man, 'Hi,' he said.

She seemed to respect the tactic and manner used.
'Hello,' she said.
'Saw you last night.'
'Did you?'
'At the jazz club.'
'Oh yes, that's right.'
'Russian?'
'Yes.'
'You speak good English.'
'Thank you.'
'May I buy you a drink?'
'I'll have some water please.'

Dexter ordered a bottle of water and another beer for himself. 'Here,' he said, passing the glass. 'What is your name?'
'Natalia. Yours?'
'Dexter.'
'American?'
'No, English. Fancy sitting down?' Dexter suggested, as he grabbed the bottle of water and went in search of somewhere to sit. After finding a booth he asked Natalia what she did for a living.

'I don't think you would believe me,' she answered.
'Try me,' Dexter said.
'Guess?'

Dexter sat back and observed Natalia for a few seconds. She was very slim and had a radiant complexion. 'Beauty therapist?' Natalia laughed. 'What? Am I close?'

'Not really.'

'Sports teacher?'

'No.'

'Ex Gymnast?'

'Close.'

Dexter said he hadn't a clue. 'Tell me,' he said.

'Dancer.'

'What sort of dancer?'

There was a pause, a sort of hesitancy as if she should tell him or not. 'Ballet.'

'Professional?' Natalia nodded. 'Where, here in Moscow?' Natalia nodded again. 'Where?' Dexter repeated. Natalia took out an identity card. She passed it to Dexter over the table. After looking at it for a few seconds he looked up. 'The Bolshoi?'

'You sound surprised.'

'I am.'

Natalia took a sip of the water. 'Why?' she said. Dexter didn't mention that he'd just driven past the Bolshoi Theatre and thought that he had to see a show there. He just said that he wondered what she was doing here. 'I love jazz,' she simply said, answering his question. Dexter couldn't quite hide the frown. 'You mean it seems a little….odd that a ballet dancer is in a club?'

'Sort of.'

'I get that a lot, as if I should be at home in bed, that's why I don't tell people.'

'Why did you tell me?'

This time Natalia frowned. 'I don't know, really, I don't know.'
'Anyway, forget that, what sort of jazz do you like?'
'Modern.'
'Miles Davis?'
'Love him, and John Coltrane.'
'What's your favourite Miles album?'
'The obvious.'
'Kind of Blue?' Before Natalia could answer a band started to play. They sounded like fusion jazz. Dexter wanted to check them out. 'Coming?' he asked, as he stood up.
Dexter really liked the venue. It was a proper jazz club, something that he'd always wanted to be involved in. One song sounded like "*Expansions,*" by Lonnie Liston Smith, one of his favourites. At the interval they went back to the booth which was empty. 'Yes, it is,' Natalia said.
'What is?'
'My favourite album.'
'Oh,' Dexter said, completely forgetting about it. 'Good piece.'
'And you, what do you do?'
'I'm here on business.'
'What sort of business?'
Dexter hated lying. He's done it, when he needs to, but in general not telling the truth isn't his thing. He looked at Natalia, she seemed so innocent, he couldn't not tell her the truth. 'Just looking at things,' he said, in a subtle way. The thing to do here was to change subject so you could avoid such things. 'Working at the moment?'
'Yes, in a production.'
'Now?'

'Yes, performing tomorrow. A new production.'
'At the Bolshoi Theatre?'
'Yes.'
'What's the production called?'
'Jewels.' Dexter said that he never heard of that one.
'It's contemporary. American, from the sixties.'
'Nice, how many Ballerinas in the show?'
'You mean production? There are three parts, The first is called emeralds, second one rubies, I dance solo in the final section.'
'What's that called?'
'Diamonds.'
'Who does the music, I mean the composer?'
'Tchaikovsky. What is wrong, you don't like him?'
'Love him, especially *"The Seasons," September: The Hunt, in G Major.*'

Dexter spent the evening with Natalia. She was good company. They spoke about jazz and art, and photography, even promising Dexter she'd pose for some snaps for him. 'Not tomorrow,' she said, as she had to prepare for the performance, but the next day for sure. 'We can go to a photography exhibition,' she promised.

At eleven Natalia had to go. It was difficult saying goodbye to her, he enjoyed the conversation. After she left, he went to the bar and ordered another beer. *One for the road*, he thought, as he went and sat near to the stage to listen to the band. Just before midnight he decided to call it a day. Nothing was planned for tomorrow as he was expecting a phone call from Viktor. He gave his compliments to the man at the door, saying how much he enjoyed the venue, band, and atmosphere.

Outside he went straight to the first taxi. 'Ulitsa Lenivka,' he said, now getting used to the pronunciation. As the car headed along the Teatra'nyy Proyezd Dexter looked at The Bolshoi Theatre. He found it a little strange that a lady he had spent most of the evening with would be performing on that stage tomorrow evening. Dexter took a quick glance into the driver's rear-view mirror. The car from earlier was not too far behind. He knew that there would be no more surveillance, not for tonight anyway. They knew where he lived, where he went and perhaps what his interests were. The level of suspicion would now be lowered. His haunch was correct, the car didn't turn into Ulitsa Lenivka, it just went straight ahead.

'Good evening Mr Spencer?' Maxim asked.

'Very good thank you,' Dexter answered. 'Good night, he added, as he made his way to the lift.

'See you tomorrow Mr Spencer,' Maxim said.

Before unlocking the door, Dexter knelt down, there was a trick he had seen in some spy movie many years ago where a hair was placed across from the door to the door frame. Dexter had tried it many times and swore by it. On closer inspection he could see that the hair was no longer there. He stood up and opened the door gently and quietly. Leaving the hallway dark, he walked slowly to the lounge. Once there he paused for a few seconds before placing his hand on the concealed pistol inside his jacket pocket. A quick step into the living room - whilst turning on the light at the same time - followed. Dexter put the pistol away and turned off the light before going to close the curtains. He looked out into the darkness and couldn't see anything of note. He went and switched the light back on before going to draw the curtains.

Someone had been in, he knew that, the question was how did they gain access and who gave them permission to do so? He took off his jacket and switched the laptop on. After a shower he made a gin and tonic and listened to *"Kind of Blue."* He had to pinch himself that he had met a Bolshoi ballerina, let alone meeting with her the day after tomorrow for some photos. He suddenly jumped up and ran to where he kept his camera, it was a similar feeling to when Perdita told him she'd seen him take photos of Leonid Andreyev. It was a feeling as if being punched in the stomach as well as feeling stupid. He took his camera from the wardrobe and opened the side. The memory card was missing. *Damn*, he thought, slamming his hand against the wardrobe door. He slumped on the sofa, trying to remember the route from the bank the other day.

He switched the laptop on and e-mailed Mike giving an update. Moscow was two hours ahead so it would be about 10:30pm in the U.K. He replied almost immediately. *Don't worry about Viktor Lebedev, he's just a manager of sorts, has no history. The one you want is a chap called Sergei Sokolova, he's a director, also travels to Holland quite a bit,* it said.

Dexter replied, saying thank you, and he'll contact him tomorrow. He didn't mention Natalia, didn't want to involve her, if someone's been in the apartment, anything's possible, they could try to hack e-mails, you never know, this is Russia. He also omitted the memory card going missing. That may be the subject of amusement after a training session or reminiscing some anecdotes down the pub or at a club, but now it could be perceived as very unprofessional. After getting into bed, he remembered something else: he'd forgotten to give Natalia his number. *Tomorrow I will focus*, he told himself, as he turned over and fell asleep.

# Chapter Sixteen

Dexter could hear the rain from under his covers as he opened his eyes. He got up and went to the window to look out. It was heavy, monsoon-like, as it pounded the pavements, cars and the river. As he made a cup of tea the phone rang, the number was withheld, which – in this business – is always a good sign. Dexter picked the phone up as he was pouring some hot water onto the teabag. 'Hello?' he said.

'Mr Spencer?'

Dexter knew who it was but pretended not to. 'Speaking,' he stated, waiting for the obvious reply.

'It's Viktor Lebedev, we met yesterday.'

'Oh yes, how are you Viktor?'

'Very good, yourself?'

'Same, thank you.'

'Mr Spencer, I met with my manager after you left, I detailed your proposal. He gave it some consideration; said he'd like to meet with you to perhaps discuss the matter further?'

Dexter had to sound a little enthused and excited. 'That would be fantastic,' he said. 'When were you thinking, considering my limited time here?'

'Are you busy today?'

'I was going to the Otkritie Arena, what time were you thinking?'

'What about 11:30 pm?'

Dexter had to think about that one, had to see if it could fit into his schedule. 'Yes, that's fine, don't have to be there until 2 pm anyway,' he said.

'Okay, thank you Mr Spencer, look forward to it.'

Dexter said goodbye and put the phone on the kitchen top. He went to the refrigerator to get the milk. On the way to the couch, he wondered if Lebedev had got the memory card and seen the photos of the bank on there? That could be a problem, he thought, the images of Tower Bridge and the Tower Hill from last week could be explained, snaps of an institution from the previous day? That's going to be a difficult one.

'Mr Spencer, your taxi is here,' Maxim said, over the intercom.

'Coming,' Dexter said.

The look was casual, but not too casual. An Oxford blue shirt over a brown merino sweater seemed to work, as did the dark grey trousers with tan shoes. It looked sporting – in a business way – which was the whole point. The fact that nobody was following the taxi was also a good sign, it meant that he was to be trusted, something you probably have to earn in these circumstances.

'Good morning,' Irina said, in impeccable broken English, it almost seemed as if the poor girl had been ordered to practice the greeting.

'Доброе утро, *(Good Morning)*' Dexter replied, with a smile.

Dexter didn't even have time to wait before Viktor raced from his office towards him. 'Mr Spencer, good morning, tea, coffee?'

'No thank you,' Dexter said.

'Please, come,' Viktor ushered Dexter to his office. He closed the door behind him and sat down. 'Please,' he said, indicating the one and only vacant chair. 'Mr Sokolova will be here soon.'

'You have a meeting at Spartak?' Viktor asked, as they waited.

'Have to check the venue out,' Dexter answered, truthfully.

'I'm more a PFC CSKA Moscow man myself,' Viktor joked, as the door opened.

Viktor stood up and greeted the incoming gentleman. 'Good morning Mr Sokolova,' he said, before introducing him to Dexter.

'Nice to meet you Mr Spencer,' he said, in impeccable English.

Dexter reciprocated the greeting. 'You too Mr ......' he said.

'Call me Sergei, please,' Sergei smiled. 'We can go to my office,' he said, as Viktor went and opened the door. 'Thank you, Viktor,' he added, as Viktor held the door open.

Dexter nodded in acknowledgement as he passed Viktor, before following Sergei to his office on the other side of the bank.

As expected, it was in direct contrast to Viktor's. This was the real deal. It was furnished in an opulent way. There were books and shelves. Paintings were on the wall in gold frames. The colour was a light grey with splashes of green and orange here and there. A leather couch was along one side of a wall. 'Sit down Mr Spencer,' Sergei said, as he took his jacket off. Dexter sat in one of the chairs, even they were different, being upholstered and comfortable. 'So, Viktor informed me of your visit, can you tell me a little more?' Sergei had that look about him, a man not to be messed with. He was probably late forties, dark, swarthy, with greying at the temples. Dexter had to be careful, he probably knew his stuff when it came to sport.

'Well, my company are looking to promote sports here. We have assets and can invest, in the right bank, that is,' Dexter stated, not being too enthusiastic. He then waited for the magic word. It came on cue.

'Cash?'

'Cash,' Dexter confirmed.

Sergei sat back. 'How much?'

'That has to be decided, but not less than a million in sterling.'

Why us?'

'Don't trust the state banks,' Dexter answered, with confidence.

Sergei nodded in agreement. 'Yes' he sighed, 'some still stuck in the past.'

'The football takes care of itself, but I think boxing will be a success here, after all Russia loves its boxers, right?'

You could hear the excitement as Sergei replied. 'We have some of the best,' he said.

Dexter knew by the tone that the proposition would be accepted, I mean, who wouldn't want to be involved in the boxing fraternity? 'I have an appointment soon, when can we make the first deposit?'

'When you are ready Mr Spencer.'

'When I return to London, I'll arrange something.' Dexter stood up. 'Nice meeting you Sergei,' he said.

'You too Mr Spencer, I hope we can enjoy much success together.'

On the way out Dexter noticed a rather striking painting on the wall. It was a young lady posing on a chair, looking sideways. It was bright and colourful 'Nice,' he commented.

'An original,' Sergei announced, proudly.

'Russian artist?'

'Pyotr Konchalovsky.'

Though Dexter had never heard of him, he feigned an interest. He walked up to the painting. 'Must be worth a bit,' he said.

Sergei came and stood next to him. He took out a cigarette and lit it. 'Millions, but you know something, I would never sell it.'

'You like art?'

'With this piece, it's not so much the art, more the history that surrounds it.'

Even though he didn't really know what Sergei meant, Dexter nodded his head in agreement. He looked at his watch. 'Have to go,' he said.

'Have a good day Mr Spencer.'

'Thank you, you too,' Dexter said, as he left the room.

'Thank you,' Irina said, as Dexter walked to the entrance.

'Спасибо, *(Thank you)*' Dexter said, halting at the door. It was raining, and heavy. He went outside, sheltering under the doorway until he saw a taxi drive past.

Maxim heard the car and came with an umbrella, Dexter thanked him, as he cowered under to keep dry from the taxi to the apartment block. 'Thank you,' Dexter said, when they reached the reception.

As Dexter walked to the lift, Maxim called his name. 'Mr Spencer?'

Dexter turned around. 'Yes Maxim?' he asked.

Maxim walked over to his desk, he reached into a drawer and held up something. 'I believe this is yours?'

It was the memory card. 'Dexter walked to the desk. 'Thank you, Maxim,' he said, without asking where he found it or got it from.

'There was suspicious behaviour last night Mr Spencer, we will always take necessary steps to protect our guests,' came the brief explanation. Dexter walked back to the lift. 'Oh, one other thing Mr Spencer.'

'Yes Maxim?'

'Some good news. A lady asked about you today. She told me to give you this, this time he took a piece of paper from his pocket. He went to the lift and gave it to Dexter, who unfolded it. It was from Natalia: *call me before you leave for London, please*, her telephone number was written underneath.

Though it wasn't professional, Dexter felt a friendship forming with Maxim. 'Do you have an interest in the arts?'

'Very much so Mr Spencer.'

'Do you know this painting?' Dexter showed him the picture he had taken of the piece in Sergei's office.

Maxim smiled. 'Portrait of Khulita Perekacho, by Pyotr Konchalovsky. Wow, Mr Spencer, where did you see this, which gallery? This is an exceedingly rare and sought-after painting.'

'The artist is popular?'

Pyotr Konchalovsky? Of course.'

'Why?' Dexter asked, trying to understand what Sergei meant when he said he was more interested in the history than the actual portrait.

'Because he was a member of a renowned group of Moscow artists.'

'Did they have a name?'

'They were called "The Jack of Diamonds."'

'Thank you, Maxim,' Dexter said, finally entering the lift. '*Russia,*' he sighed, as the antiquated lift rattled its way to the second floor.

Inside the apartment Dexter kicked off his shoes and relaxed on the sofa. It wasn't even 12:30 pm, *not bad for a morning's work*, he thought, pleased with the progress thus far. He realised that he needed a couple of more days in the Russian capital, tomorrow was too early to leave. There were sights to see, and things to do, he had to take this opportunity. Anyway, he had made many inroads and had leads Jasper would be more than delighted with. He plugged in the laptop and e-mailed Mike to say that he had met Sergei Sokolova. He then e-mailed Jasper to say that he was staying two more days.

'Going to the Otkritie Arena at 2 pm, booked a tour, would you like to join me?'

'Don't you remember what I told you yesterday?' Natalia asked.

Dexter suddenly remembered. 'Of course, good luck with tonight's performance,' he said.

'What time are you leaving tomorrow?'

'I'm not,' Dexter announced, in a triumphant way. 'Staying for another two days.'

'Then we can meet tomorrow afternoon if you want? Go to a photography gallery.'

This was music to Dexter's ears. 'Where? You have one in mind?'

'Not off hand, but I'll find one, you can have a look as well, if you're not busy.......' Her voice trailed off.

'Natalia?'

'Was thinking.'

'About?'

'Why don't you come and see the performance tonight? That's if you want?'

'If I want? Natalia, I'd love to. But you don't sound too sure about it.'

'To be honest, on the first night, I don't invite friends or family, but.….'

'But?'

'Well, this is different, I guess. The actual performance starts at 8 pm, but be there earlier, go to the box office, I'll leave a ticket there. What's your second name?'

'Spencer, Dexter Spencer.'

'Okay Dexter, hopefully see you later, meet me by the stage door about half an hour after the ending.'

Dexter said he would, before saying good luck again and terminating the call. After a quick change into something more casual he decided to walk to the nearest metro station: Kropotkin kaya. Exiting the lift Maxim said there was a situation: 'Similar to the other day,' he said, nodding his head in the direction of the window.

Dexter understood what he meant. 'Got it,' he uttered, as he put the rucksack on his back.

Aware of the man following him, Dexter grabbed a coffee on the way. He could have given him the slip, but what's the point? He had nothing to hide. Once inside the station Dexter felt like he was truly in Russia. It's the same wherever he travels in the world, only when he is amongst the workers - the people who travel to and from their occupations - does it feel like he's in the country. There was a change at Lubyanka before continuing to Spartak. *Spartak metro station is something else,* Dexter thought, as he disembarked from the train. There was a slight football theme, but what impressed most was the light and cleanliness of it. Outside was less impressive, there was nothing to note about this suburb in the northwest part of the city. As Dexter approached the stadium, he turned around 180% to observe the bleak landscape. The man was at the station on his phone, *probably told to just sit and wait*, he thought, as he went inside the entrance to meet his personal tour guide.

Nicholai was waiting by the reception desk. A blond man - probably late thirties – he seemed more than pleased with his new guest. 'Not many English travel here?' he said, eagerly shaking Dexter's hand.

'I'm surprised,' Dexter replied, a little sarcastically.

'You English, so funny,' Nicolai said, before becoming more formal and professional. 'So, welcome to the Otkritie Arena Mr Spencer.'

'Pleasure,' Dexter said. 'One question?' he added.

'Of course.'

'Is photography allowed?'

'For tours, yes,' Nicholai replied.

Dexter took out his SLR camera. 'Ready when you are,' he said.

The tour was interesting. It was a new stadium and like the metro stations, efficient and well kept. The players' changing room was good, as was the tunnel, pitch and the monument to the Starostin brothers. Dexter even got Nicholai to take a picture of him sitting in the dugout, but it was the press lounge and the luxury box that Deter really wanted to see. 'Nice view?' Nicholai asked, as Dexter seated himself in a prime location overlooking the pitch.

'Very nice,' he purred, snapping away.

'The cream of Moscow sits here,' Nicholai announced proudly.

'Can you see the Spartak metro station from here?' Dexter asked.

'Of course, you can see everything from here. Come, let me show you.' Dexter followed, as Nicholai took him to a window. 'I'll let you guess where the station is,' he smiled.

It wasn't that difficult. The man was waiting outside the entrance, in the same spot as where he was before. Dexter zoomed in and took a few snaps. 'Do like panoramic shots,' he said.

On the way back to reception Nicholai was showing off his impressive knowledge of English football. *If only we reciprocated the same detail*, he thought, listening attentively. 'I love football,' he concluded, as they reached the desk.

'Which team do you like in England?'

The answer was predictable. 'Chelsea,' Nicholai said.

'Thank you for everything,' Dexter said, as they shook hands.

'You too Mr Spencer, thank you for coming.'

Dexter could see Nicolai was sad to see him go. He felt the same way sometimes, there are some people who you just enjoy their company, and you don't want to see them go. There had been many times when the thought of not seeing someone again – especially someone you meet in another country - was too much for him. Then again, maybe that's the reason why you enjoy their company in the first place, who knows, it's still sad though. Dexter tried to recall when it last happened, he suddenly remembered: it was Alina – the jazz singer in Paris, not too long ago. As Dexter walked from the stadium he turned around. Nicholai was standing just inside the reception doors. He waved. Dexter waved back, before turning around and walking to Spartak metro station.

The man threw his cigarette on the floor then abruptly entered the station when he noticed Dexter approaching. On the platform Dexter looked at a booklet Nicholai had given him as part of the tour. It was the history of the club, how they were formed, and who were the notable players to have worn the red and white shirt of Moscow's most decorative club. It was a good read on the way back to central Moscow. It was a nicely presented piece of literature and must have looked important to an observer, almost as if he had just had an important meeting with the cream of Moscow.

As Dexter exited Kropotkin kaya and walked home, he noticed the man had gone, his job obviously completed. Sergei would ask what he witnessed. The man would say he saw Dexter take the train to The Otkritie Arena, enter the reception, stay for an hour, leave, wave to a member of staff and read what looked like an important booklet on the train back. Dexter smiled. *It must have looked good*, he thought.

'What did you think Mr Spencer?' Maxim asked.

'Nice stadium,' Dexter said, walking straight to the lift. He was a little tired, he'd absorbed a lot of information up to now. He now needed to go and rest before the trip to the Bolshoi.

In the room Dexter checked out the images. There were some good ones of him in the luxury box. Nicholai wasn't that bad a photographer. He looked closely at them, familiarising himself with the interiors, just in case he was asked any questions. The man at the station was important as well. He zoomed in on his face and took a picture with his phone. It was a face he hadn't seen before. After switching the camera off he took out the memory card, just in case.

'Taxi for you Mr Spencer,' Maxim said, a little while later.

'Coming,' Dexter replied.

He took a look in the mirror. The light blue brushed cotton shirt from Budd London looked cool with his suit jacket and dark blue jeans. After a splash of Penhaligon's cologne he locked the door, again placing a piece of fine hair across the doorframe. Instead of the lift, Dexter decided to mix things up a bit, opting to take the stairs. Dexter asked Maxim what the situation is like?

'Normal Mr Spencer,' he replied.

'Pleased to hear that,' Dexter said.

'Well, if I don't see you in the morning, have a safe flight Mr Spencer.'

'I'm staying on for two more days Maxim.'

Though it was unprofessional, Maxim smiled. 'You must like Moscow,' he said. 'Can I ask you a question Mr Spencer?'

'Of course.'

'The music you play in the evening, who is it?'

'The Who, Quadrophenia, can't live without it.'

Maxim asked how to spell it as he wrote it down. 'Thank you, Mr Spencer,' he said.

Dexter said no problem, before asking what do you give ballet dancers after a show?

'Flowers Mr Spencer.'

'Any particular ones?'

'Roses,' Maxim replied, as the sound of a horn was heard.

'How do you say Florist in Russian?' Dexter asked walking to the door.

'Флорист *(Florist).*'

'Thank you, Maxim, have a good evening,' Dexter said, as he jumped into the waiting taxi. 'A Florist first please driver,' Dexter said. The driver looked at him, a little confused. 'Флорист,' Dexter said.

The driver nodded his head, before starting the engine. Dexter was pleased that his pronunciation was understood. He was also pleased that after looking into the rear-view mirror, he wasn't being tailed. Seems as though he had finally won the trust of Sergei.

'Dexter Spencer,' Dexter repeated, in a monosyllabic tone, for the second time to the lady at the box office. This time she understood, handing him a white envelope with his name written on the front. The exterior of the theatre is impressive enough – especially at night-time when it's all lit up - but nothing prepares you for your first experience of walking into the auditorium. Though a lot smaller than he imagined, Dexter was in awe of the place. The gold and red interiors blended perfectly to create a luxurious feel. Dexter's seat was in the first circle and just to the side of the stage. He sat down and took in the atmosphere, waiting for the performance to begin. Dexter had never been a ballet person, he never really knew anything about it, but since travelling around Eastern Europe and Russia, he'd seen how respected and how much it was a big part of their cultural heritage. Suddenly the low murmur of the crowd was replaced by silence as the lights went down.

Emeralds took about half an hour, Rubies twenty minutes, both had short intermissions. Dexter had goosebumps when he heard Tchaikovsky's Symphony Number 3 in D Major. Natalia floated onto the stage like a butterfly. She had all the poise and grace of a top ballet dancer. Dexter couldn't keep his eyes off her, he was transfixed as he followed her every move. She was dressed in white and was immaculate for the thirty minutes she performed.

Dexter stood and joined in when the dancers came out to acknowledge the standing ovation at the end. Even though the light was on in the auditorium, Natalia didn't look up once, instead choosing to soak up the accolades, *she deserved it*, Dexter thought, continuing to clap He gave Natalia a little time he joined the rest of the punters in the bar afterwards. The flute of champagne he treated himself to was very expensive, Dexter didn't mind, this was a once-in-a-lifetime opportunity, *have to savour it,* he thought. After half an hour he made his way to the stage door. A crowd had gathered, waiting to meet the stars they'd just seen on the stage. The anticipation was similar to how a football player gets treated in Italy or South America, such was the passion. A few of the dancers came out, photographs were taken, and flowers were given, as they politely chatted with the fans. Natalia emerged after a while and Dexter stepped back. She saw him and smiled, before signing autographs. 'Thanks for waiting,' she said, as she came over.

'I thought you were brilliant,' Dexter said. 'More roses?' he asked, handing her the bouquet.

Natalia laughed, as she took them, keeping them separate from the rest. 'Thank you for coming,' she said.

'What do you do with them?'

'Keep them.' She looked at them. 'I'll put them in water when I get home,' she said.

'Thank you for the invite, really enjoyed it, have always wanted to go.'

They walked around the front and sat by the fountain. Natalia was treated like royalty. She apologised for the interruptions as people were in awe of this ballerina. 'How are you getting home?' she asked.

'Taxi,' Dexter answered.

'Me too, come on, let's go.'

As they walked to get a taxi Natalia said she would meet Dexter tomorrow. He gave her his number. 'Don't rush,' he said, knowing she had to rest.

'I'll find an exhibition, we can have some lunch,' she said, as a taxi pulled up.

Dexter opened the door for her. 'That'll be great,' he said. After saying goodbye and closing the door, he watched as it drove off into the Moscow traffic, before hailing one himself.

Maxim was at the desk when Dexter arrived back at the apartment block. 'How's the situation?' he asked.

'Normal Mr Spencer,' came the reply.

Dexter was tired. He said goodnight and took the stairs to the second floor. Before unlocking the door, he kneeled to check the hair. It had gone. *So much for the normal situation,* he thought, putting the key in the lock, and opening the door. Continuing the evening's good fortune, he made a swift gin and tonic, before sitting down and switching on the laptop. He wrote to Jasper, explaining the morning's events with Sergei at the bank. As he waited for the reply, he played Quadrophenia on his laptop and sat back. Tomorrow was his last day, there were a couple of things he had to do to round things off.

Jasper got back, saying Sebastian had agreed to bankroll the deal. He would transfer an advance of two hundred and fifty thousand. Dexter was to collect from an allocated bank in the morning. This time the money was going to be tracked so they would see where it was going and how it was invested. Dexter wrote a brief reply, acknowledging the e-mail. He finished the drink, turned up the music a little, before deciding to make another. "The Real Me," sounded so good Dexter had to increase the volume a little.

# Chapter Seventeen

Dexter woke up at 6 am on the dot. Though a little hungover, the first thing he did was go to the laptop. Jasper had sent over the details of which bank the money would be deposited. He added that it was a state bank that had a net profit of ninety-four billion dollars last year so it wouldn't look suspicious. Dexter wondered about security, travelling around Moscow with a quarter of a million in cash isn't the best of moves. Not wanting to go through Maxim, he looked for nearby taxi firms. Writing down the number of one, he went and took a cold shower to liven up. After eating there was a couple of hours to spare before he could call Viktor. Listening to a Russian language lesson his phone rang. It was a Russian number. 'Hello?'

'Dexter?'

'Natalia?'

'Good morning. Did you sleep well?'

'Not bad,' Dexter answered truthfully. 'You?'

'Woke up at 5 am.'

'Probably because of last night, the adrenaline.'

'You're right, it happens. So, would you like to go to an exhibition?'

'Would love to, have to be in the afternoon though.'

'That's fine, means I can rest a little, let me find something. I'll call you later.'

Dexter put the phone down. It was nearly 9 am, he called the RIB, hoping someone was there. 'Русский Международный Банк' *(Russian International Bank).*

Yes, Dexter thought, getting to his feet. 'Доброе утро, можно мне поговорить с Виктором Лебедевым?' (*Good morning, can I talk to Viktor Lebedev?*)

'Кто это?' *(Who is this?)*

Dexter recognised the voice. It was Irina. 'It's Dexter, Englishman, came yesterday.'

'Wait, one moment,' came the instruction.

After a few minutes Viktor came to the phone. 'Mr Spencer?'

'Viktor, good morning. I am leaving in a couple of days, tomorrow I am busy, so I need to make a deposit today, is that okay?'

'No problem Mr Spencer.'

'Will have to be this morning.'

'Cash?'

'Cash.'

'I will be here.'

'Good, thank you, see you soon.'

Dexter punched the air. He had to tell Viktor he was leaving in a couple of days as opposed to tomorrow as a safety buffer just in case anything went wrong. He had one clean shirt left. It was a light grey one from DAKS in Jermyn Street. After taking off his t-shirt he looked into the large gold-framed mirror above the fireplace. Despite no training for a few days, he looked in good shape, sometimes it's good to take a break, but not for too long. He went and opened the curtains. The coast was clear, so to speak. The shirt went perfect with the jeans and perfect for the glorious sunny day that he could see was going to happen.

He called the taxi and charged the phone while he waited. He told the driver to wait on the main road, there was no need to come to the door, he would see when it arrived and would come out. Ten minutes later he noticed the car pull up. He grabbed his camera, put in in the rucksack, unplugged his phone then locked the door. 'Good morning Maxim,' he said, passing through reception.

'Mr Spencer, good morning sir.'

'Can't stop, in a rush, have a good day.'

'You too Mr Spencer,' Maxim uttered, to a fleeting Dexter, who was already out the door.

The driver could speak a little English, so Dexter did not have to explain details too much. One thing he didn't do was mention the word bank. Instead, he named a shop around the corner and told him to wait for him there. 'A few minutes,' he said, closing the door.

The receptionist was expecting Dexter, telling him to take a seat. A few minutes later a silver-haired man in his early fifties took Dexter into a room where he counted the cash in front of him. 'Two hundred and fifty thousand, sterling,' he said. As requested it was in fifty-pound notes. They looked new so took up less space. The man looked on in amazement as Dexter placed them neatly in his rucksack as he was handed each bundle. When that was full, he put the rest in the bag he'd bought some groceries from. Dexter put the rucksack over his shoulder and picked up the bag. 'Thank you,' he said. Before the man could answer Dexter was walking out the door. Dexter got in the back seat and mentioned another shop around the corner from the RIB. He paid the driver the fare and gave him a tip. 'Спасибо,' *(Thank you)* he said, before getting out of the car. He went into a shop until he saw the car drive off in the direction of the city centre. Once out of sight, Dexter bought a bottle of water, then headed to the bank around the corner.

As he approached the door, he saw Irina get up and walk to the back. Dexter took a seat in the reception area, before Irina returned with Viktor. 'Mr Spencer, good morning,' Viktor said. 'Would you like a hand?' he added, referring to the bag Dexter was carrying.

'It's okay, can we go somewhere?'

'My office,' Viktor said, leading the way.

As the cash was being counted Sergei came in. He had some luggage with him. 'Just came to say hello Mr Spencer. I have to go away for a while, Viktor will look after you.'

'Anywhere nice?'

'Unfortunately, it's for business, not pleasure,' Sergei lamented not answering the question. 'How did the meeting go yesterday?' Dexter looked a little puzzled, not recalling any meeting. 'At Spartak?'

'Oh, yes, briefly discussed a few things, in the initial stages, but they are very keen,' Dexter answered, seeing that Sergei was impressed.

He handed Dexter his business card. 'Keep me updated. I should be in London in a few weeks.'

'Business or pleasure?'

Sergei lit a cigarette and inhaled. He then waited a few seconds. 'Both,' he answered, exhaling a mass of deep blue smoke.

Viktor rushed to open the door for him. 'Have a good journey Mr Sokolova,' he said. After closing the door Viktor came back and attended to Dexter. 'Now, where were we?' he smiled.

Dexter suddenly remembered his camera. 'Wait,' he said, running to the door. Sergei was talking to Irina at the desk. 'Mr Sokolova?'

Sergei turned around. 'What is it Mr Spencer?'

'Sorry, if you wouldn't mind.' Dexter held up his camera. 'I need a picture?'

Sergei laughed. 'A picture? What for?'

'Well, I know it sounds a bit stupid, but I always take photographs of business ventures, especially something like this. Will show my bosses, anyway, it's not only the business side, I have such good shots of Footballers, Boxers, and Golfers. You like golf? Maybe we can organise a golfing tournament here, now that's big money. Here let me take your case.' Dexter pushed the luggage behind Irina's desk. He saw the travel label tied on the handle. Departure was from Moscow; the arrival was Eindhoven.

'Hurry, my car is here,' Sergei said, adjusting his tie.

Viktor was at his office door. 'You as well Viktor,' Dexter shouted, beckoning him over. He gave the camera to Irina. 'All you have to do is press this,' he said, indicating a button. Dexter stood in the middle as Irina took a couple of shots. 'One second guys,' he said, as he checked the images. 'You are a natural Irina,' he smiled.

Dexter wheeled Sergei's case to him. 'Thank you, Mr Sokolova, have a safe trip.' Sergei gestured with his hand as he walked out to his waiting car. Dexter turned to Viktor: 'Shall we finish?'

Viktor was beaming. The photoshoot had obviously gone to his head. 'Of course, Mr Spencer,' he said. After the cash was counted Dexter said he had another appointment. 'Where to this time Mr Spencer?' Viktor asked.

Dexter really wanted to say to meet a ballerina of the Bolshoi but had to think about Natalia. He could risk her, and besides, he had to be respectful, not everyone was as keen for publicity as Sergei and Viktor. 'Just an artist friend, nothing exciting I'm afraid,' he replied.

As he was leaving there was a knock at the door. Viktor went to answer. 'Yes?' he asked.

'It's Michail,' came the muffled reply.

Viktor opened the door. 'Good timing,' he said.

Michail walked in and looked at Dexter, who held out his hand. 'Dexter Spencer,' he said.

'Michail Andreyev.'

'Michail will be working with me,' Viktor announced. 'Though his English isn't that great,' he added.

'Another member of the team?'

'You could say that' Victor frowned.

'This calls for a photograph,' Dexter said, bringing out his camera again. 'Have to set the self-timer.' He put the camera on the desk. 'Quick, we have twenty seconds,' he added, as the three of them huddled together. Dexter checked the images. 'Great,' he smiled. 'My bosses will love this. Anyway, have to go. I'm leaving for London the day after tomorrow, so hopefully we can meet before then?'

'That will be possible Mr Spencer, anytime,' Viktor said, as he and Michail began to collect the cash from the table.

'Goodbye Irina,' Dexter said, as he passed through the reception.

'Goodbye Mr Spencer,' she replied, with a smile.

'Hey, big improvement,' Dexter said, commenting on her pronunciation.

Back at the apartment Dexter downloaded the images. He sat back and looked at them. He liked the compositions as much as the content. The settings were almost perfect. The shots had captured the moment. They were all smiling, happy with their new acquaintances without knowing what the other was really up to: or did they? Though Dexter had said that he was leaving the day after tomorrow, did they know the truth? Were they letting him convince them? He knew that now cash had been exchanged he had to be extra careful. The hair had gone again so someone was checking the room. Today and tonight vigilance had to be observed. He looked out the window, the situation was normal. He set up the speakers and played Suede as he took a shower. "*The Beautiful Ones*," sounded eerie as he stood there, thinking about Natalia whilst keeping his eye on the door. The phone rang as Dexter was drying himself. He quickly ran to the lounge to answer it. 'Hello?'

'Dexter, it's Natalia.'

'Hi Natalia, how are you? Rested?'

'Yes, I got a little more sleep. Still want to meet?'

'Of course, I do,' Dexter responded, immediately and without hesitation.

'Great. Let's meet midday at The Arts Centre in Winzavod.'

Dexter had been there before. It was a cool and arty part of town. 'No problem see you soon,' he said.

Maxim asked where he was going, something he had never asked before. This was strange, unusual - as well as unprofessional. Dexter had to just be normal, play the part, so as not to arouse any suspicions. This is Russia, and anyone can be bought, at any price. 'Bit of sightseeing,' he answered, holding up his camera.

Dexter left the building. Nothing seemed to be amiss, the situation seemed normal, maybe Sergei had been convinced, or maybe now he had the money he didn't really care.

The exhibition was in an old winery building. The photographer was Igor Posner. He was Russian, from St. Petersburg, but went to America to study. The images were different, purposely being slightly out of focus. Dexter liked them. Natalia said she needed a coffee. 'I know I shouldn't, should be drinking lots of water but....'

Dexter smiled. 'Don't worry, treat yourself,' he said.

'So, what have you been up to today?' Natalia asked, as they sat outside a café.

'Not a lot, just a visit to the bank, then to drop something off, little boring really,' he answered.

'What was it you said you did again?'

'Visiting, I like Russia, haven't seen as much of it as I'd like to, but still enjoy coming, even for a couple of days.' Dexter tried the coffee, as expected, it was good. 'Have you been to London?'

'No. I go mainly to New York; we have ties with The New York Ballet Company. Been to Paris, Athens, Beijing, but never London.'

'You'll like it. The Royal Ballet is in Covent Garden, The English National Ballet has a new home, in the East End.'

'And Sadler's Wells?'

'That's a venue, there are many. Did you like Paris?'

Natalia tilted her head backwards as she answered. 'Loved it,' she exclaimed.

'Heard the French invented ballet,' Dexter joked.

'True, a lot of people think it comes from here. 'Need to send someone a text, excuse me for a moment,' she said. A few seconds later Dexter's phone made a noise. He ignored it. 'Your phone,' Natalia said.

Dexter reluctantly took out his phone, there was a text from Natalia. *"There is a man to your right in a blue shirt, he was watching me before you arrived, and has been looking ever since,"* it said.

"It's okay, I'll look in a minute. Thank you," he replied.

They spoke about the photography exhibition and their love of photography. Dexter asked if he could take some pictures of her? 'Sure,' she said. 'Here?'

Dexter took out his camera and focused on her face. She was pretty, one of these dark-haired ballerinas he'd only seen on television. He took a couple of shots. 'Love that noise,' he said, referring to the quick succession of the shutter. 'Reminds me of that Duran Duran song, "Girls on Film," you know it?' Natalia turned her head from left to right, smiling, then from right to left not smiling. 'Okay let's exchange sides,' he said.

'Okay,' Natalia obliged.

Dexter got the man in the background and set the focus on him, taking a few snaps before concentrating on Natalia again. 'Nice,' he said, as they went back to the previous seating arrangement.

'He's coming,' she whispered.

Dexter heard what she said but continued to click the button without saying anything. The man walked slowly past the table, and into the café. Dexter saw him head towards the bathroom. After a few seconds he stood up. 'Excuse me,' he said.

There was no noise as Dexter opened the bathroom door slowly. The man was in the cubicle, talking on a phone. Dexter closed the door, stood at the side, and listened. He couldn't quite decipher what was being said, so he pressed record on his mobile phone. After a few minutes the man flushed the toilet and opened the door. As he walked to the mirror he saw Dexter in the reflection, but it was too late. The arm came from behind and around the throat. Dexter's right leg swung around, toppling the man off balance. As he tried to steady himself to retaliate Dexter had him up against the basin, head against the mirror, facing him. 'Who are you? And why are you following me?' he asked, quiet and assured.

The man spoke in Russian for a few moments before ending with 'I no speak English.'

'Last time and be quick, who are you?'

'Okay, leave me, I tell you.'

With the right hand pinning him up against the wall, Dexter patted him down with his left. In the waistband he felt something. He took out the gun and quickly emptied the bullets into the sink. Dexter kept the gun as he loosened the grip. 'And?'

'My name is Pavel.'

Dexter tightened his grip as he took out some documents from the inside pocket of his jacket. There was a driving licence. 'Pavel Arsenyev?'

'That's me.'

'What are you doing following me?'

'I was sent.'

'By whom?'

'By no one.'

Dexter picked up one of the bullets from the basin and inserted it into the magazine. He spun it around before pointing it at the man's head. 'You better be quick, my coffee's getting cold.'

'I was sent by Viktor.'

Dexter knew this wasn't true. How did Viktor know about Natalia? There was only one person who knew about her. 'One last time,' Dexter said, pulling back the hammer.

'Okay, Maxim.'

'That's better. What's the reason?'

'He told me about the girl coming to the apartment and giving you her number. He recognised her from the Bolshoi, wanted to know what was happening with you two.'

Dexter didn't believe him, but this wasn't the time or place to debate. He took out a few fifty-pound notes. 'Now you tell Maxim you lost track of me, okay?'

The man smiled. 'Of course,' he said.

Dexter took out the bullet from the magazine and collected the others from the basin. 'Here,' he said. The man fixed himself in the mirror. 'One more thing my friend.' The man looked at Dexter in the mirror. 'I'm here for a couple more days.' He handed the man a couple of more notes. 'No more following today, okay?'

'Sure.'

After the man left, Dexter fixed himself up. He took a couple of deep breaths before re-joining Natalia. 'Where did you go?' she asked.

'Had to wait.'

'Some good news.'

'Which is?'

'That man has gone.'

'Has he?' Dexter looked around. 'So he has,' he said, with a wry smile.

'He just walked past, smiled at me, said have a good day, why was he so happy I wonder?'

'May have recognised you.' Dexter took a sip of the cold remaining coffee. 'You must get recognised, being a member of the Bolshoi?'

'This is my first major role, so apart from after last night's performance no, not really.'

Dexter remembered Pavel saying that Maxim had recognised her. 'Never?' he asked.

'Only from people that go to ballet.' She admitted, taking the last sip of her coffee. 'Well, have to go and prepare.'

They both waited a few minutes before standing up. 'Are you taking a taxi?' Dexter asked.

'Think I'll take the metro,' Natalia replied.

For some reason Dexter felt a little uneasy about her choice but didn't say anything. 'I'll walk with you,' he said.

Kurskaya metro was no more than a fifteen-minute walk. On the way Dexter told her that he was leaving in the morning. 'Do you want to come tonight?'

As much as he wanted to Dexter declined. 'Have to prepare to travel,' he said.

'I understand. There's talk of the production going on tour, London will definitely be included, depends how it's received here first though.'

'Well, if last night's reception was anything to go by, I'm sure it will be successful.'

'That reminds me, have to buy *Argumenty i Fakty (Arguments and Facts)* tomorrow, see the review,' Natalia said.

Dexter walked with her inside the foyer. 'Well, good luck tonight,' he said.

Natalia held out her hand. Dexter kissed it. 'Thank you,' she said.

After saying goodbye Dexter watched as she went into the platform area. *What a station*, he thought, taking in the splendour before walking out of the station.

Deciding to walk home, he rested on some steps just outside the station. He felt a little sad as he looked towards the station, thinking of Natalia. He'd love to stay and chill out with her, go to some jazz clubs as well as art galleries. As he turned around, ready to go, he noticed something, there was a man hurrying towards the entrance. It was Pavel Arsenyev. Dexter hastened as fast as he could, almost breaking into a jog. He had to buy a ticket first, after which he headed to the platform. As he heard the doors closing, he ran to the train, but unlike the London underground the doors didn't open. He banged on the side of the train as it departed.

Outside he called Natalia, but couldn't get a reception, so he sent a message: *call me as soon as you get this, it's urgent,'* it said.

Dexter's relaxing amble on his last day in Moscow had to be put on hold as he went back to the steps, waiting for his phone to ring. After half hour he tried again, this time it rang. 'Natalia?'

'Yes, Dexter, just arrived home, was about to call you.'

'Did you get my message?'

'Yes, what has happened?'

'That man who was at the café, after I left you, I saw him walking into the station.'

'Oh, I didn't see anyone.'

Dexter had to decide whether he should tell her why he's in Moscow, after giving it some thought, he decided not to. She had to perform tonight; he didn't want to cause her any worry. Anyway, Pavel might have been rushing to get home, thousands of people use the metro. 'Okay, was just a bit worried, that's all, may have been a stalker.'

Natalia laughed. 'Don't be Dexter, that sort of thing doesn't really happen here, not in ballet anyway.'

'Well, have a good performance, I'll call you in the morning before I leave.'

'What time is your flight?'

The departure was 08:40 am, but Dexter added a few hours. '2:40 pm,' he said.

'Okay, call me then.'

Dexter felt relieved after saying goodbye and hanging up. Now he could enjoy the stroll back to the apartment.

He paused a few times along the river, taking it in, looking into the water. It was starting to get cold and he decided to head straight back to the apartment.

'Good afternoon Mr Spencer,' Maxim said, as Dexter walked through the door.

Dexter remained calm as he replied. 'Good afternoon Maxim,' he said. When am I booked in here until, have forgotten?'

'Let me see.' Maxim took out a logbook from a drawer. 'The day after tomorrow Mr Spencer.'

'That's not long, only one more full day here. Dexter sighed. 'Any suggestions what I can do tomorrow?'

'There are many things to do Mr Spencer. Besides photography, what are your interests?'

'Architecture,' Dexter promptly replied.

'Do you like shopping?'

'Sometimes.'

'Then maybe you should visit The GUM,'

'Been there,' Dexter said, in reference to the opulent shopping mall on Red Square.

'Then what about The Sandunovsky Bath House?'

'You know what, after today I could do with some pampering, excellent idea,' Dexter said.

'What has happened today Mr Spencer?' Maxim asked.

Dexter walked over to the desk, putting both his hands on the top he leaned over. 'A lot, but I did learn one thing though.'

'Which is?'

'That it's a small world, and there are some people you can never trust.' Dexter straightened himself up. 'Know what I mean?'

'For sure Mr Spencer,' Maxim nervously responded.

Dexter walked to the lift without saying anything. The situation had now changed, you could feel it in the air. The wait for the lift to arrive seemed to take longer than usual, in reality it took the same time, but the ambience had shifted, had taken on a different perspective.

The hair had gone. It didn't bother Dexter anymore, the only thing he had to make sure of was keeping himself safe. *It was going to be one long night*, he thought, as he opened the door.

It was time for a blast of gin and tonic, accompanied by Quadrophenia. "*I am The Sea*", sounded good as Dexter headed for the shower. Leaving the door ajar he kept a careful eye on the hallway. He was being observed, he knew that. All he could do was carry on regardless, act normal, see how it plays out. He brought the gin with him, taking sips as he lathered up some Truefitt and Hill sandalwood shower gel and invigorated himself.

The hair across the laptop wasn't there either, but there wasn't anything on the hard drive. An important rule is this business was to transfer the data before deleting it. After checking the door to see if it was locked, he took out the memory card from the camera. The images of Natalia were tempting, but first was business. The photos of Sergei, Michail and Viktor looked good. Even better was the RIB sign in the background. That was unintentional but added to it. Dexter wondered if they knew and played along with it? Or would they be angry that they had been duped? Maybe neither, maybe they thought that Dexter was who he said he was, a promoter from London with bags of cash and a way to meet sports stars, something that seemed to enlighten them.

He had captured Natalia naturally. Her face was bathed in the dusky Moscow sun. He particularly liked the side shots and one where she's holding up the cup - about to take a drink of coffee - and smiling. The fact that Pavel was clearly visible in the background was a bonus. After saving, he deleted them from the memory card. The only ones left were from the bank and of Natalia.

He sent Jasper an e-mail, saying he was returning tomorrow and would come and see him the following day for an update. After sending an e-mail to Mike saying that he was looking forward to some training, he logged out. He also sent an image of Pavel, asking if he knew of him. You never know who knows who in this game. Sitting back, he thought about the training, and though it had only been a few days, he felt rusty. Putting the drink down, he changed the music to traditional Chinese and practised some Tai Chi. He felt more centred after. The Qi Gong had left him focused and relaxed. Putting Quadrophenia back on he made another drink before arranging a taxi for the airport. 'Corner of Ulitsa Lenivka and Volkhonka, 3 am,' he said, to the controller. Dexter went out to get something to eat. Maxim wasn't at the desk when he left or when he returned.

Back in the room Dexter looked at the time, it was 8 pm. The plan was simple: stay in, stay awake, pack the suitcase, and get to the airport.

Jasper and Mike both got back with replies. Jasper kept it brief. *Great*, it said. *Will go to Ronnie Scott's.* Mike's was more detailed: *Pavel Arsenyev, met him a few times, ex KGB, they had to let him go, a bit clumsy, got caught out on a few jobs. Doing the rounds as a private hire. Only thing he's got going for him is that he's determined, so expect another visit from him. Stay safe and hopefully see you at training.*

Dexter spent the evening wishing he had gone to the Bolshoi, but he would have been too tired to deal with the inevitable. Dexter looked at his watch later it was now 2 am, time to leave soon, he thought as pulled the curtains open a little and lay on the couch. The light of the streetlamps, filtering through the gap added to the eerie silence and waited. On cue, he heard a noise. Rolling from the couch, he gingerly tip-toed to the front door. The light from the hallway under the door was suddenly blocked by a shadow. Dexter had a good idea who the uninvited visitor was, so had to be clever. There was a gentle rap on the door. 'Mr Spencer?' Dexter didn't say anything. 'Mr Spencer?' A few seconds later a key was inserted into the lock and the handle turned. Dexter stepped into the bathroom at the side and waited.

Dexter switched the light on. 'Looking for me?' he asked, as he launched into a side kick. The sheer power and speed sent Pavel tumbling. The gun was still in his hand as he fell. Dexter was faster with the next move, one foot landing on the wrist, the other on the neck. 'Well?' Dexter knew the question was futile as Pavel could hardly utter a word. Squeezing on the wrist with his heel, Dexter released the gun from Pavel's ailing grip. 'Make any sound and my foot will sink,' he said, once again unloading the cartridge, leaving one bullet in. 'You just don't listen, do you?'

Acknowledging Dexter's request Pavel nodded his head as much as he possibly could, which – given the circumstances – wasn't that much. Before loosening the grip, Dexter searched his pockets. Some of the cash was left. Dexter was caught in a dilemma, especially after what Mike had said. I mean this guy was probably down on his luck and would take any job. Dexter knew it wasn't personal, he could be anyone. 'How much is Maxim paying you?' Dexter asked, as he stepped back. Pavel held up a few fingers. 'You got kids?'

'Three,' Pavel answered.

'Here,' Dexter said, throwing the money back. 'Where is Maxim?'

Pavel shrugged his shoulders. 'Don't know,' he uttered.

'Does Maxim know Viktor?'

'Yes.'

'Sergei?'

Pavel nodded his head. 'Yes.'

They spoke a while about football and boxing. Dexter then got the telephone, dropped it at Pavel's side, and pointed the gun at his head. 'Tell Maxim, you will be coming down in five minutes,' he said, dialling reception. There was no answer, so Dexter dropped the receiver before having to do something, he really wasn't too fond of. Sensei Tibbs's speciality was how to render someone unconscious for about an hour with one blow. Dexter had only used it once before, and it worked. Pavel couldn't be trusted, even when you pay him. 'Here Dexter said, holding out his hand to help him up. Pavel accepted and as he was half standing, he received a palm strike to the temple area. Dexter caught him as he collapsed before moving him to the couch. After making sure he was safe and breathing he took out the last bullet and threw the gun on the table before wheeling his suitcase to the lift.

'Mr Spencer?' Maxim asked.

'Good evening Maxim. You seem a little surprised, everything okay?'

Maxim stood up. His tone changed. 'Leaving us?'

Yes,' Dexter replied, honestly.

'Any particular reason Mr Spencer?'
'Unwanted guests.'

Maxim came from around the desk and approached Dexter. 'I'm afraid you cannot leave Mr Spencer,' he said, reaching into his jacket pocket.

'Really, why's that?' Dexter asked. Before Maxim could answer Dexter launched into another of Sensei Tibbs's specials, this time a double-spinning kick. The first kick took out the gun, the second – a strike to the head – took out Maxim. Dexter bent down to pick up the gun. 'Very disappointed,' he said, taking out the bullets, before throwing the weapon towards the semi-conscious Maxim. He looked at his watch, it was 2:55 am. 'Adios amigo,' Dexter said, as he wheeled his suitcase towards the door.

The taxi was waiting on the corner. 'Domodedovo?' he asked, as Dexter approached the car.

'да,' *(yes)* Dexter answered.

The driver got out and opened the boot. 'Разрешите,' *(Allow me)* he said, taking the suitcase.

As the engine was ignited Dexter pointed to the Ulitsa Lenivka. 'This way,' he said. The driver understood and drove slowly down towards the apartment. 'Wait,' he said, as he opened the door and got out. He went to the front of the building and threw the bullets. Looking upstairs he could see Maxim in his apartment. Dexter turned around and got back into the taxi. 'Погнали,' *(Lets go)* he said.

The drive to the airport was interesting. Moscow in the early hours is like no other, there was an eerie feel to it, especially the outskirts. Like London it was a tale of two cities, the only difference is that there is some wealth going on in London. The suburban landscape of Moscow seemed pretty grim in comparison. Dexter was going to miss Moscow; he'd grown to like it. Suddenly remembering

Natalia, he sent a text to ask how the performance went. Given the time, he didn't expect an answer until later in the morning.

'Спасибо,' *(Thank you)* the driver said, as Dexter handed over the fare, a tip, and the loose change he'd acquired over the past few days.

Dexter reciprocated.'Спасибо,' he said, when the driver gave him his suitcase.

Even though it was in the early hours the airport was still quite busy. Dexter sat and waited until check-in time. He was getting tired and was thinking about home when an announcement was made. First it was in Russian then in English: The 08:40 am flight to London was delayed. It was now leaving at 12:40 pm. Dexter sighed. *Knew it was too good to be true,* he thought as he stood up and took his jacket off. After taking a sweater from the suitcase and putting it behind his head he threw the jacket over himself before somehow managing a two-hour uninterrupted sleep. Feeling a bit groggy he sat up and went to the bathroom where he threw some cold water on his face.

On the way to the check-in desk Dexter noticed that the Argumenty i Fakty was on sale. Remembering Natalia saying that there would be a review in there he bought a copy. He rolled it up and tucked it under his arm. *Something to read on the plane,* he thought, as he went and checked in.

After the plane made its way upward into the sky, Dexter settled back and opened the newspaper, looking for any pictures of the Bolshoi and its dancers. Near the back there was a photo of Natalia. He smiled, as he looked at her dancing during the performance of Jewels. 'Speak English?' he asked, the man sitting next to him.

'Yes,' came the answer.

'Could you tell me what this says please?' Dexter asked, pointing to a caption under the photograph.

The man took the newspaper. 'Bolshoi ballerina misses last night's performance,' he said, handing the paper back.

Dexter took another look. *No*, he thought, *that can't be true.*

He felt helpless, knowing that he couldn't phone her for at least another four hours.

150

## Chapter Eighteen

*London*
As soon as he could he phoned Natalia, there was no answer. He left a message, saying to call him as soon as possible. Dexter took the Heathrow Express to Paddington then the Bakerloo line to Oxford Circus where he changed to the Victoria southbound to Vauxhall. 'Good afternoon Dexter,' Terence said, greeting him at the door. 'How was it?'

'Was good,' Dexter answered, not wanting to give too much away.

'How do the Concierges compare?' Terence asked, enthusiastically.

'Good question. Let's just say a little different,' Dexter tactfully replied.

'Need any help?'

No, I'm fine thanks Terry. Was up early, flight got delayed, bit tired.'

'No problem Dexter, you go and rest.'

Dexter turned around just before he got to the lift. 'Any news Terry?'

Terence had to think for a minute. 'No Dexter, none,' he said.

Dexter didn't even bother to open his suitcase. He put some Miles Davis on the turntable, took a shower, made a gin and tonic then dived on his bed. It was mid-afternoon and the day was still young, but Dexter knew he had to rest. Not long after the phone rang, thinking it may be Natalia he picked it up and answered it. 'Hello?' he said, in some sort of vain hope.

'Dexter?'

'Jasper.'
'You back?'
'Yeah, not long, flight delayed for four hours.'
'Up for a bit of Ronnie Scott's?'
Dexter sat up. 'Tonight?'
'10 pm?'

Already Dexter felt more invigorated. 'See you then,' he said. Sitting back, he thought of Natalia and tried calling her again. He left another message, asking her to call him.

Dexter walked into the legendary venue at 9:55 pm exactly. He was still on duty and Jasper was still paying him, so he had to be on it. Autumn was on its way, and the evenings were getting a little colder. The black cashmere sweater complimented the smoky grey suit jacket. He took a seat next to Jasper, who shook his hand whilst beckoning the barman over at the same time. 'Gin and Tonic for my friend and…....'

'The Bullshot?' the bartender asked.

The answer was without hesitation. 'Go on then,' Jasper said. As the bartender went to mix up the drinks he turned to Dexter. 'Well, how was it?'

'Let's just say eventful,' Dexter replied, moving his stool closer to Jasper.

The drinks arrived and Jasper picked them up. 'Let's find a table,' he said, leading the way to a table not too far away from the bar. 'So, evidence?'

'Photos of the manager, assistant manager and Leonid Andreyev's brother Michail.'

'Jolly good. Bring them tomorrow.'

Dexter knew Jasper was old school. He was IT savvy, kept records online, but also kept to the traditional method of the business. He wanted hard copies, physical photographs, paper files and such. 'I'll bring them tomorrow,' Dexter said.

'How was the apartment?' Dexter relayed the previous day and evening. Jasper had a little trouble digesting it, asking Dexter to repeat himself a few times. 'Dexter, what have I said about women and business, you could have blown the whole thing.'

Dexter ignored what Jasper had just said. He frowned. 'Still confused about the connection between Pavel and Viktor, whom he sent him when I met Natalia,' he said. 'Was he working for Sergei?' He took a sip of the gin and tonic. It tasted good. 'And Maxim? He changed after a while.'

'I would imagine the man who followed you had a word with him, offered some money, then he sees a Bolshoi ballerina ask for you, tells him, who tells Sergei, who hires Pavel to tail you,' Jasper said, logically.

'So, they are aware that I'm not really a sports promoter but an agent? If so, why did they go along with it, why not say no business to begin with?'

'Cash is an aphrodisiac. It seduces, makes people's perception a little wobbly.' Jasper took a gulp of The Bullshot. 'That's why we use it,' he said, struggling with the words.

'What happens if they did play along to get the money? How are you going to get it back?'

'That's the least of our problems,' Jasper said, as the band were about to play. 'Now we have this, we can work on Nasser and his connections to them. 'Ready for that one?'

The band started to play. The song was a cover: "*Feeling Good*," by Nina Simone. Dexter listened for a few seconds before answering. 'Of course,' he replied.

After a few more drinks they called it a night. Dexter needed a night out on his home turf. He needed to see and feel the familiar surroundings. After Jasper jumped into a cab, he walked down to Piccadilly Circus. The London air felt good and refreshing against his skin. Such was the sensation he decided to continue to Green Park, Victoria then over the bridge to Vauxhall.

Dexter slept well. He woke feeling refreshed after the uninterrupted slumber. After a coffee he unpacked his suitcase. Some clothes were thrown in the washing machine, the others ready for the dry cleaners. Next it was the darkroom. The images of Natalia looked even better. He watched as they dried, wondering if she was okay. Another pleasing factor was that you could see the RIB sign behind Sergei and co. That was one of the magical qualities of photography: the unexpected.

'Good to be back Dexter?' Terence said.

'Very good,' Dexter answered, truthfully, as he walked through reception to hail a taxi.

'Where to Gov?' the driver asked.

Dexter savoured the destination. 'Mayfair please,' he said.

Jasper was pleased. 'Good work,' he said, commenting on the photographs.

'Sergei said he was coming to London in a few weeks,' Dexter said. 'I asked the reason, he said business.'

'Probably wants to meet with Nasser. You'll have to find out when.'

Dexter was still concerned that Sergei knows he's not who he says he is. 'If he tells me.'

Jasper put the photos into a brown file and tied it up. 'You know as well as me, there are so many coincidences in this game. Some people know other people and so on. Always remember what the job entails. Everybody is looking after themselves, it's their livelihood. That Pavel chap may know one thing but won't disclose it to say someone such as Sergei even though he's paying him. Know what I mean?'

'I do,' Dexter said, noting the tone and look on Jasper's face.

'I would say that Sergei thinks you are a bona fide sports promoter who hasn't a clue who you really are, and that Maxim, Pavel and Natalia are a separate issue,' Jasper concluded, throwing the file in a draw and slamming it shut.

Dexter took the hint. Enough had been discussed for today. 'I'll keep you updated,' Dexter said, as he made his way to the door.

Dexter felt like an art exhibition, he needed to cleanse himself of the previous few days and start afresh. Art, sculpture, and photography helped him to do this. He enjoyed the concept of starting out as a blank canvas. He walked towards Piccadilly and the Royal Academy to see Kapoor works again. This time it was something different, which was as good as seeing it the first time, if not better.

He took lunch at the same table. Drinking Earl Grey after he thought about Uba, what she was doing, and when he would see her. He knew Cairo would be soon. Jasper was probably busy organising the trip, putting together the itinerary as well as personal details. He smiled, thinking that Uba may be his wife for a while. It was a pleasant thought, in fact very pleasant. Sitting back Dexter took stock. Of all the jobs, why did he choose this one? Then again, he wouldn't change it for the world. He got up and walked down Piccadilly, taking a right down St. James and into Jermyn Street to buy a shirt.

'Perdi?'

'Dexter?'

'Yes. How are you?'

'I'm good. How was Moscow?'

Dexter was economic with the details. 'Raining, but nice. Any news?'

'On Nasser and Andreyev?'

'Yes.'

'Not really, haven't noticed anything unusual. You?'

'Yes, a little information I found out. Can we meet?' When?'

'Tonight, same time and place as last time?'

'See you then.'

Dexter jumped in a cab, there was some time left before meeting Perdi but he wanted to rest a little at home first. He tried to call Natalia, this time it didn't even ring, going straight onto answer phone. There was nothing online about her not showing up for the performance the other night, or even if she had returned. He searched for any review, again there was nothing. Dexter looked at the three shirts he'd bought. One was navy blue, one pale blue, the other white. He hung them up with the others, thinking they'd look nice in Cairo. After hitting the bench press, he showered and took a taxi up to the Edgeware Road.

'Same place?'

'As last time?' Perdi asked, looking pleased to see Dexter.

'Why not,' Dexter said, walking towards the Lebanese café.

After ordering coffee and sfouf they went and sat down. 'So,' Perdi said, 'what's the news?'

'Sergei's coming to London soon and…….'

Perdi had to interrupt. 'Sorry, who's Sergei?' she asked.

'Oh, sorry, Sergei Sokolova I think owns the RIB - or is high up there - that is also the sister branch of the AIB.'

'Heard of that, is it in the Netherlands?'

'Amsterdam, where Nasser is based a lot of the time…….'

'I don't understand.'

'I haven't finished,' Dexter said, before continuing. 'Leonid Andreyev used to work there.'

'Really!' Perdi exclaimed, as the coffee came.

'And - this is the interesting bit - Nasser specialises in diamonds.' Dexter grimaced as he took a sip of the dark liquid.

Perdi frowned, looking a little perplexed. 'What's so special about diamonds, that's what Amsterdam is famous for,' she said.

'Well, that's where we think the money is being invested.'

'The money from my uncle?'

'Would have been hashish a few years ago, now it's minerals, sounds more glamorous as well.'

'So where is it going to be invested?'

Dexter wasn't going to disclose Cairo at this point, he'd said enough. 'That's what we need to find out,' he said, convincingly.

Perdi sat back. 'Wow, how cool.'

'What is?'

'Your job, must be exciting?'

Dexter sighed. He pondered whether to relay the Moscow trip, but how exciting it would sound the mention of cash, guns and ballerinas may be a little too much. 'Can be,' he humbly answered. Dexter got straight down to business. 'When Sergei comes, he may visit your bank. If you hear anything, let me know.'

'Do you think they are trying to take it over?'

'Definitely will be trying to place more of their people in there, that's for sure.'

'They have to be stopped,' Perdi said, a little emotionally.

'That's the whole point. Who handles the selection process for any job interviews?'

'Nasser.'

'Then they'll start the same process in another bank, and so on and so on.' Dexter could see that Perdi was thinking about Sebastian, so left it at that. 'Here comes the cake,' he said, welcoming the timely arrival.

The coffee and sfouf complemented each other. Dexter was glad he had discovered it and would make this a regular in his routine. He finished before Perdi before attending to the coffee, observing Perdi discreetly as she took her time. Dexter estimated her age to be early to mid-thirties. The well-spoken voice was definitely due to a public-school education, as was the relation to a top London banker. 'Good?' he asked, as Perdi finally finished.

'Very,' she said, taking some coffee. 'Coffee's good as well.'

They spoke for a while about banking. Dexter didn't really know that much about it but was getting there. That's one of the assets of the job. Whatever the assignment, you go through an intense learning process of the dynamics, becoming just as knowledgeable as someone who has a career in it. Dexter also liked that you quickly forget it as you move onto the next case. Perdi asked whether Dexter was married. 'That's personal,' he said, keeping the professional boundaries intact.

Perdi respected – and understood – Dexter's reluctance to disclose personal details. 'Fair enough,' she said. 'Anyway, guess I better be going.'

Dexter walked her to the bus stop. 'Thank you Perdi,' he said, noticing her bus approaching.

'How close are we to getting them?' she asked.

'Getting there,' Dexter answered.

Perdi smiled. 'Hope so,' she said, before getting on the bus.

## Chapter Nineteen

'One more!' Sensei Tibbs ordered, sensing the lack of practice.

Dexter struggled as he went for the extra press-up. 'Oss Sensei,' he yelled.

'That's more like it,' Sensei Tibbs remarked, as Dexter got to his feet before running to join Mike for some sparring.

The training was just the tonic for Dexter. They say a week is a long time in politics, but it's just as relevant for Karate. Dexter was feeling it after as he walked to the car with Mike. 'How was it?' Mike asked.

The first thing Dexter mentioned was the altercation with Pavel and Maxim. 'Don't tell Sensei though,' he said, knowing that wouldn't go down well. Sensei Tibbs is a stickler for not fighting. *'Always walk away,'* is his ethos. Dexter knew he wouldn't but had to make sure.

'Of course, I won't,' Mike confirmed. 'So, how was it?' he repeated.

'Went according to plan. Got some nice evidence. 'Just a bit worried about Natalia that's all,' Dexter admitted.

'She'll be fine. If you dance for the Bolshoi you are like royalty, no one will take the chance. If anything, they may have asked her about you, but that's about it.'

Dexter felt a little reassured by what Mike said. 'Hope so,' he said.

Mike wanted to talk a little more so invited Dexter to sit in his car for a while. He played Chopin's *"24 Preludes, Op. 28: No 15 in D-Flat Major, "Raindrop."* 'Nice eh?'

Dexter knew what was coming next. The piece was always a clue. 'Sad though,' he said.

'Reminds me of our apartment in Caracas,' Mike sighed. 'Used to play this before going to bed sometimes.' There were a few seconds of silence before Mike inquired about the next move.

'Waiting for Egypt now.'

'That will be exciting.'

'Yeah, looking forward to it,' Dexter said. 'Will have a female companion.'

'One of them?' Mike joked, drawing on his experience when he had to work as a team. 'Sounds fun.'

'I've met her, knows her stuff by the looks of it. Swedish Somali.'

'Uba?'

Dexter turned and looked at Mike. 'You know her?' he frowned.

'Of course.' Mike leant over. 'She's good, one of the best.'

Dexter took his word for it. Mike had met and worked with them all. 'Small world.'

'Very. Heard she's in Amsterdam at the moment.'

'Doing what?'

'Probably the same as what you were doing in Russia.'

'How did you know about Pavel?'

'A contact in Ukraine used to work with him. Didn't really have much to say about him, which says it all really.'

'Still wondering what he and Maxim were up to.'

'Desperate, trying it on.' Mike laughed. Dexter didn't mind – anything to take his mind off Andrana – but still asked why. 'Trying to kidnap a Bolshoi dancer,' he said, in between bursts of laughter. 'Must have thought it was Christmas when he saw her walk in the apartment block.'

Dexter joined in the merriment. It was quite amusing and comical. 'But why did Pavel mention Viktor?' he asked, seriously.

'Listen, they all know each other. Probably spoke with the guy who was following you, who Viktor definitely sent.'

'That's true. Anyway, I'm done, need to sleep.'

'And we were going to have children,' Mike said.

'Give her a call, she may have separated from whoever she married.'

'Why did I let her go? Look at me, once was married to a beauty queen, now I'm single.' Mike banged the steering wheel in anger.

'Mike, Listen, you're still young, you have plenty of time.'

Chopin's *"Raindrop"* Came to an end, the ambience changed, it wasn't as sad. 'When you fall in love, you'll realise Dex,' Mike said, in a more sober manner.

'Can't say I'm looking forward to that one,' Dexter said, opening the door to get out.

'There will be nothing you can do about it,' Mike stated, prophetically, igniting the engine.

Dexter walked to his car; his footsteps sounded loud against the empty car park. He looked around before unlocking the door. There was no one to be seen. Whatever the circumstance, you had to be always alert. You make enemies in this game, that's certain. Dexter had known a few acquaintances who had met with suspicious and untimely endings. Once the forensics and Police know the profession, they seem to shut the case. The drive home was anxious, the river looked a little more restless. Back home Dexter put on some Charlie Mingus and sat on the balcony with a gin and tonic. He focused on Westminster Bridge whilst thinking about what Mike had said. Dexter didn't know what love is or was. He couldn't form a relationship that Mike had with Andrana anyway, wouldn't even know where to start. The mix wasn't right in the drink, there was more gin than tonic. Charlie Mingus made him think. Natalia was stunning, but there was no spark, same with the others he had met on assignments. Maybe that was the problem: it was work-related, not personal. Sure, there were the one-night stands and flings, but nothing near to a relationship. *So, how did Mike fall into that one? One that even after all these years continues to consume him.* He took a deep breath, *no way, not me*, he thought, struggling to swallow the last of the drink.

'Yes, that's correct Dexter, the day after tomorrow.'
'Where am I going to meet Uba?'
'She'll be waiting for you at Frankfurt,' Jasper said. 'Documents arriving tomorrow evening, I'll call you before then with instructions,' he added, before saying goodbye.

Dexter put the phone down. He was excited. The last part of a job was always satisfying. Once the evidence was handed over to Jasper and he was satisfied in passing it over to the Crown Prosecution, it was job done. This time he would take some time off, treat himself to a holiday somewhere remote like Iceland or Scotland, somewhere a little cooler, where he could do some walking and fishing in solitude. Jumping out of bed, he made some strong coffee. Today, he decided was going to be a relaxing one. It was going to be coffee, weights, shower, breakfast then an exhibition. Tomorrow – after an afternoon resting – will be reserved for a visit to the Royal Opera House for a spot of ballet.

'Hot and busy, but I like it,' Mike said, when Dexter asked him about Egypt's capital.

'Decent jazz clubs?'

'Oh, you'll be surprised. Cairo has everything,' Mike answered.

Dexter was choosing something to wear for the ballet as he was speaking to Mike. 'Can't wait,' he said.

'Have to be careful there though Dex, it's a little different to here or say Russia. Rules are different, if you see what I mean?'

Dexter did, he knew what Mike meant. It was the Police. They could be bought, very cheaply as well. Morocco was like that. The Police treat tourists and visitors with respect, but they can be bought and the only way to stop them giving you a hard time was to pay them off. For them it was a win, win situation, but that's part of the deal. Sometimes it was scary, sometimes fun. Dexter enjoyed both. 'I understand Mike,' he said.

'Well, have a good one. Say hello to Uba, mention Mike from Belgrade a couple of years ago. Trained together.'

'In what?'

'Karate.'

'She does karate, what grade?'

'One higher than you.' There was silence. 'Dex?'

'Yes, I'm here, sorry.'

'Mike laughed. 'I know how you feel, but you have something in common, try and do some training.'

'Will do Mike. If you hear anything, let me know.' Dexter put the phone down and went online to look for an exhibition. It wasn't long before he decided to take his camera and head somewhere to capture something new.

'See you later Terry,' Dexter said, as he passed through reception.

'Dexter, looking casual, where you off to?'

As nice and professional as Terence was, Dexter never disclosed locations or destinations with him. 'Just a walk along the river, see where it takes me,' he answered.

'Nice day for it,' Terence said.

He was right. It was a pleasant morning, sunny, with a nice breeze. With his rucksack on his back Dexter headed to Vauxhall station, destination: Hampstead.

Dexter could see the allure for painters, poets and the like. There was something about this part of the capital. He started by photographing some red phone boxes on Heath Street. The sunlight illuminated the vivid red. Feeling a little creative he held the door open as he snapped the receiver and box. They brought back memories from a few years ago when it was advised not to use a mobile - as they can be traced – and to use a payphone. He captured shadows from the window frames into the shots. Dexter always looked forward to developing the unusual and spontaneous. For some reason they were the ones that came out the best, giving the most satisfaction.

As it was a weekday it wasn't too busy, so Dexter found himself somewhere open and quiet. Throwing off his bag he prepared with some light stretching, before setting up the stance and going into the Qi Gong set, he's learnt in China. It took twenty minutes and felt good. The 108-form followed; this involved a little more movement but still incorporating the breathing technique. Dexter tried to make it twenty minutes but finished at just over fifteen.

He sat down on a fallen tree trunk after. Looking onto the Heath Dexter felt relaxed. In two days, he'd be in some bustling metropolis, so he had to appreciate the current surroundings while he could. Reaching to his rucksack he took out some fruit and a book: *The Power of Now*.

'Fancy the ballet?'

'When?'

'Tomorrow, if you are free that is.'

'I'd love to, never been to the ballet before,' Perdi said.

'Bit of a novice myself. Only been once, and that was a couple of days ago.'

'In Russia?'

'Yes.'

Bet it was an enjoyable experience.'

'It was. 'Let me see what's on, I'll call you later.'

Dexter walked through the Heath, along Pond Street, catching the tube at Belsize Park. 'Good walk Dexter?' Terence asked.

Dexter couldn't quite relay the day so far into words. 'Amazing,' was the best he could come up with.

'That good?'

'And it hasn't finished.'

Dexter checked to see what the performance was. He picked up the phone. 'The Sleeping Beauty.'

'Sounds fabulous. Did you say tomorrow?'

'Yes.' He checked the time for the performance. '8 pm.'

'Where shall I see you?'

'What's the nearest station to you?'

'Notting Hill Gate.'

'See you at 7 pm at the entrance.'

Even though she would have to rush Perdi agreed to the time and place. 'See you then,' she said.

Dexter called up an acquaintance saying he needed a couple of tickets. 'See you outside Bow Street Police Station at 7:30 pm,' the man said.

For some reason Dexter felt like going out, but knew he had to rest. Making a drink he disappeared into the sanctuary of his darkroom. He was right, the images of inside the phone box looked cool. The monochrome composition captured that feeling he related to earlier, the one of nostalgia and danger. When dried he put it into a mount and frame he keeps to one side for the special ones. *Definitely one for the kitchen*, he thought.

Dexter prepared for the relaxing evening ahead. After making some food he went to the lounge, putting on some Thelonious Monk. Halfway through the phone rang. It was Mike. 'You didn't say too much to that girl, did you?'

'Which girl?' Dexter asked, trying not to give the impression there were so many he couldn't remember which one he was talking about. 'Perdi?'

'The ballerina.'

'Natalia?'

'Yes.'

Dexter was a little surprised but knew he hadn't. 'No, was careful with her for some reason. Told her I was visiting, why?'

'Was talking to a contact there, I mentioned Pavel and he mentioned the ballerina.'

'Is she okay?'

'She's back performing. But he told me that she hadn't long broken up with a boyfriend.'

'She didn't say anything about that, then again, we didn't get that close, just chilled out in a jazz club and art gallery. Who was he?'

'Some guy called………'

'Maxim?'

'That's it.'

Dexter wasn't surprised. Nothing shocked him in this business. Although he was pleased he didn't disclose anything to Natalia, he was also a little angry he'd been taken in. 'Strange combination,' he said.

Turns out he was a dancer himself but got injured so had to give it up.'

'Coincidence of him knowing her.'

'Happens.'

'Indeed. One last thing Mike, you said Uba was in Amsterdam, has she left?'

'Went back to Sweden today.'

'What was the reason for her going there anyway?'

'Told you, surveillance and to record Sergei being there.'

'She didn't deposit any money, though did she?'

'No, just a few photos.'

'Thanks Mike,' Dexter concluded.

He was pleased to hear Natalia was back performing. *Did she know Pavel when they met me for a coffee?* Dexter wondered. He sat back. Or had he unintentionally got mixed up in a feud between two former lovers? In a way, he hoped that was the case. Dexter kicked back and relaxed for the rest of the evening, listening to music and drinking wine.

Dexter leisurely laid in bed the following morning, something he rarely did, and for that reason it was quite enjoyable. Having to fight off the urge to go for a run he got up to make coffee. As it was being brewed, he went to the lounge and opened the curtains. Another glorious sunny day, he thought, looking eastward along the Thames. After putting on a dressing gown he took the moka and a cup onto the balcony where he sat down, faced the rising sun, and closed his eyes. He thought about Cairo and Uba. His take was that Nasser had some sort of business there that launders cash and diamonds. It would be interesting to know how the profits were spent. It may have been the anticipation, or the coffee, but whatever it was, Dexter felt a knot in his stomach.

The Jag purred its way over the Chelsea Bridge as Dexter headed to Notting Hill Gate tube station. He went around Sloane Square twice, just for the fun of it, before flying through Knightsbridge. 'You look nice,' he said, complimenting Perdi on her navy blue outfit.

'Thank you,' she said, getting into the car. 'Looks a nice production,' she added, referring to the Sleeping Beauty. Tickets must have been difficult to get?'

'Not really,' he answered, navigating one of his favourite roads: the Bayswater Road. After handing over the car to a valet at The Savoy Hotel, they walked the short distance to The Royal Opera House. 'Wait here, I'll be three minutes,' Dexter said, before crossing the road to Bow Street Police Station.

'Alright Dex?' Chequer said.

Dexter cut to the chase. 'How much?'

'For you….' Chequer looked across at Perdi. 'Is that lovely lady with you?' Dexter nodded. 'For you, a hundred.'

Dexter took out his wallet. 'Don't suppose you take Roubles, do you?'

'Afraid not, only sterling tonight,' Chequer joked, looking for two good seats. 'Here, stalls,' he said.

Dexter handed over the cash and took the tickets. 'Thanks, have a good evening.'

'Enjoy the show,' Chequer shouted, as Dexter crossed the road.

'Who was that?' Perdi asked.

'Just someone I know. Ready?'

The interiors were remarkably like the Bolshoi Theatre with red and gold being the dominant colours. After sitting down Dexter provided Perdi with an interesting piece of information. 'The Sleeping Beauty was the first ever production here, 1946,' he stated.

'It is very nice,' Perdi admitted, as she looked around the auditorium.

The performance was for approximately two and a half hours including a twenty-minute intermission where Dexter treated himself and Perdi to a flute of champagne.

Dexter felt satisfied after. *Expensive, but money well spent,* he thought, as they took a little stroll through Covent Garden Market. 'Looking forward to tomorrow?' Perdi asked.

'I try not to think about it, but now you've mentioned it, yes, I am.'

'Must be exciting.'

'Can be.'

'Dangerous?'

'Can be,' Dexter replied.

'How long do you think you'll stay there for?'

'That I have no idea. To be honest I don't really know what I'm going there for except to see where Nasser's business is.'

'There'll be more.'

'What makes you say that? Has Sebastian told you anything?'

'He doesn't mention anything, not even to my father. I suppose he does not want to take any chances. I know something's going on because I work at the bank, if I didn't, I wouldn't have a clue.'

'Sounds a very humble man.'

'He is. Worked hard to get where he is, and ……'

'And what?'

'I'm not going to have anybody ruin it.'

'They won't. It's a shame you couldn't find out more about Nasser.'

'He's very secretive. Doesn't say a lot to anyone except Andreyev. They leave together sometimes, walking towards Park Lane, don't know where they're going.'

Dexter did but didn't say anything. The Cairo venture would be the last, Dexter couldn't ruin it now. The stakes are too high. If there are diamonds involved, it could go deeper. Diamonds can be dangerous collateral. If Dexter mentioned The Playboy Club Perdi may take it upon herself to do some investigating, such was her interest in the glamorous side of the business.

'I'll drop you at the station,' Dexter said, as he suggested going home. It was getting late and he needed to be there to collect the itinerary and documents, something he did enjoy, as there was a little glamour to it.

'That will be great, thank you,' Perdi said.

The West End at night was fantastic. Driving up the Haymarket then turning left into Piccadilly with the roof down was a thrill. It didn't take long before they reached Notting Hill Gate station. 'Well, thank you for joining me,' Dexter said as he pulled up beside one of the entrances.

'That was an amazing evening, thank you.' Perdi looked at Dexter. 'Please stay safe,' she added.

'I will. And you too, don't take any chances with Andreyev and Nasser, as tempting as it may be. We're nearly done, and your uncle will have peace of mind.'

Perdi smiled and opened the door. 'That's all he wants,' she uttered, quietly.

'I know,' Dexter concurred. After Perdi closed the door he put his foot down, accelerating towards Holland Park.

'Courier came for you,' Terence said. 'Be back in an hour.'

'Thanks Terry, send him up.'

'Will do.'

About an hour later there was a knock on the door. Dexter looked through the spyhole. It was the same courier as last time. The courier seemed a little nervous. 'Mr Spencer?' he asked, having to go through the formalities.

'That's me,' Dexter replied, taking the package. 'Thank you.'

Dexter walked into the lounge and put the package on the coffee table. He knew he had to have an early night but couldn't resist one last gin and tonic and some Quadrophenia. Jasper said that Cairo would be extremely hot as well as humid and to dress accordingly so Dexter would select the appropriate attire after looking at the itinerary.

The visa was a standard tourist one for three months. Five hundred Egyptian pounds and some tourist maps to make him look the part. Dexter opened one up and looked at it. Looking at a picture of the Pyramids he became excited, for one thing was certain, he was going to pay them a visit, no matter what. The ticket was a return to Cairo, departing Heathrow at 2:40 pm. Dexter was pleased with the time, meant he could pack in the morning. With a stopover at Frankfurt - where Uba should be joining - it should take four to five hours. He was looking forward to seeing her – not to mention being a boyfriend. *Perks of the job*, he thought. Sitting back, he raised his glass, *cheers*, he said, aloud, taking a sip of the London gin.

## Chapter Twenty

'Where to this time?' Terence asked, as Dexter wheeled his suitcase through the reception area.

Dexter was cautious. 'Just a little break for a few days,' he replied. The case was hotting up - there was a lot at stake - so Dexter had to be extra careful. He pointed upstairs. 'And...'

'Keep an eye on the apartment?' Dexter nodded, without saying a word. 'Will do, any mail will be put away and any visitors will be noted,' Terence said.

'Thanks Terry. See you soon,' Dexter said.

'Have fun.'

'Try my best,' Dexter smiled, nervously.

Dexter was well ahead of time. It was something he had to work towards. It wasn't enjoyable rushing around and being late. It used up too much of his energy. He found being early and on time better for him. At Heathrow there was ample time to browse for a magazine. He chose two publications: Men's Health and British GQ. After putting them into his hand luggage, he went and checked in.

Dexter watched the plane from the business lounge. He loved British Airways; it was a brand that carried a certain class money couldn't buy. The flight to Frankfurt was short and sweet. Dexter had a conversation with the passenger next to him about why they should bring back one of the icons of British design: the Concorde. He was well rehearsed on this topic, as he had discussed it many a time, always learning something new. This conversation's nugget of information was that only twenty had been built, something Dexter didn't know. He was also impressed that the man had travelled on one. The only sighting Dexter had seen was when it had been dismantled and travelled on a barge down the river Thames on its way to Scotland. The man said that there was one on display in New York. Dexter had heard rumours that there could be one displayed on a platform above the Thames between the London Eye and Westminster Bridge. *Could you imagine that*, he thought, *seeing the Concorde, a supersonic jet from your apartment? Cool, or what?*

There was barely enough time for a quick flick through the Men's Health magazine. He needed a good run, now he had a partner, if she turns up for the flight that is. Many an Agent has got cold feet at the last minute and cancelled. Dexter couldn't blame them, some – like this one – can be dangerous. The thought of adventure and glamour is one thing, the reality, another. It was an acquired taste, no matter how much you get paid. For Dexter though, it wasn't only a job, it was a way of life.

The man said goodbye after landing at Frankfurt International. 'Nice to talk to you,' he said, gathering up some personal belongings.

'You too, all the best,' Dexter reciprocated, not really concentrating. His thoughts were on who will occupy the seat next.

It didn't really take much for Dexter to act the boyfriend part. 'Darling,' he shouted, waving when he saw Uba appear by the cockpit.

This was a cue for Uba to get into the relationship mode. 'Coming darling,' she yelled.

Dexter got up and let her take the seat near the window. 'I know it's your favourite,' he said.

'You remembered,' she said, squeezing past Dexter and settling into the seat.

They both knew that they could be being observed - this is a game of cat and mouse – and as far as they were concerned, they were. Dexter had to wait for a visit to the bathroom to survey the other passengers. 'How was work?'

'So glad it's finished, really need this little break.'

Dexter sat down and took out his phone. 'Never did get your number,' he whispered. Uba wrote it down on a piece of paper. 'Thanks,' he said, sending her a text: *Are you being followed?*

*Not as far as I know,* came the reply.

Dexter knew this meant could be. Reaching for his hand luggage he took out British GQ. Uba did likewise only hers was Deutsch Vogue. Waris Dirie - the Somali supermodel turned activist - was on the cover. 'Been through a lot,' she said.

'Was a Bond girl,' Dexter commented, recalling the movie "The Living Daylights". 'Timothy Dalton, so underrated,' he added.

'What?'

'Timothy Dalton, underrated,' Dexter repeated, hinting they were supposed to be together.

'Oh, of course darling, my favourite was Roger Moore……...as you know.'

After the flight took off and you could unfasten your seatbelts Dexter said he was going to the bathroom. Waiting until someone passed, he got up, purposely walking slowly behind them, taking note of anything suspicious. The stereotypes had long gone. Now it wasn't someone wearing sunglasses smoking a cigarette whilst reading a newspaper. It could be anyone. Through experience Dexter could nail it down though. It would probably be female, late twenties, early thirties. Given the case, origin would be Russian, Dutch, or Egyptian.

'Is there a queue darling?' Uba asked when Dexter returned to his seat.

It was another chance for Dexter to note anything odd. He looked back down the aisle. 'Only three people darling,' he answered.

Uba got up. 'See you in a minute,' she said.

Not a lot was said for the rest of the flight after she returned. Dexter checked out some British fashion, Uba looked at Germany's next batch of up-and-coming models to watch out for.

Dexter loved touching down, especially somewhere new. Even before disembarking he could smell and taste Cairo. The aroma was rich and steeped in history. Cairo International Airport was clean and well maintained, it gave a good impression. After collecting their luggage Uba headed for the taxi rank. Dexter didn't argue, they could be under observation. They couldn't give away the fact that they hardly knew each other. 'Leave the bargaining to me,' Uba whispered, as they exited the terminal towards one of the white taxis. Dexter handed her the itinerary as they approached the first car at the rank. 'كم ثمن الزمالك؟' *(How much does Zamalek cost?)*

'خمسون'.'م' *(M'.'fifty')*

'أربعون'. (.*'Forty'*)

'خمسون'. (.*'fifty'*)

Uba closed the door. 'Let's go darling,' she said, walking away.

The man got out. 'حسن40' *(Good)* He shouted.

'Let's go,' Uba said, handing over the luggage, "اين في الزمالك؟ سأل. (*Where in Zamalek?*)

'El Gabalaya Street.' Uba replied, as she and Dexter got into the back seat.

Dexter understood that bit. It was where the apartment was. 'Everything okay darling?' he asked, as they began to head towards Cairo city centre.

'Yes, thank you darling,' Uba answered.

Though working Dexter took a few minutes to enjoy the moment. He'd waited for this for a long time. The driver was playing Egyptian music, it was hot and sweaty, and cars were beeping their horn. Dexter sat back and closed his eyes for a few seconds. As he opened them, he looked sideways at Uba and smiled. He had a feeling he was going to enjoy this one.

The centre of Cairo was as congested as Dexter had imagined. The clock was ticking away, building up the fare. Uba gently reminded him that he could go as slow as he wants, as a fixed price was agreed. Catching sight of the River Nile for the first time was an experience. No rivers are the same. The Thames is different to the Moskva, which is different to The Seine, which is different to the Hudson. Zamalek was a sort of island sandwich between the Nile in the centre of Cairo. El Gabalaya Street ran along the western side of the Island, the apartment – ironically - was facing the British Council, situated on the other side of the Nile. Jasper had done the same as Moscow – renting the apartment for a week – open ended. The driver got out and fetched the luggage. Uba said. شكرا لك (*Thank you*)

As the driver got back into the car Dexter leant inside the window and passed a few Egyptian pounds.'شكرا لك (*Thank you*) he said, trying to remember Uba's pronunciation.

'Thank you,' the driver smiled.

'You're welcome,' Dexter said. *Oh well, not for the want of trying,* he thought, joining Uba outside the gate.

There was no concierge, the property manager came straight out and opened the gate. He greeted them in English. 'Abanoub,' nice to meet you both,' he said, looking around. 'Baahir?' he shouted. A few seconds later a young boy came and joined them. 'Help the couple with their luggage.

Baahir somehow managed to skilfully navigate three suitcases into the compound, up some stairs and through the entrance door.

'Let me show you your apartment,' Abanoub said, escorting them to the lift that took them to the fifth floor.

The apartment was modern, spacious, and clean. Jasper had tactfully – and respectfully - rented a two-bedroomed property. Uba thanked Abanoub, saying that will be all. 'If there's anything you need, please,' he said, handing his business card to Dexter, said, شكرا لك *(Thank you)*

'Quick cup of tea then I need to rest, only got back from Amsterdam yesterday,' Uba stated, after Abanoub and Baahir hastily exited the apartment. She checked her phone and started typing. A few seconds later Dexter received a text. *We will discuss arrangements later, must check for any devices first,* it said. Dexter nodded in agreement.

As Uba went to make some tea Dexter went onto the balcony, pausing as he leant over. There it was, right in front of him: the River Nile. It looked a deep green. Uba joined him about ten minutes later with some Egyptian tea. It was black and sweet – thanks to the added cane sugar. 'Enjoy darling,' she said, as she stood next to him.

'Lovely, isn't it?' Dexter asked, in reference to the vista.

'Very nice,' Uba answered. 'We needed this break didn't we darling?' she added.

'Sure did,' Dexter replied, taking a sip of the bitter beverage.

'Anyway, my love, I'm going to shower, unpack and rest. If you need any more tea, there is some in the pot. See you later.'

Dexter finished the rest of his tea. 'Sounds like a good idea,' he said.

Dexter waited a few minutes before walking to the kitchen. As he began to look for some more sugar, he received a text. It was from Uba. *Checked the kitchen, do the balcony. I am doing my bedroom - then bathroom - do yours after,* it said.

Dexter poured the tea and added some sugar before going back to the balcony. It was 8 pm, and the aftermath of the Egyptian sunset was still powerful. Though just missing the golden hour, Dexter felt it, it had an energy, that's for sure. Standing on the balcony he looked out, the Cairo Tower was within touching distance. He then wondered how long they would be here for. The assignment was quite simple; they had to locate Nasser's investment company and look at its inventory, see what's being invested and from where, should take a few days at most. They didn't want to be hanging around for too long. Dexter could use the relationship as going sightseeing, drag it out a bit, as well as making it look good. Knowing that a balcony is where people eat and relax – as well as talk – there was a quick scan. A strategically placed plant at the end caught his eye. After finishing his tea, he casually walked behind it and knelt. Having a careful forage, he felt something plastic. Without removing it he took a closer look. It was a miniature camera, he'd seen the same ones in South Audley Street, Mayfair. He got up and walked back to collect his cup. Before going to the kitchen, he sent a text. *Found something on balcony,* he wrote.

After washing his cup, he collected his case and went to his bedroom. He could hear Uba in the shower as he passed the bathroom. The bedroom was massive and had a nice view over some gardens. Knowing Uba would be awhile, he started to unpack. 'Finished darling?' he yelled, hearing the bathroom door open.

'All yours my love,' came the reply.

The bathroom had an aroma that Dexter missed. You can keep your own bathroom as clean as you want, but there is nothing more comforting than when you share that space with a woman. This is what Dexter missed. He lived alone, which – given his occupation – was good and to some extent a necessity, but he would love to experience this more often. Maybe this was what Mike missed about Anandra. The shower was cool and refreshing. The shower gel Aaran added to the proceedings. The scent of sea salt, rockrose and myrrh replaced the more feminine aroma left by Uba. The towels were real Egyptian cotton, the real deal. 'What we having to eat tonight love?' Dexter shouted, as he passed Ubas room.

Uba opened the door. 'We can order something or take a walk to the supermarket, come back and cook,' she said.

Dexter was easy. 'Up to you, I'm easy,' he said, continuing to walk to his room.

After choosing some faded Lacoste jeans and a light blue cotton shirt, Dexter checked the room for any devices.

After being satisfied it was clear he ventured into the lounge area and waited for Uba.

'I think we should walk to a supermarket,' Uba suggested, as she sat on one of the sofas.

'Agreed,' Dexter stated, knowing that – as of yet – this wasn't the most confidential of places to discuss business.

On the way down they met Baahir. Dexter asked for a good, cheap, local place to eat. 'Cairo Kitchen,' he said. 'El-Aziz Othman,' he added, proceeding to give directions.

The air was warm and kind as Dexter and Uba ambled to the Cairo Kitchen. Dexter felt good. This was in direct contrast to Moscow where he was on his own, here he had Uba, it made a difference.

The choice of the day was baked chicken and potatoes. Dexter chose a cola as a drink, Uba went with bottled water. As they waited for the food Uba got straight down to business. 'So, what's the agenda?' she asked.

'Quite simple really. Nasser has a business here. He's using cash siphoned off from banks he has staff placed in, running through here and investing in diamonds.'

Uba took a sip of water. 'Diamonds are big business here in Egypt. The Armenians run it. It's no big deal if we inquire about them. No one will think anything suspicious.'

'But we don't know where or how Nasser is sourcing them from before he sends them to Amsterdam. Did you see any outlets there?'

'There were a couple. More are planned.'

'We have to nip this in the bud. Behind it all is exploitation and political corruption.'

Uba nodded in agreement. 'You mean here, in Africa?'

'Yes, Angola, Congo, South Africa. What about Somalia?'

'No, nearest would be Tanzania.'

'Can you imagine the bribery and backhanders that go on.'

Uba sighed. She had grown up with politics. 'Something close to my heart,' she said. 'And one of the reasons I took this job.'

The food came. There were many side dishes of vegetables and beans. Dexter enjoyed everything on display. He loved Arabic food. 'We can take it easy for a couple of days, while we look for where his office is, then make some inquiries regarding investment.' Dexter explained the injection of cash into the RIB. 'The money has been tracked. If we can get them to hand some of it over here in Cairo, that'll be a huge stride towards conviction.'

'How are we going to do that?'

'Maybe ask for exchange from the Egyptian pound into sterling. They'd agree because they will charge you interest.'

Uba sounded surprised. 'Me?'

'I'm the one who deposited it in Moscow. Can't take that chance.'

Dexter thought about the case. It had started out as some rogue employee syphoning money from an employer into a political issue. The next stage was that the diamonds were more than likely used to buy weapons used for military coups and civil war. He took a sip of the cola. 'You are okay darling?' Uba asked.

'Yes, fine thank you my love,' he replied, now knowing that he had to be incredibly careful. It had moved to another level: a dangerous level.

The food had re-energised them. There was a spring in their step as they walked a different way back to the apartment along the 15 May Bridge main road. Back in the apartment Uba held out her arm to stop Dexter unlocking the door. 'What?' he whispered.

Uba knelt and picked up something from the tiles. She held it up between forefinger and thumb. It was a hair. 'Someone's been in,' she said.

Dexter took the lead, quietly opening the door. He then went and checked his door, it was the same, the hair was missing. He looked at Uba, shrugging his shoulders. They couldn't say anything. Uba went to her room, Dexter did likewise. He didn't bring his camera - so he didn't need to worry about that – and the laptop seemed fine. He took it to the lounge area and plugged it in. A few minutes later Uba appeared, holding her laptop. She smiled, still not saying anything, as she sat on the other sofa.

Dexter emailed Jasper, saying they had both arrived safely and asking for the name and address of Nasser's business in Cairo. Dexter missed having a gin and tonic. This was the perfect night for it. He got up to make some tea. 'Shall we sit on the balcony darling?' he asked.

Uba was typing away. 'One minute, let me finish this.'

Dexter went to the kitchen and made some Egyptian tea. He carried the tray outside to the balcony where Uba was sitting. 'Here my love,' he said, placing the tray on the table.

'Was thinking, we can go to the Khan Al-Khalili market tomorrow,' she suggested.

'Good idea. So many exciting things to do here, shame we won't have the time.'

'Need to buy some cosmetics as well,' Uba added.

They drank the tea in silence, gazing out into the star-studded Egyptian night. The Nile looked a dark shade of emerald green as it nestled beneath the sky. Dexter thought its stories would be of a different context to the Thames. Though both bodies of water were used for trade and commerce, the dynamics were different. 'Time for bed,' Dexter announced, collecting the cups.

Uba yawned. 'Think I'll join you,' she said.

After washing the pot and cups Dexter checked his emails. Jasper had replied, giving the details of Nasser's business. Uba had gone to her room so he sent a text. *Change of plan for tomorrow, got Nasser's address.*

*We can do both, sweet dreams,* came the reply.

Before going to sleep Dexter checked for a jazz club. He found one. Switching off the laptop and light he got into bed, tomorrow was going to be an adventurous day, that was for sure.

## Chapter Twenty-one

'Good news,' Dexter declared, the following morning. 'It's near the market.'

Uba was stretching in the lounge. It was impressive. 'There's some coffee in the pot darling,' she said.

'Did you hear what I said?'

'Yes, I did,' Uba replied, holding a finger tightly to her lips. Dexter poured some coffee, then went onto the balcony. It was going to be another hot one. Uba joined him. 'Sleep well darling?'

'I did. You?'

'Yes,' came the answer, before she retreated to the lounge. 'We'll have to leave soon,' she shouted.

Waiting for the shower Dexter did some stretching himself. Mike had recommended doing some training with Uba. *Maybe tomorrow*, he thought, as he practised his roundhouse kicks.

As they passed the reception area Baahir appeared. 'Car?' he asked.

Uba replied "لا، شكرا" *(Thank you)*

'We are walking?' Dexter asked, as he closed the gate.

'See how we get on.'

The premises were just before the Khan Al-Khalili off Gohar Al Kaed. Dexter left Uba, saying he'd meet her at the market. He didn't want to go inside without her, it would ruin the first-time experience, so he wandered around the vicinity. About an hour later a text came. *I am outside the Naguib Mahfouz Coffee Shop, where are you?*

Dexter asked a man where the Naguib Mahfouz Coffee Shop was. 'Around the corner, on the left,' he explained.

Dexter said'شكرا لك' *(Thank you)*

He then replied to Uba: *Five minutes.*

'Second coffee of the day,' Dexter sighed, as the owner placed some strong, steaming coffee in front of them.

'Sugar?' he asked.

'Please,' Uba answered, before turning to Dexter. 'You're on holiday, treat yourself,' she smiled.

After the man had left Dexter asked how it went. 'Well, I said I needed some sterling for a cosmetics business here. Very international, Cairo, you know.'

'What do you mean?'

'The man who I dealt with was Russian.'

'Name?'

'Michail. He was genuinely nice, said to return tomorrow for the exchange.'

'Second name?'

'Wait.' Uba took out a business card from her bag. 'Michail Andreyev.'

'How much?'

'Said I needed five thousand, said he couldn't do a deal unless it's ten thousand at least.'

'Interest?'

'We'll discuss tomorrow.'

Dexter felt like celebrating. 'Pastry?'

'Of course,' Uba replied.

'You must be careful now, they tailed me in Moscow after visiting the bank.'

'They weren't expecting my visit. By the time they ask someone I'd be gone.'

The coffee was thick and sweet, it complimented the pastries. 'What made you use a hair on the door yesterday?'

'Saw it in a James Bond movie,' Uba smiled.

For the first time in a while Dexter laughed. He needed it. Uba just sat and observed as he just let it go. 'You are funny,' he concluded.

The walk around the Bazaar wasn't that interesting. Sure, it was bright and colourful, but - through no fault of the traders - a little too touristy. A little like contemporary Camden market, historic, but has lost a little of the magic. Uba said she needed to visit the nearby Al-Hussain Mosque. Unfortunately, Dexter wasn't permitted to enter, so he stayed at the café and waited.

They took a taxi back to the apartment. On the way Uba said that she had searched for any devices in the morning and found nothing. Dexter said he had done the same.

Uba checked the door, she smiled as she removed the hair. On the bedroom doors the hairs were intact. Uba said she was going to rest a little before going to a cosmetics shop. 'But first……,' she beckoned Dexter with her finger, as she went onto the balcony. Dexter watched as she ripped up the camera behind the plant then tossed it into the corner. 'Now, we can talk,' she added.

Dexter watched as she went to her room. He got his laptop and went back to the balcony. For some reason he felt free, liberated. Maybe it was because of the camera, maybe that he was thawing out from London and Moscow, or that he had company. Slowly but surely being with Uba made it a little easier. After relaxing a while, he emailed Mike, giving an update. The reply was - as expected - immediate. *Glad to hear it. Do some training with Uba, highly recommended*, it said. Dexter looked for a jazz club, it didn't take long. There was one in the Kempinski Nile Hotel Garden City, it was nearby as well, just on the other side of the Nile. 'Yes!' Dexter exclaimed, aloud.

Uba entered the room. 'What?' she frowned.

'Jazz club tonight.'

Uba didn't respond. 'Going for a shower, then shopping,' she announced.

Dexter missed being called darling, or love, it was endearing, he was beginning to understand why some people need relationships. 'Will you escort me?' he shouted.

'Of course, darling,' came the reply.

Dexter wished he had brought his camera, he felt like taking a few shots, but knew that photography was a sensitive issue. Around the Pyramids would be okay, but everyday life in the street? That could be problematic. Uba came and said goodbye. 'Won't be long,' she said. 'Need anything?'

'Water, cheese, bread.'

Uba laughed. 'Yes boss,' she joked.

'Uba?'

'Yes?'

'Tomorrow, can we do some training?'

'What sort of training?'

'Karate.'

'How do you know?'

'The way you were stretching this morning.'

'After a morning run?'

'The morning after having something to eat and listening to some jazz?'

'See you later.'

'Later what?'

'Darling!' came the answer, bellowing down the hallway. When he heard the door close. Dexter went back to the balcony. The afternoon heat was now searing. Looking out over the Nile he pondered the case so far. If

Uba could take the cash from Andreyev and it was the marked one he had deposited in Moscow, the case would take a quantum leap. It would be a major step towards prosecution. The gang would be rooted out and rounded up and face justice. Only problem was that it would only be a temporary reprieve before it happened again, such was the lure of diamonds and cash. Dexter sat back in the shade with his hands behind his head. It didn't seem to bother him, after all, it was work, paid the bills, and where else would he get the chance to spend a few days in somewhere like Egypt with a stunning woman he was going to a jazz club with? He played Quadrophenia on the laptop. The angst was still there, but a little different. The only problem that presented itself at the moment was when to sunbathe under the sun-drenched Egyptian sun. The answer was quite simple; 5 *pm*, he thought.

Uba returned a few hours later. Dexter got up to help her with the bags. 'How you going to get these through the airport?' he asked, placing them against the wall in the hallway.

'Where there's a will………'

Dexter finished the saying. 'There's a way.'

He liked how she had used the trip to buy something that may be difficult to purchase in Sweden. 'Guess what?'

'I'm listening.'

'I was followed.'

Dexter knew it had been a little too easy so far. This changed the mood. 'Do you know who by?' Dexter inquired, seriously.

'Yes.'

'And?'

'Baahil.'

'You had me worried there,' Dexter admitted.
'Curiosity, probably.'
'Let's hope so. If Andreyev sees me, well....'
'If it is, will be a coincidence, don't you think?'
'What will be?'
'I was followed in Amsterdam, you had the same in Moscow, it's as if someone knows where we're staying and passing on information, don't you think?'
'Dexter shook his head. 'No one knows, only Sebastian, I haven't told anyone, have you?'
'Only your friend.'
'My friend?' Dexter looked puzzled. 'Who?'
'Michael.'
'Mike?'
Dexter went into the lounge and sat on the sofa. 'No,' he said.
Uba switched her laptop on. 'Can't trust anyone in this business,' she said.
'Agree, but I've known Mike a long time. He's solid.' It was 5 pm. Dexter got up. 'Going to soak up a little sun,' he said.
'Have to write a couple of e-mails, see you in a minute,' Uba said.
Dexter placed the lounger towards the sun. He thought about Mike. *Absolutely not,* he confirmed. He didn't tell him exactly where in Moscow he was, and he hasn't told him where the apartment is in Cairo. Baahil was a houseboy, nothing more. Forget it. After putting on some Miles Davis, he stripped down to his shorts and - like a tom cat - sprawled out on the lounger. The sun instantly felt good, taking any concerns away.

Not long after Dexter heard a scraping noise, looking up he saw Uba had moved the other lounger beside him. 'You like the sun?' he asked.

'I'm from East Africa, of course I do,' came the terse reply.

After half an hour Dexter turned over. It was the turn of his back to receive some rays for thirty minutes, after which, fifteen minutes on each side, then done. 'Going to take a shower,' he said, looking at Uba. There was no response. He observed her for a few seconds, he couldn't help it. Sleek and slim, flawless. Bone structure to perfection.

She opened her eyes, knowingly. 'Go on then,' she said, closing them.

Dexter got up and headed to the bathroom, looking forward to the cold shower.

The shirt was black, it complimented the charcoal grey linen trousers. This will be a one-off. He had to savour it and look the part. He waited for Uba in the lounge and wasn't disappointed when she appeared. The attire was a combination of black and olive green: chic and classy. Even Baahil had to do a double take, as he lingered in the garden area. 'Car?' he asked, in vain.

The reply was prompt. 'No,' Uba said, before closing the gate to hail a white taxi from the street.

The lounge bar was on the top floor of the Kempinski Nile Garden Hotel. It wasn't really a jazz bar as such, more of a cabaret. The interiors were soft and luxurious, but the special feature was the panoramic view over the Nile. After the meal they sat back and relaxed as a singer sang covers of some jazz classics. Dexter asked about tomorrow's meeting, was Uba looking forward to it? She said she was. The reply was eager, as well as political and humane.

'They are putting quite a network in place,' Dexter summarised, discussing how Nasser and Sergei's network is growing.

'We will stop it,' Uba stated, in a determined manner.

Dexter ordered some coffee and sweets. 'What's the motivation?' he asked, taking a sip of the coffee when it arrived.

'Greed.'

Dexter had always been curious why this happened. Sergei ran a couple of banks. One specialized in quality diamonds. Nasser held a good position in a bank and an investment company here in Cairo, both were comfortable. Why risk everything? Dexter had seen it before, but not on this scale. The singer sang *"Ain't Nothing Like the Real Thing,"* by Tammi Tyrell, as he looked over the Nile, pondering his own motives. Uba was right, it was the money. He got well paid for something he enjoyed doing. It was never boring - and sometimes dangerous – but there had to be something else, something hidden. He had always felt that politicians – even if you disagreed with them or not – generally went into politics to help people and society. It suddenly dawned on him that maybe this was another reason for his career choice, that he wanted to serve justice, which is a way of helping people who have been wronged. The song played in the background. Marvin Gaye never got over Tyrell's death. He thought about Mike and Andrana, wondering whether it would be a good idea to give him an update or not.

Dexter asked Uba when it would be a good time to leave. 'The day after tomorrow,' she said. 'Then again, you never know what might happen,' she added. Dexter knew what she meant. Anything can happen at any time, but a big part of the trip was to see the Pyramids of Giza. This was something he had to witness. He asked Uba if she would be interested in visiting the site tomorrow after the meeting. 'Yes, I would, been there before, would be nice to go back, but as I said, anything can happen.' The rest of the evening was spent not really saying a lot. The vista over the Nile was distracting, which suited Dexter.

Back at the apartment the hairs were still intact. Uba retired to her room, Dexter stayed in the lounge, sending Jasper an email asking for money to be transferred for tomorrow's transaction. The reply was immediate, giving details of where to collect the cash: The Central Bank of Egypt. He sat back, thinking of the Pyramids of Giza. He would wait for the sunset there, feel the energy, recharge before returning to London the following day.

## Chapter Twenty-two

The workout was good. Mike was right about the recommendation, Uba was good, very sharp. It was all there: power, technique, and the speed. Her kicks were impressive, high and accurate.

Even though it was a short walk to The Central Bank of Egypt, Dexter and Uba took a taxi. If you are collecting five thousand Egyptian pounds you must look the part. Baahil offered his services again, Uba quickly declined them. Dexter felt for him. He seemed harmless, maybe he had a little infatuation with Uba, nothing more, it's not every day you get to witness a five-foot-eleven Somalian presence. Then again, after Moscow, no one is to be trusted.

Uba waited in the car as Dexter went to collect the cash. Again, Dexter placed it neatly into the rucksack. 'شكرا لك *(Thanks)* he said, putting the bag over his shoulder.

The manager replied','شكرا لك, ماشاء الله *(Thank you, God willing).*

The morning sun was searing, beating down on Dexter's back as he left the bank and headed to the car. Uba asked the driver to head back to the apartment. Dexter handed the bag over on the way. 'Good luck,' he said, before getting out. Uba was focused, not saying anything. Dexter watched as the taxi reversed and went back in the direction it had come from. He then walked to a nearby supermarket to buy some groceries for lunch before taking to the shade to walk back to the apartment. 'Where is your friend?' Baahil asked, as Dexter walked through the door.

'Shopping,' Dexter replied, with a smile. 'You know women.'

Baahil looked at the shopping bags. 'Help?' he asked.
'No thank you,' Dexter answered.

'You are lucky man,'

Dexter noticed Baahil looked a little worried. He knew the look, having witnessed it many times. He kept it short and sweet, continuing to the stairs شكراً *(Thank you)* he said.

'Mr Spencer?' Dexter didn't stop to answer as he hastened up the stairs. 'Mr Spencer, I need to talk to you for a while,' Baahil shouted from the bottom of the stairs.

As predicted, the hair was missing. Baahil reached the top of the stairs. 'Anyone in here?' Dexter asked.

'Maybe cleaner,' came the nervous reply.

Dexter beckoned to Baahil to stay where he was as he gently inserted the key before slowly opening the door. Standing just inside the apartment he could hear a noise from the lounge area. Dexter leaned against the door that led to the lounge. 'Hello?'

Abanoub appeared from the balcony. 'Mr Spencer?'

'What are you doing here? Who gave you permission?'

'Mr Spencer, as the house manager I need to make regular checks, just to see if anything requires any maintenance work.'

'You need to ask permission.'

Abanoub walked towards the door. 'Apologies Mr Spencer,' he announced, opening the door.

After the door closed Dexter checked both bedroom doors, the hairs were still intact. He then went to the balcony and checked the plant; the camera had gone. After a quick search Dexter was satisfied a new one hadn't been installed. He went to the kitchen to make a coffee before plugging in the laptop and listening to Quadrophenia. "I'm One," sounded poignant and different as Dexter sipped the coffee, looked out over the Nile, and waited for Uba's call.

'Dexter?'
'Uba?'
'It's Uba.'
'I know. Are you okay? Did you get the money?'
'Yes, coming back now. See you in ten minutes.'

Dexter knew that if the notes were the same as the ones he had deposited in Moscow, it would be a massive step towards bringing them down. The cash had been marked with infra-red detected watermarks by both British and Russian intelligence. The Russian authorities were keen on the case because laundered money can be channelled anywhere; including funding the Taliban in neighbouring Afghanistan. There was an election coming up so it would look good to be seen as getting a grip on such matters.

Dexter turned the music off when he heard a key turn in the front door. Uba entered the lounge and threw the rucksack next to where Dexter was sitting on the sofa. 'Going for a quick shower, then we'll go to the Pyramids,' she said.

As Uba went to collect some clothes from her room Dexter went to the kitchen. 'Hungry?' he shouted.

'Yes,' came the reply, accompanied with the closing of the bathroom door.

Dexter knocked up one of his specialities: an onion and cheese omelette with bread and a side salad. He put them on the table with some fresh fruits and waited for Uba. 'Lunch ready,' he hollered, as a reminder.

He had to think what to do with the cash as he waited. Abanoub would more than likely make another maintenance check. Dexter hit on a good idea, he would hide most of it somewhere in the apartment and take a few of the notes with him, just in case

'So, how did it go?' Dexter asked, as they sat at the table.

'Not too good. They have suspected something now.'

'What makes you say that?' Dexter asked, sucking on an orange Uba had sliced.

'Andreyev made me an offer. To begin with.'

'And?'

'Then he took a phone call, saying who he was with. He described me.'

'You speak Russian?' Uba nodded her head, as Dexter continued. 'What happened next?'

'I made sure that we did the transaction straight away, so I had the money. He asked if I was interested in investing in artefacts, that's where the money is,' he informed me.

'Art?'

'Sphinxes.'

'Sphinxes?'

'I said I may be interested. He was about to elaborate when the phone rang.'

'Who was he talking to?'

'Someone called Yulia.'

'So, what's the problem?'

Uba went on to explain that a couple of years ago they were working on an assignment together. Yulia got greedy, was informing the other side about the surveillance and intelligence. She got caught and thrown in jail. 'I was the main witness,' Uba, sadly reflected. 'It was hard facing your colleague - who you had got to know and admire – and testify against them,'

'How do you know it was her? Yulia is a popular Russian name.'

'She was on loudspeaker; I could recognise that voice anywhere. When she asked Michail who he was doing business with he mentioned my name. She asked him to describe me, which he did.'

'What did Michail do?'

'After she shouted not to deal with me, he slammed down the phone and rang to lock the door.'

'How did you get out?'

Uba held her hand up. There was swelling and a cut alongside the outside of the right hand. 'The training session this morning came in useful,' she smiled.

'Do they know about me?' Dexter asked.

'Not yet, and they couldn't follow me, I ran for a block, then hailed a taxi that parked around the corner and walked the rest of the way.'

'Well, Cairo is a big city, plenty of hotels, they'll never find us before leaving tomorrow. Dexter then asked if Uba was okay?'

'*Shaken, not stirred,*' Uba answered.

Dexter dressed down for the much-anticipated visit to the Pyramids. A polo shirt, beige chinos with baseball cap and sunglasses was the casual choice. Uba wore a full-length olive-green dress, and a black headscarf. Before leaving Dexter thought it would be courteous to send Mike an email – he didn't send one yesterday. *Everything is running smoothly so far. Now going to fulfil a lifelong dream: off to visit the Pyramids of Giza, will fill you in more later,* he wrote.

'Sphinxes?' Dexter uttered, as he closed the door. 'These people never learn, do they?'

'Never,' came the terse reply.

Baahil was watching Arabic television. 'Car?' he asked.

This time Dexter took the reins. 'No thank you Baahil, won't be long, just going for a little walk,' he said.

The sun was unbearable, but it was the last day and Dexter had to see the sunsetting behind the Pyramids, that was a must, so had to be endured. They jumped in a taxi, who seemed to know where they were travelling to. 'Giza?' he asked, in near-perfect English.

Dexter replied', نعم *(Yes)*.

Uba closed the door and looked over at him, smiling. 'Very good darling,' she said.

It never took Dexter long to pick up a language. People were always surprised how on arrival he couldn't say a thing to a few days later when he could start to have a conversation. Problem is, he always forgot on his return to the U.K., which was a good thing as far as he was concerned.

The car crossed the El Galaa bridge and navigated its way through the sun-baked backlog of vehicles until they hit the Charles De Gaulle. Uba pointed out the Russian Embassy on the left. Once on the El Haram it was straight to the Giza Necropolis. Dexter paid the driver and walked with Uba to the site. He closed his eyes as Uba guided him. They came to a halt. 'Okay, you can open now,' she said.

Now there are some things that you can prepare for and some things – no matter what – you can't. This was one of them. Dexter slowly opened his eyes and there it was, right in front of him: The Great Sphinx of Giza. It was smaller than he imagined, but just as impressive. In the few minutes it took to walk closer Uba had rejected ten or so requests for souvenirs and camel rides. After what was quite a walk along a tarmac road to see one of the Pyramids they returned in front of the Sphinx and sat in the shade. Dexter thought of Andreyev's proposition about investing in Sphinxes. Maybe it wasn't such a bad idea after all. 'What exactly did he mean?' He asked.

'Didn't get the time to discuss,' Uba replied.

Before Dexter could say anything else. He heard a voice. 'Uba Ahmed?'

They turned around. There was a tall, slim blond woman with another man. The man was Michail Andreyev. 'Yulia Kotova,' Uba said, getting to her feet.

'Been a while.'

'Yes, it has.'

Yulia walked towards them. 'Been waiting for this.'

With his baseball cap, a bandana wrapped around his nose and mouth - to keep out the sand – and sunglasses, Andreyev obviously didn't recognise Dexter. He addressed Uba. 'What is it you want? Who do you work for?' Michail asked, whilst holding back Yulia with his arm.

'I needed some sterling, that's all,' Uba calmly replied.

'She's lying,' Yulia spat, brushing aside Michail's arm and moving a little closer. 'She works for the government; she is a spy.'

Before Uba could say anything, Yulia ran and jumped in the air with a scissor back kick. It caught Uba by surprise and knocked her to the ground. 'I want the money back,' Michail insisted.

'Uba looked up as she knelt on the sand. 'Impossible,' she stated.

Yulia came forward and launched into a front kick. This time Uba was quicker, managing to roll over to one side whilst jumping onto her feet – both executed without the use of her arms. Yulia was persistent, this time it was a punch. Uba stepped to the side, catching the hand and managing to step under and deliver a counter blow to the side of the face. This time it was Yulia's turn to hit the deck, but not for long. She wiped her mouth and looked at the blood smeared on her hand. This time there was a trio of roundhouse kicks. Uba managed to evade the first two but wasn't as successful with the third. 'The cash,' Michail repeated, as she crashed to the ground.

Aware of the attention the fight was bringing Dexter intervened. 'We can meet later,' he said.

'Who are you?' Michail asked.

'We want to start a business here in Cairo, a perfume business, we need ed sterling as collateral, but if you need it that bad, we can return it.'

'When?'

'Same time tomorrow?'

'He's lying,' Yulia said, this time walking over to Dexter.

Dexter took a step back. 'About what?'

'Tomorrow.'

'Look, the Police,' Dexter said. As Yulia turned around Uba swept her legs, upending her. You could hear the crash as she landed. 'Oldest trick in the book,' Dexter reminded her, as he grabbed Uba's hand and hailed a passing taxi. 'Tomorrow morning,' he shouted, quickly getting in and driving off. He looked behind as Michail attended to Yulia. 'You okay?' he asked, seeing that Uba was a little concussed and disorientated.

They both put on a brave face as they entered the apartment block. Abanoub was fixing something on the desk with a screwdriver. 'Good afternoon,' he politely said.

Do you think Abanoub is okay?' Dexter asked, as he opened the apartment door.

'I'd say so,' Uba said.

'Me too,' Dexter agreed.

Uba took to the sofa as Dexter offered to make some coffee. 'How did they know where we were?' she asked. 'Did you tell anyone?'

'No,' Dexter frowned.

'Well, I didn't, but they knew.'

Dexter had a rethink as he made and brought the coffee into the lounge. He retraced the morning's events. Except for the taxi driver, Abanoub and Baahil, he hadn't spoken to anyone, and even with them he hadn't mentioned where they were going. 'Strange,' he said.

'What about on the phone?'

'E-mail?'

Dexter looked at Uba. 'Only..........'

'Mike?'

Dexter was speechless, he continued to gaze at Uba. 'No, it can't have been him, surely. Why would he do that? He's a friend, I've known him for years, know everything about his life.'

'Including Andrana?'

'How do you know about Andrana?'

'Dexter, maybe I should have told you before, but I've worked with Mike, and guess what?'

Dexter took a sip of the coffee. 'What?'

'He was on the case with Yulia as well.'

Dexter sat with his head in his hands. He had heard enough. 'Tell me another time,' he said.

'It's okay, they won't find us here, unless..........'

Dexter took another gulp of coffee before standing up. He took the hint. 'Let me check my e-mails,' he said. After plugging in the laptop, he turned to Uba. 'Here, listen:' *Hi Mike, hope you are well. Just back from a rather eventful visit to the Giza Necropolis. Now safely back in our hotel we are staying at in the centre of Cairo. Will update you in the morning.* He turned the screen towards Uba. 'Sound okay?'

'Yes. If he's in contact with Yulia, she'll think it'll be a Hilton or something. Give us a bit of time. We need to book our flights.'

'There's one at 12:40,' Dexter said.

'I'll get that one,' Uba shouted, from the bathroom.

Dexter booked his. He wouldn't mind staying in Cairo a little longer, but it was now too risky. Mike may contact Jasper, asking where he is staying. 'Booked it,' he said, as he passed the bathroom.

'I'll do mine when I'm finished,' Uba shouted. 'What seat?'

Dexter went back and checked. '24a,' he answered.

Remembering that they didn't check the front door to see if anyone had entered, he rushed to the bedroom. The hair had gone, and – after a frantic search – so had the bag with the cash. Leaning against the wall he sighed. *How was he going to explain this one*? He returned to the lounge, waiting to tell Uba. 'Booked it, 24b,' she announced, sitting down. Intuitively picking up something was amiss she asked Dexter what was wrong.

'The cash,' he replied.

'No? Sure, you haven't mislaid? Forgotten where you put it?'

'Don't worry, I have an idea who's responsible, and I'll get it back.'

Uba smiled as Dexter called downstairs. 'Baahil? A problem with the shower. Come tomorrow morning, 9 am, fix it.'

'Is he coming?' Uba asked. Dexter nodded. 'Have to plan a surprise,' she added.

The rest of the evening was spent drinking tea and talking about different countries and their politics. Uba was passionate about the latter. Her sense of the injustices was strong. Dexter got the impression she would have taken this job for nothing; such was the depth of feeling. It was an early call for bed, there was packing to do. If everything went according to plan, there would be a swift exit to the airport.

## Chapter Twenty-three

The knock on the door was exactly on time. Dexter got up to answer as Uba drank some coffee on the sofa. "Who is it?' Dexter asked.

'Baahil, come to have a look at the shower.'

Dexter opened the door. 'Morning,' he said.

Baahil did not reply, he just walked straight to the bathroom. 'What's the problem?' he asked, checking and turning on the taps. 'Seems to be working okay.'

As he turned around Dexter pointed the pistol at his forehead. 'Money please?'

Baahil held his hands up. 'Mr Spencer, what are you doing?' he asked.

'About to shoot you through your head if you don't hand back the cash.'

'Mr Spencer, please, calm down, I don't know what you are talking about.' Dexter knew the next stage was always the convincing part. It required no words. He slowly pulled back the trigger. 'Okay, put the gun away.'

'Where is it?'

'Downstairs, I'll show you, come.'

'No, you won't. Tell me where it is, that's all you need to do.'

'It's better I show you; I can't explain in English.' Dexter pulled the trigger back to the maximum. 'Okay, It's in the spare room at the back of the office.'

'Keys?'

Uba walked in as Baahil retrieved the keys from his jacket pocket. 'Which one?' she asked, taking them from her hand.

'That one,' came the reply, singling out one of the keys.

'Back in a minute,' Uba stated.

As they waited Baahil looked ashamed. Dexter asked if Abanoub had anything to do with it. The answer was inevitable: 'No,' Baahil said.

Uba returned with the bag, gave back the keys and counted the cash. It was all there. Dexter told him to leave, 'Not a word to anyone,' he said, not looking forward to what he had to do next. The thud of the pistol against the head meant the job had been done. Dexter supported Baahil as he collapsed into his arms. After carrying him to the bedroom he laid him on the bed. 'Sorry,' Dexter uttered, feeling a little guilty. He placed the spare Egyptian pounds he had left on the bedside table next to him. 'Ready?' he asked Uba.

They wheeled their suitcases from the lounge to the front door. The taxi was waiting. The manager was waiting at the Central Bank of Egypt for Dexter as he walked in. The transaction was swift and simple: Dexter deposited the cash, and it was sent via courier back to the U.K. He had taken photographs just before leaving, so everything was recorded. The manager asked about the missing money. Dexter said it was expenses, taking the reciept.

'شكرا لك'
شكرا لك'
رحلة آمنة' the manager replied ', *(Thank you)*

The drive to the airport was one of relief and reflection. This always happened when Dexter was departing a country. The journey to the airport always brought up emotions and this was no different. It had been an eventful few days to say the least. Dexter had finally made it to Egypt, and that was something. The driver played some Arabic music. The beat was hypnotic. Dexter sat back, knowing he would return to the land of the Pharaohs; there was unfinished business, he still hadn't seen the sunset over the Pyramids. Looking over at Uba he felt safe, secure that in this business of deceit he could trust someone. It would never happen again - as most assignments are solo – but it had been an experience that was for sure.

On the flight they discussed the situation so far. Uba told him about Amsterdam, and that she had traced to where Nasser diamonds were being purchased. The next step would be to find out which country they were being sourced, before the polishing and presentation took place for buyers such as Nasser who paid good money. She had photographs as evidence. 'I'll rest at home for a few days then do some research,' she said.' This was what she was interested in, this is where the exploitation begins. The diamond industry is notorious for it. 'Don't tell Jasper yet,' she added. 'That's between you and me.'

When the plane touched down at Frankfurt Airport Uba got up to collect her hand luggage from the overhead compartment. Dexter noticed the swelling on her face, as well as the cut on her hand. She had been in a battle, led from the frontline. 'You okay?' he asked.

'It's fine,' she answered, as she put a rucksack over one shoulder and carrying her laptop 'Well, Dexter, been a pleasure.'

Dexter knew he would see her in London once the case had gone to court. She would be there in the courtroom awaiting the sentencing, that's for sure, seeing justice prevail. In the context of everything entwined with this assignment, the injuries were minor.

'Have to go back to the Somali restaurant,' he said.

Uba smiled. 'Sure,' she said, before turning and making her way towards the exit door.

Dexter knew she wouldn't turn around. It wouldn't be professional. He was right, she didn't.

Heading towards London Dexter flicked through the GQ magazine. There were some nice watches. He had a thing for watches. The Tag Heuer he was wearing had done its job. Though still working to perfection, it was time for another one. He always treated himself after a job, though to say this one was almost over was an understatement to say the least.

There's something about British airports Dexter doesn't quite like. He could never put his finger on it, but there was something there. Sometimes he thought it may be the slight dampness of the place, even though it could be good weather, it always seemed a bit chilly. The walk from the plane to customs wasn't the most enthusing either, again was always cold or soulless. He wasn't in any rush so chose the underground over the Heathrow Express. The Piccadilly line did at least manage to feel a little more comfortable and homely.

'Dexter!' Terence exclaimed, catching sight of his favourite resident. 'Good trip?' he asked, opening the door.

'Good….' Dexter looked at his watch for confirmation. 'Evening,' he added. 'Wasn't bad, thank you.'

'Good to see you back Dex,' Terence stated, this time closing the door and walking back to his desk.

'Good to be back,' Dexter sighed. 'Tired though. See you tomorrow, Terry.'

For some reason Dexter was tired so he savoured the unlocking of his home, sliding the suitcase to the corner, putting on some Dave Brubeck, then hitting the shower was savoured to say the least. Then came the time for a gin and tonic and hitting the balcony in his dressing gown. *What a couple of days*, he thought, looking out onto the Thames whilst reflecting on Cairo, Uba, the Pyramids and just about everything else that had happened. It was in the latter stages of dusk, *'still the best sunset,'* he said aloud, not wanting to think about having to miss the sun as it disappeared behind the Pyramids.

## Chapter Twenty-four

'Fantastic Dexter, see you nine,' Jasper said.

There wasn't any need to go to the office, basically there wasn't anything to handover, no photos or anything on surveillance. Uba had the images and would send them. The task was to make certain that Nasser did have a business in Cairo, and that it was linked to the RIB. The cash would prove the link between the two, and that – along with Uba's evidence – would be strong enough. 'See you then,' Dexter said.

He was looking forward to meeting Jasper, he was good company, especially at times like this. Dexter was still a bit wired, and to be in the wrong company wouldn't be a good idea at the moment. The suspicion and distrust were still there.

Dexter decided to do some shopping so headed to Old Bond Street. Even though he hadn't been paid in full, he needed a dose of retail therapy. With Dolce and Gabbana shirt and trousers the next stop was the Royal Arcade to look for a watch. The choice was difficult, coming down to either a Jaeger or Breitling, after careful consideration – and not wanting to spend too much – the latter was purchased. After a coffee and buying a book at Waterstones Dexter headed home.

Lifting the weights felt good and helped clear the mind. A run in the morning would definitely be welcomed. After a shower and a bite to eat Dexter went to jump in a cab for the West End. 'Looking good Dex,' Terence commented.

Dexter mustered up a smile. 'I try,' he said.

'It's raining.'

'Oh no,' Dexter said. He was wearing his new shirt and trousers and didn't want them to get wet. Terence went to the door and chose an umbrella. Dexter wasn't so sure, he didn't like umbrellas, was always losing them, and besides, didn't look classy, especially when entering a club such as Ronnie Scott's. Then again, he didn't want to be burdened by a coat. 'Go on then,' he sighed, accepting the rather large umbrella.

On the way he stared pensively out of the window. The raindrops were cascading down the side of the window with the city lights blurred and distorted behind them. Dexter could identify, he wasn't at the beginning of a job – or near the end – he was in the middle, and it was how he was feeling. He had the experience to know that this was how it was. You get caught up with the characters and personalities. It was a good thing; meant you were on top. Problem is sometimes you can become attached, it happened in Paris with Alina, now it's Uba. He thought of Mike and Anandra, he was beginning to see the reason Mike always went on about her. 'This okay gov?' the driver said, snapping Dexter out of thinking too much.

Dexter didn't know where he was so had to wipe the window. He was outside Ronnie Scott's in Frith Street. 'Yes, this is fine, thank you.'

Dexter paid up the money, opened the door and quickly ran to the entrance. The black shirt got a little wet, not too much though. As he went to pay, he stopped, taking a deep breath: he had forgotten the umbrella.

'Dexter,' Jasper announced, as Dexter approached the bar. He beckoned the bartender over. 'Gin and tonic and…....'

'The Bullshot?'

'Please,' Jasper said. He turned to Dexter, stood up and extended his hand. 'So good to see you.'

Dexter shook his hand. 'You are happy,' he asked.

'Very, wait.' He went and got a spare chair, 'please,' he said, placing it alongside the bar. Dexter sat down and they both waited for the drinks to arrive. Jasper thanked the barman and continued. 'Excellent work. Also received an e-mail from Uba this morning outlining the work you guys did. This is a major step.' He paused to take a sip of his drink. Dexter followed suit. He had waited all day for this. The blend of gin, tonic water, crushed ice and a slice of lime never tasted so good. *Must have been the Saharan heat*, he thought, waiting for Jasper to continue. 'This all looks really good, will stand up in court and get a conviction.'

'These guys do need locking up,' Dexter said. 'They are growing their empire everyday by the looks of it. 'Did Uba mention Sphinxes?'

'Sphinxes?'

Uba obviously hadn't. 'Nothing,' Dexter said.

'As I was saying, this looks really good. The person who hired me will be incredibly pleased.' Jasper took another sip of The Bullshot. 'Can I get you something to eat?'

'I've eaten, thanks anyway,' Dexter replied. 'So, what next?' he asked.

'Well, the cash will be handed over to Scotland Yard tomorrow, they will do a forensics test, hopefully it will be the same cash you deposited with them in Moscow. Then I'll give them the photographic evidence showing the main players. I expect statements will then be required before they send to the Crown Prosecution to see if there's a case, which, I'm sure there will be.'

'If there is then arrests will be made?'

'Hopefully,' Jasper answered, knowing that sometimes the process can be lengthy as well as unpredictable. Bribery is not unheard of in these cases.

Dexter pondered for a while. 'Jasper, you've been in this business a while. Have you heard of a man named Michael Goman?'

Jasper frowned. 'Michael Goman, Michael Goman…. Ah, yes, if it's the one I'm thinking of, yes, a chap who used to work for the government. Once based in Venezuela I think.'

'That's the one, what do you know about him?'

'Sacked,' came the terse answer.

'What for?'

'A couple of things. Messed up a big job in Russia once, God, that one didn't go down too well, but the main one was suspected of being involved in the death of a banker here.'

'In London?'

'Yes, was on a job tracing missing funds from the Vatican. Poor chap who was the suspect committed suicide, well, allegedly, shall we say. Was a big story, got leaked to the press, so they had to let him go.'

'Where was the suicide supposed to have happened?'

'Westminster Bridge. Another one?'

Dexter finished off what he had left and passed Jasper the glass. 'Please.'

'Nice guy Mike, but not for business I'm afraid.'

'Why?'

'Like a lot of agents that lose their career, became disgruntled, ended up selling information to the other side.' The drinks arrived. 'Why do you ask?'

'Nothing,' Dexter replied, wondering how far Mike went with disclosing any information. He was seeing him at training tomorrow, would ask him.

Jasper was adamant about making Dexter feel appreciated. 'Well, if I can't buy you to some food, let me treat you to an evening at Aspinall's?'

Dexter couldn't resist this one and accepted. 'Done,' he replied, as they both held up their glasses. 'Cheers,' he said.

It was still raining when they left Ronnie Scott's and took a taxi the short journey to Curzon Street. Aspinall's was – ironically – directly opposite Globalink International. Dexter didn't care, he wasn't going to hide from anyone for one simple reason: there wasn't any need to.

Jasper knew the doorman and walked straight to the desk where he showed his membership and signed himself and Dexter in the book. *'Don't come here enough,'* he whispered as they made their way to The Club Room. Dexter marvelled at the interiors, he'd been to some swanky places, but this was up there. 'Blackjack? Roulette?'

'Blackjack,' Dexter answered.

After making themselves comfortable in the plush red velvet seats they settled down for some serious gaming. Dexter's first card was an ace, his next was a king. 'Stick,' he announced. Jasper busted. The dealer decided to call Dexter's bluff, sticking on twenty. Dexter took delight as the dealer moved the chips in his direction. He had a certain knack for this game. There wasn't much skill involved but had the knack anyway.

After a few games they moved to the roulette wheel. This was all about luck, not something that appealed to Dexter. He believed in a little of everything, skill, luck, and bluffing, it was a good mix and made it exciting. Dexter split with Jasper for a while, choosing for some baccarat as Jasper opted for some poker. The table overlooked Curzon Street and Globalink. From his seat he could see into the building. He thought about Perdita, wondering if she had any news. Baccarat came easy to Dexter, he'd played it in Cannes and Turin, and wasn't bad at it. There were a couple of people seated at the table as Dexter sat down. The croupier dealt the cards and the fun started. The lady to his left was French and seemed well-versed in the game, the gentleman on the right - American - less so.

The main thing was that Dexter enjoyed it. He didn't win, and he didn't lose, it was fun, and a break from the seriousness of the case. Although it may not show, it can take its toll, Jasper understood this, he'd seen it before, and wanted to keep his finest in good shape. After another gin and tonic, they both left the club. Jasper lived in Richmond and said he was going past Vauxhall and the taxi could stop off there.

'Thanks Jasper,' speak to you soon,' Dexter said, as he was climbing out of the back.

'Will do Dexter,' Jasper acknowledged.

Dexter didn't even have the energy for a shower, after taking his shoes, socks, shirt and trousers off, he collapsed on the bed.

The sound of the phone startled him. 'Hello?'

'Dexter?'

'Who is it?'

'Perdita.'

'Hi, was going to call you later.'

'Thought you might be back. Can I see you? Have some news.'

'Same time and place?'

'See you then,' Perdita confirmed.

Dexter put the phone down and squinted as he looked at the clock. After a few seconds he made out the time: 07:05. *Six hours sleep, not bad*, he thought, kicking the covers off, before making his way to the bathroom. The cold water felt good splashing against the face. After a quick comb of the hair, he put on his running gear.

The pounding of the pavement felt good. The rain had continued into the early hours but had abated, leaving the pavements fresh and clean. Battersea Park was lush and green. The London Peace Pagoda as always looked magnificent. A man was doing some Tai Chi next to it, absorbing the energy. Dexter would practice tomorrow, tonight was karate, he was looking forward to not only the training but also seeing Mike. On the way back he passed the spot where he first saw Uba, even though it was just over a week ago, it seemed longer.

This time Dexter suggested a walk around Hyde Park, he was in the fitness zone, and wanted to squeeze it. Perdita agreed on one condition. 'What's that?' Dexter asked.

We can get a takeaway coffee and sfouf?'

Dexter laughed. 'Deal,' he said. As soon as they entered the park and walked past Speakers Corner Dexter got down to business. 'What's the news?' he asked.

'Someone has left the bank.'

Dexter took a bite of the sfouf. 'And?'

'He's in accounts, will need replacing.'

'Got it. Nasser will be hiring.'

'That's right.'

'When?'

'We need someone straight away.'

'That's a good thing. He'll obviously bring in someone he knows, we can find out who he is, do a check and build a stronger case.'

'Oh, something else. I was a bit naughty.'

Dexter knew what she meant. 'What did I say? You have to leave it to us, if you make a mistake it could cost us everything, and your uncle will lose everything.'

'Couldn't help it.' Dexter stopped, took a sip of the coffee, and waited to hear what she had done. 'I stayed late at work the other day. As I was leaving, I noticed Nasser and Leonid together, they were walking ahead.'

'Down Curzon Street, towards Park Lane?'

'Yes, so I followed them. Outside the Hilton they met with another man. Was strange.'

'Why?'

'He looked the spitting image of Leonid. Looked like he could be his brother.'

Dexter thought of Michail. 'Only with a beard?'

'Yes, how did you know?'

Dexter ignored the question. 'Where did they go from there?'

'To the Playboy Club.'

'Interesting, but please, from now on, no more, okay?' Though a question, it was more of an order, Dexter was serious, there was no way he was putting his life on the line for some stupid amateurish mistake to mess it up. He waited for the reply. 'And?'

'Okay, just seemed like fun and glamorous.'

'Far from it, total misconception,' Dexter tersely stated.

Perdita realised she'd upset Dexter. 'Sorry,' she uttered.

He put his arm around her. 'It's okay.' Perdi looked up at him. 'I'm thinking of your uncle, he's invested a lot of money into this, we just want justice done.' After a few seconds he realised that he was holding her in his arms. She didn't seem to mind: neither did he.

'Good to see you Dexter,' Mike said, as Dexter walked into the Dojo.

'Thanks Mike,' came the tepid reply.

Sensei Tibbs was on form. The level was raised. He used Dexter to demonstrate some blocking and attacking techniques. No holds were barred as Dexter felt the controlled strikes pound against his body. Sparring was with Mike, this time it was Dexter's turn to display his skill set. 'How was training with Uba?' he asked, in the changing room.

'Good,' Dexter replied.

'Is there something wrong?' Mike inquired, as they walked to their cars.

Dexter stopped. 'Mike, what's going on?'

'About what?'

'The only person who knew about going to the Pyramids was you, me and Uba. Someone told Michail and Yulia we were going.'

Mike laughed, nervously. 'Come on Dexter, you think it was me? What about Uba? You trust her? Come on man.'

'I don't know who to trust. What concerns me is the same happened in Moscow and Uba didn't know about that.' Dexter paused, thinking whether to mention what Jasper had told him last night about the banker for the Vatican, he didn't want to get him into trouble. 'Mike, why did you leave MI6, what was the reason?'

Mike's persona changed. He became a little irate. 'What are you talking about Dexter? Why are you coming out with stuff like that? What's wrong with you?'

The car park was deserted but Dexter wasn't going to back down now. He let Mike have it. 'Why did you tell Yulia where we were going?'

Mike didn't answer, he was about to say something, but decided not to. He walked to his car, opened the back door and threw his holdall in the back. Slamming the door, he got into the driver's seat, started the ignition, then put his foot down sharply before driving erratically up the ramp towards the barrier. Dexter could only stand and watch as the car disappeared into the night. He had no choice than to say what he had. Mike now knows that he needs answers: the ball is in his court.

Walking back to his car Dexter felt a little uneasy. Before unlocking the door, he looked around, thinking that something doesn't seem quite right. The first bullet ricocheted of a pillar next to him. He ducked behind the vehicle as the next one followed suit, only coming a little closer. He managed to open the door and take the pistol from under the seat. Seeing in which direction the bullets were coming from Dexter ran to the next pillar, again only just managing to dodge the fire. Crouching down with his back on the pillar he waited. After a few seconds silence a car started and quickly drove off. He ran in the direction and onto the main road. With the car out of sight Dexter tucked the revolver into his waistband. He heard a voice. 'Everything okay?'

It was Sensei Tibbs. 'Yes Sensei,' Dexter replied, hoping Sensei hadn't witnessed what had just happened.

'Thought I heard what sounded like gunshots, guess they were fireworks, oh well, see you next week.'

'Oss Sensei,' Dexter said, a little relieved.

Sensei Tibbs then walked to the bus stop. Despite being offered a ride, he always took the bus. *Nothing worse than being stuck in a car and traffic jam*, he used to say.

Dexter found the bullet cases. He picked them up with a handkerchief and put them in his pocket. The gunman wasn't supposed to kill him. It was a warning shot. Dexter couldn't be bothered to decipher who it could have been, one thing he could be sure of though: it definitely wasn't Mike.

## Chapter Twenty-five

'Came from a Makarov,' Jasper explained, holding one of the bullets between forefinger and thumb. 'Strange choice of weapon to use, especially nowadays with sleeker models on the market,' he added, passing it back to Dexter.

Jasper was a logistics expert when it came to weapons and their arsenal. Having served Her Majesty on many continents as such, his eye for detail became highly thought of. 'Which country?' Dexter asked, curious.

'Russian made. Designed by Nicolay Makarov, 1948. Been used in many wars, and in fact is still used today in Afghanistan.'

'Interesting,' Dexter said, wrapping the spent ammo in the handkerchief.

'It's a beautiful piece of machinery, very Soviet Union. I'd say whoever fired it was a bit of a connoisseur, someone who enjoys weapons as a form of culture, like you appreciate art.'

'Speaking of which.' Dexter looked at his new watch. 'Have to get to an exhibition.'

'I'd say someone who has been to Afghanistan,' Jasper suggested, as Dexter opened the door.

'Thanks Jasper.' Dexter closed the door then skipped daintily down the stairs and out into Shepherd Market. There was a Terence Donovan exhibition at some private gallery in Cork Street. He was a big fan of the swinging sixties, loved its array of music, art, and film. The exhibition was a set of portraiture prints that showed the stars of the decade. The one of Sean Connery was good, as was Sophia Loren but Dexter's favourite was the shot of Twiggy with the Union flag as a backdrop. There was time for a quick coffee at Waterstones before Dexter headed back to Vauxhall.

The walk was welcomed, as was the phone call Dexter received as he stood on the bridge in St. James Park. 'It's Mike,' the voice said.

'Hi Mike.'

'Sorry about last night, was emotional.'

'I understand, but you have to see it from my point of view, you could have got us killed Mike.'

'I know, I'm sorry. Listen, about what you asked last night, There's something I need to tell you.'

Dexter knew it couldn't be done by telephone. 'Want to meet?'

'Tomorrow?'

'Sure, where and what time?'

'Let me think, I'll text you later.'

'No problem,' Dexter said. After hanging up he looked at the phone before putting it in his pocket. For some reason there didn't seem to be that many tourists around. After walking and spotting a discreet tree Dexter took his jacket off and began to practice his Qi Gong set. It felt invigorating straight away and continued to do so until the end. Putting his jacket back on he noticed an observer. This always happens when you do Tai Chi, for some reason it attracts people. Dexter didn't mind, in fact he liked it as not only was it a compliment but was also good for the mind, it taught you to not be distracted. In ancient China the masters always recommended their students to practice in the local market, *probably for that very reason,* Dexter thought, noticing the man quietly shuffling away.

In contrast to what happened in the previous two evenings this one consisted purely of lifting weights, drinking water and listening to Quadrophenia, after which

– funnily enough – Dexter had one of his best night's sleep for a while.

Dexter had switched his phone off before sleeping so received the text from Mike the following morning: *1 pm*, it read.

'*That's fine. The London Eye,*' Dexter replied.

After a run and shower, Dexter settled down at the laptop, listening to some Charlie Byrd. He searched for The Bolshoi and read a review. Natalia was back performing. Doing well, said the review, adding that she is a star for the future. This was good news for Dexter, he had thought about her every day since returning from Moscow and was a little worried. It put his mind at rest, knowing she was okay.

It was a bright day, though a little chilly. *Autumn is on its way*, Dexter thought as he took the short walk to one of London's famous landmarks. Mike - punctual as ever - was waiting in nearby Jubilee Park. Dexter joined him on the bench. 'Ever been on it? He asked.

'You know what? I never have,' Mike admitted, gazing at the mechanics of it.

'Strangely enough, neither have I,' Dexter said. 'Perfect day for it.'

'Let's do it,' Mike said, standing up. As they both walked from the booth to the capsule, he turned to Dexter. 'Regarding the question you asked.'

Dexter had many but stuck with the obvious: 'Why you left MI6?'

'It became too much, the work, the marriage,' Mike said, as they were escorted into the large white pod. Dexter didn't say anything. There was a pause as he waited for Mike to continue. 'Got into financial problems.'

'Gambling?'

Mike shifted his glance from Dexter and stared into the River Thames, as they began to slowly make their way up. 'Yes, been going on a while, that's why Anandra left, she couldn't take it either.' There was a pause. 'In hindsight I don't blame her. I must have been an absolute nightmare to live with.'

Though sympathetic, Dexter got straight to the point. 'So, you started taking money?'

Mike took a deep breath. 'Once it starts it's difficult to stop, it's like they've got something on you, as if you are in their pocket and they control you.'

Dexter looked at Westminster Bridge. 'You were investigating a banker from the Vatican?'

Mike was surprised. 'How did you know?' he asked.

Dexter turned and looked at Mike. 'You know as well as me what a small world this game is Mike.'

'That was another reason, though I didn't do anything wrong, I promise. I was just doing my job.'

'I believe you,' Dexter said, nonchalantly.

Mike became a little defensive. 'It's the truth.'

'I believe you,' Dexter repeated. Not wanting to press him on the so-called suicide Dexter needed to know other more important things. 'Where were you gambling Mike?'

'All over,' came the vague reply.

'Specifically?'

'Had a couple of *favourite haunts*, so to speak.'

The capsule was reaching the apex of its purpose. The vista was breath-taking. Dexter took a few minutes to digest the scene. He could see his apartment. With a pair of sharp binoculars, he could see inside, *something to think about,* he thought. 'Which were?' he continued.

'Golden Nugget.'

'And?'

'The Playboy Club.'

'So, you met Leonid?'

Mike got a little nervous. 'Like you say, small world.'

'What have you said to him Mike?'

'We were talking one night at a table. He knew someone I knew. Said if I needed a little money there was something on offer.'

Dexter continued to press. 'Which was?'

He said that there were some diamonds coming into Hatton Garden, and did I know anyone to pass them too.'

Dexter knew that Mike had contacts for such things. 'How did we come into it?'

'We were talking about the Netherlands, and where they came from. I didn't know what he was doing at Globalink, he never mentioned where he worked. When I found out that you were assigned this, it was too late. I was already in on it.' Mike took a deep breath. 'I kept everything down to a minimum though, I promise. I had to give little snippets, such as telling them that you and Uba were going to the Pyramids to make it look good.'

'You could have got us killed Mike.'

'I'm sorry. Yulia was after Uba, she wanted revenge for what she did to her.'

'Uba was a witness. She went to jail because she passed on information, got greedy.'

'I'm not greedy Dexter, you know me. If it wasn't for the gambling, I never would have done this. It's all pure coincidence that you got dragged into it.'

The pod started to descend down the other side. Canary Wharf was clear and visible, as if you could touch it. 'So, what are you going to do now Mike?'

'Don't tell Uba, I know she's one for justice.'

'She already knows Mike; it was her who told me.'

Mike began to chew his nails. 'Damn,' he uttered, shaking his head.

'There is one thing you can do though, something that will save you from going to jail.'

Mike looked at Dexter. 'No, I can't do that, they'll finish me off.'

The capsule finally reached the end. 'Like the banker?' Dexter asked, as they walked back on land.

Sitting back on the bench Mike agreed to testify against Leonid and Nasser. He hadn't met Sergei, but heard he was coming. As Dexter got up to leave, he asked what really did happen to the banker from the Vatican? 'Don't really know, that's the truth,' came the inevitable answer.

Back at the apartment Dexter played some Quadrophenia. Things were hotting up. He wasn't going to say anything to Jasper about Mike for the time being. The next step was to await Sergei's visit. Mike said that he will let him know when that will be.

## Chapter Twenty-six

A few days had passed, and Dexter had tried contacting Mike to see when Sergei was coming to London. There was no answer. He also didn't show up at the karate lesson. One day after visiting a gallery Terence was reading a newspaper at his desk. 'Another one,' he said, as Dexter passed.

'Another what?'

'Suicide.'

'Where?' Dexter asked.

'Westminster Bridge. Why choose there?'

'Let me see,' Dexter asked.

Terence folded the paper and passed it to Dexter. 'You can keep it, finished with it anyway,' he said.

Dexter didn't want to seem too keen on the story, so just casually placed it under his arm. 'Read it upstairs after dinner,' he said.

As soon as he closed the door Dexter opened the newspaper, scouring for the story. His fear was founded as he read the mini headline on page five:

***Ex M16 spy found hanging from Westminster Bridge***, it said, in bold text. The story continued with details: Michael Goman, 36 from London Bridge was found hanging from under Westminster Bridge in the early hours. Police say that there is no evidence of foul play and are looking for no one else in connection with the incident. The case has been referred to the coroners for cause of death.

Over the years Dexter had learnt and been conditioned to keep his feelings under control. It was a big no no to show your feelings - they could be exploited and give the game away – but this affected him. He collapsed on the sofa, paper still in hand. If only he had an opportunity to tell him that he understood the trauma of gambling addiction, and how it can alter your sense of morality. Dexter knew he wasn't responsible for the shooting outside the karate club last week. Guilt came into the reckoning. Was he too hard on him, adding to the pressure he already had? He was going to miss sparring with him. The walks to the car after training had gone – he clicked his fingers with little enthusiasm – like that. No more heartfelt stories about Anandra. *Life can be so cruel* he thought. Having to get a grip Dexter sat up, threw the paper on the table, and went to make a gin and tonic, this time with a little more emphasis on the former. After selecting some Herbie Hancock for the turntable, he went onto the balcony, staring at Westminster Bridge. It was eerie and had lost its attraction. A thought entered his head: Maybe – like the Vatican banker - it wasn't suicide.

'What's wrong?' Perdita asked, as they sat in a deck chair in Hyde Park.

'Nothing, it's okay,' Dexter replied, holding the cup of coffee to his lips.

A few minutes silence followed. 'Tell me.'

Dexter didn't want to discuss the reason. It was personal. 'Nothing,' he repeated. 'What news do you have?'

'Sergei, he's coming.'

'When?'

'Two weeks.'

'How do you know?'

'Was speaking Leonid at lunchtime, said that a former colleague was coming over, quite sure it will be Sergei.'

Dexter concurred. 'I'm quite sure as well,' he said.

'What are you going to do?'

'About Sergei?'

'Yes, how are you going to apprehend him?'

'What have I said?' Perdita looked at him in a childish way, like a young girl who's been naughty. 'Leave the logistics to us.'

As they walked towards the Serpentine Perdi said that she was sorry to hear about Dexter's friend.

'Dexter didn't understand. 'What friend?'

'Michael.'

Dexter had to stop. 'What do you know about Michael?' he asked.

'When I followed Leonid and Nasser to the Playboy club, they met up with him outside The Hilton.'

'How did you know it was him? 'Dexter inquired, as they continued walking. 'It could have been anyone.'

'A friend of mine works there, as a hostess. I meet her for lunch sometimes when she works in the evenings and sometimes for a drink when she works the afternoons.'

'Look, Perdi?' Dexter sighed, stopping again as he held her arms. He looked her in the eyes. 'Please, no more, as I've said, you could put this whole thing in jeopardy.' For some reason, Perdi fell into Dexter's arms. It was unexpected, and something Dexter found a little difficult. It wasn't a greeting hug, this was a little more, all he could do was reciprocate. It felt nice, warm, and in some ways, he needed it just as much as she did. 'How did you know about Mike?'

'Saw it in the paper. The name, I asked Sofia who the man was with Nasser and Leonid, she said Michael Goman...'

Dexter interrupted her. 'But how did you know that I knew him?'

'My Uncle told me.'

'What?'

Perdi took her head from Dexter's chest and looked up. 'A man who he's hired to investigate all this told him.' *Must be Jasper,* Dexter thought, still holding Perdi close to him. 'Don't be angry,' Perdi added, nestling her head in his chest once again.

'I'm not angry,' Dexter stated, just a little surprised.

'Good,' Perdi said.

Dexter had his arm around Perdi's shoulder, she had her arm around her waist as they continued the walk to the Serpentine. 'Shall we watch the sunset?' He asked.

'Would love to,' came the answer. As they sat and watched the ducks being fed Dexter asked what else Leonid had mentioned. 'Only that he was enjoying London, said Amsterdam was good, but London was better, more opportunities here.'

'Anything about Russia?'

'Just that he served in the army. Perdi sat up as she recalled the conversation. 'Actually he seemed quite proud of that, seemed to relish telling me about what he specialised in.'

'Which was?'

'Firearms. Was in a special firearms unit and deployed somewhere.'

'Did he mention where?'

'Afghanistan.'

'I want you to be extra careful now,' Dexter said, with an assertive tone. 'These are dangerous people if they suspect you are seeing me it could be fatal.'

'You mean kidnap me, like in a James Bond movie?'

'I'm serious.'

The sunset was nice. It was one of those late summer turning to autumn ones. It was all surreal as Dexter gazed out onto the water as it shimmered on the Serpentine. He was lost, but in a good way. He thought about Mike, and, if anything had finally come to understand why he mentioned Anandra all the time.

Dexter could have stayed in the warmth of Perdi's arms for longer but had to get back. They walked hand in hand through Kensington Gardens to the Bayswater Road. The Irony wasn't lost on Dexter as he passed the Russian Embassy to take the tube from Notting Hill Gate. 'I'll text you when I get in,' he said. There was one last hug before he ran down the steps. 'And remember what I said, leave it to us now,' he shouted, on the way down.

The karate club was shocked. Sensei Tibbs wasn't his usual self. Dexter had to break the news to him beforehand. After was even worse. No more Mike in the changing rooms, talking about Anandra, saying how much he missed her. No more walking to the car park and talking about assignments. Though Dexter parked in the usual spot, he decided to take a different route to reach his car. Nothing seemed suspicious as he walked around the front. Maybe the other night was a warning, it happens. If it was a trained Russian sniper who had worked in Afghanistan, they would have taken him out, that's for sure. The drive home was sombre. Dexter closed his front door, threw the kit bag in the corner, slowly got undressed then threw the duvet cover over his head. He didn't have the spirit – or energy - to do much more. He briefly remembered Hyde Park and Perdita the other day. This provided a brief smile before he thought of Mike again. *Life can be so cruel*, he thought.

## Chapter Twenty-seven

'Sorry I didn't get back to you, but I've been busy,' Uba said.

It was the following morning and Dexter hadn't slept that great. 'That's fine,' he acknowledged.

'Sorry to hear about Mike. Was shocked. We had our differences sometimes, but always got on. Any Coroner's report?'

'As yet nothing.'

'I have an idea what they'll say.'

'Me too, but we'll have to wait and see. If they say they're not looking for anyone else, you can be sure of the verdict.'

'What do you think Dexter?'

'About the suicide?'

'Yes.'

'He had problems, but I don't think he would do such a thing.'

'Me too. When I said I was busy I looked into Sergei and Nasser's history there.'

'Find anything?'

'Spoke with a contact who said that Sergei brought Nasser into the RIB.'

'Leonid?'

'He came after from RIB. Then Nasser got a job in London as an investment banker before moving to Globalink as a consultant and director.'

'Before seeing a gap and bringing Leonid over?'

'Exactly. I also found out there was someone who was starting to buy diamonds from the same source as Sergei in Amsterdam and putting them on the London market for less.'

'Do I know him?'

'His name was……. wait, I have it here somewhere. Richard Banks. Heard of him?'

Dexter hadn't, but he had a strange feeling about this one. 'One second Uba,' he said, as he went to the intercom in the hallway pressing the reception button.

'Dexter?'

'Good morning Terry got a question. That banker that was found under Westminster Bridge, can you remember his name?'

'Damn, one second, yes, I remember, Richard something…...'

'Banks?'

'That's it. Why?'

'Nothing just wondered. Thanks Terry, that's all.'

'Uba, still there?'

'Yes.'

'Listen, it's a long story. Try and find out as much as you can about him before you come to London.'

Uba understood that Dexter couldn't explain by phone, he had to see her and speak face to face. 'Hopefully won't be long.'

'Hopefully,' Dexter said, before saying goodbye.

Sitting back, he thought of Richard Banks. Now there was another take. Was he taking money from the Vatican to finance the buying of diamonds? Much the same way Leonid is doing at Globalink? *Another time* Dexter thought, knowing that bringing Sergei, Nasser and Co before the courts was what he is being paid for. Knowing they were being investigated - and how ruthless they can be - Dexter checked up on Perdi. 'Just seeing how you are,' he said.

'Dexter?'

'Yes,'

'Dexter, I'm frightened.'

Dexter was concerned. 'Of what?'

'I don't know. Leonid's not talking to me. I think they may suspect something.'

'We don't know for sure,' Dexter said, not really knowing what to say. He tried to reassure her. 'Just act normal, keep doing the same things.'

'I found out when Sergei's coming.'

Dexter sat up abruptly. 'You do?'

'Next Thursday.'

'Thought Leonid isn't speaking to you?'

'My uncle told me. Said there will be interviews taking place for a new director, and that Nasser has recommended someone.'

'Which means he's in.'

'That's how it works I'm afraid,' came the rueful response.

Dexter knew that this would be a good time to haul them in. *The evidence would be strong enough,* he thought, but it wasn't his decision. That honour belonged to Jasper, Dexter was just an employee, paid to do a job, and that's it. All the legalities were not his remit. He would have to find out where Sergei would be staying, and who would be escorting him. He explained to Perdi that as much as he wanted to, meeting her wasn't an option. 'Way too risky,' he explained.

Perdi understood. 'Not long left,' she said.

'Not long at all,' Dexter concurred.

After saying goodbye, Dexter called Jasper. He didn't want to disclose the information but had to. Jasper would then be able to prepare the evidence for the Serious Fraud

Office so arrests could be made. 'Have to get moving!' Jasper exclaimed, in an upbeat tone.

The way it came across was that he already knew. This was one part of the job that irked Dexter, the part when he felt his services were done with, and that he wasn't being disclosed any information, and wasn't needed anymore. This changed when Jasper said that he needed photographic evidence of Sergei, Nasser and Leonid together. Dexter was already thinking about the location. Snapping them outside the Playboy Club would be a dream, not only professionally, but personally. That one would be dedicated to Mike; it was the least he could do. He quickly rang Perdi again and suggested gently asking her friend who works there about times and dates.

Thinking – and talking – about photography gave Dexter a thirst for an exhibition. It didn't take long for a decision to be made, Patrick Lichfield it was. Dexter put on Quadrophenia and took a shower, knowing that for modern art and culture, London is the best.

'Poor man,' Terence lamented, as Dexter dashed through the reception.

'Who?' he asked, having to slow down a little.

'That poor banker, Richard Banks.'

'I know, sad,' Dexter said.

'Just made me think of him when you asked the other evening. Remember when it happened, was walking over the bridge when the police were there.'

'Wasn't it taped off?'

'A little, traffic still going over though. Strange, I was looking over the side of the bridge but didn't see anything.'

'You mean no body?'

'No, nothing. Then that one the other day, what is it with that bridge?'

'So, you think nothing could have happened?'

'Who knows Dex? funny old world we live in.'

Dexter continued to the door. 'Certainly is,' he concluded.

Deciding on a walk to clear the head, Dexter deliberately avoided Westminster Bridge; though it was visible from Millbank, he didn't look. He thought about what Terence had said, could it really have been a hoax? Maybe Mike was still alive? As positive as it sounded, *it was possible,* Dexter thought.

The gallery was in between the Embankment and Covent Garden. It was one of those townhouses painted a dark shade of grey. Being of aristocratic ilk, Lichfield would have approved. This neck of the woods has history when it comes to the upper classes and nobility. The River Thames was pushed back so the well-heeled of the day could disembark from their boats without too much bother to visit the theatres, coffee houses and other forms of entertainment of the day.

Dexter identified with much of the work. There were images of Mustique, and though he hadn't been to the actual island itself, he knew the Caribbean well. It was somewhere he loved, be it for work or pleasure. The jet set of the 70's was there: Mick, Bianca and Marsha, all smiling and carefree. The ones of Cuba were interesting. Dexter loved the place. The jazz was amazing, as were the people. Being an agent or spy was difficult though. They suspected you straight way, but the thrills and spills you encountered on the job were worth it. One was locating and rescuing a daughter of an American tycoon, now that was a particularly crazy one, Dexter even had a chuckle thinking about being pursued through the backstreets of Havana. He had a couple of lucky escapes there, that was for sure. On a personal note, one of Dexter's plans was to retire to the Caribbean someday. Where exactly though, was another matter. Before leaving he paid particular attention to a black and white shot of some escalators in a metro station in Moscow. He remembered travelling on it to the football stadium and meeting Sergei for the first time. He was looking forward to meeting him once again, only this time the circumstances will be different.

The exhibition was uplifting and much needed. Dexter took a stroll up to Covent Garden and had some lunch al fresco style. In the mood for a stroll after having a coffee Dexter walked past the Royal Opera House. Looking to see what was on as a treat for Perdi, Dexter had to do a double take as he looked at one of the posters, there was a new production coming: "Jewels" - by The Russian Bolshoi Ballet Company - will be making a London debut in October.

On the way home Jasper called. 'Come to the office tomorrow, midday, with all the photographic evidence,' he said, in an upbeat mode.

This was a good sign, it meant that the assignment was moving into the latter stages. Dexter poured a gin and tonic; he felt a little sad this was the case. He had enjoyed it so far, was pleased with his work. Sitting looking at Chelsea Bridge he marvelled at the setting sun whilst thinking about Perdita. He had feelings for her. Maybe it was the right time to take the plunge. A bachelor lifestyle is okay, but it has an expiry date. Dexter was in his mid-thirties now, he had to think of starting a family, and considering someone else. Compromise would be difficult to begin with, having to share would not come easy to a man who does what he wants, when he wants. She knew his occupation as well, which was a bonus. She would understand his absences and security issues. If it came down to it, he would give it up, it would be difficult, but he would. He couldn't risk a family's safety no matter what the reason. He took a large gulp of the gin, *maybe it was time for some peace of mind, learn another vocation, move somewhere, start a new life,* he thought.

'Good work Dexter,' Jasper said, as he sifted through the developed images.

The sound of the prints being shuffled made a pleasing sound. It sounded tangible, had some substance. Dexter acknowledged the compliment. 'Thank you,' he said.

Jasper placed them on his desk. Some were overlapping as he struggled to choose the ones, he thought would be the most incriminating. Dexter had his own preferences, but it wasn't up to him. Was a good thing really, for when it comes to photography his mind can sometimes take over his heart. 'What do you think?' Jasper asked, after narrowing them down.

There were a few definite ones such as the ones taken at the RIB and of Pavel. 'Shame I couldn't take any in Cairo though,' Dexter lamented.

'On that note,' Jasper said, reaching into the drawer and taking out some smaller prints. Jasper handed them to Dexter.

Dexter was surprised, they were of Cairo. 'Uba?' he said aloud.

'Told you she was good,' Jasper remarked, with a wry smile.

Dexter went through them, naming the captured moments: 'Though I never went there, must be Nasser's office.' He laughed when he saw one of Abanoub and Baahil. 'I remember this one,' he said, seeing the cash from the bank. 'How did she manage to get these in?' he asked himself, looking closely at various shots of the fight at the Pyramids. 'Do you know any of these?' he asked, indicating Yulia and Michail.

'This one is known to us,' Jasper replied, pointing at Yulia.

'Thought as much,' Dexter said, remembering what Uba had said. Though barely a couple of weeks, it seemed a lifetime. 'Here,' he added, handing the photos back. Jasper didn't even bother to look up as he took them, so engrossed was he deciding on which ones would nail them. 'Did you hear about Michael Goman?'

'I did, such a shame, pleasant chap. Now let me see, this one…….'

Dexter went and sat on the edge of the desk. 'What do think happened?' he asked.

'They said suicide, poor man was so beset with problems.'

'Do you believe that?'

This time Jasper looked up. The tone was delivered in a more serious tone. 'Look, Dexter, I have to prepare these for the Serious Fraud Office.'

Dexter sighed. 'No problem, have some stuff to sort out anyway. Guess we're nearly at the end of the road?'

'Not quite there yet Dexter, you have the experience now. Until there's a conclusion, anything can happen.'

Dexter stood up and walked to the door. 'True,' he concurred. He looked over at Jasper - who was still immersed in sorting out the prints – before opening, then closing the door behind him.

The walk down the stairs was lonely. Dexter knew by Jasper's reaction that the case wasn't over. Dexter perked up as he hit the street. It was lunchtime and Shepherds Market was busy. *In fact, it's probably far from over*, he thought, mingling in with the crowd.

## Chapter Twenty-eight

The training was a tame affair. No Mike meant sparring someone else, which was fine, it was after that Dexter struggled with. The walk to the car was just as lonely. There was some good news though. According to Sensei Tibbs a higher grade had contacted the club and was to start training in a couple of weeks. Leaving the car park Dexter noticed a car he hadn't seen before parked on the road, just a little way down from the gate. It was a black Audi with smoked windows. For some reason he had a funny feeling about it. It was one of those feelings you pick up as you go along, comes with experience. Dexter called it a gift, a sixth sense that can literally same your ass. More importantly was that it rarely proved to be incorrect. When it saw Dexter's Jaguar it switched its lights on. *Time for a much-needed spin,* Dexter thought, as he slowly exited the car park. At the first set of traffic lights, he looked in the rear-view mirror, the Audi was a couple of cars behind. It was too early to make assumptions, so Dexter decided to take a detour, taking the first left, then right, then left again just to make sure. Because of the darkness, seeing who the driver was proved difficult, but he or she showed some fine driving skills. Dexter decided to up the level, put them to the test, so he headed towards Chelsea Bridge. The purpose was to lose them, Dexter didn't want any confrontation, apart from not being in the mood for it, it was unprofessional given the stage of the assignment.  any confrontation. The logic was simple, they wanted to see where he lived. Mike wasn't around anymore to give them any information, so they had to go back to basics. It brought back memories for him. In the early days he spent a lot of time following suspects all around London for different reasons. At the lights just before the bridge Dexter made sure it came directly behind him so he could take note of the licence plate: NO12 ONE. Dexter had a photographic memory - it was one of the skills he had in his armoury - but for evidence he had to take a picture. He turned around and ducked between the two front seats, taking a quick few shots.

The lights turned green as Dexter put the camera under the passenger seat. It was the cue for some excitement over his favourite bridge. It wasn't a long or wide bridge, so it had to be quick. It started as a one-two-three – as Dexter calls it - where you overtake one car, weave to the inside of the next, then repeat again. It was now the halfway mark and a glance in the rear-view mirror showed the Audi was keeping up. This time it was one-two-three with a three-point turn ready to travel in the opposite direction. Again, the Audi kept up until straight later the first three-point turn Dexter did another one, followed by a one-two-three then flying through an amber light at the end of the bridge before turning right into Grosvenor Road. Dexter slowed down as he looked back to see the Audi screech to a halt at the red light. A wry smile followed before turning left into Lupus Street.

Back at the apartment there was a cause for a little celebration. Dexter still had it when it comes to dexterity behind the wheel. He sat on the balcony looking back at Chelsea Bridge and what had happened earlier. This time the blame couldn't be placed with Mike. After taking a larger than usual sip of the gin his thoughts became a little more cynical: *or, could it*?

'Sergei's here,' Perdita announced, in an upbeat voice.

'I know,' Dexter responded.

'You do?'

'Well, I don't know for sure, just a feeling,' he answered, not wanting to disclose the previous evening's incident. 'How do you know?'

'My friend who works at the Playboy Club told me. Is his name Sokolova?'

'That's him.'

'Just thought I'd tell you.'

'Would she be able to find out where he is staying?'

'I'm sure they have to give details if they come as a guest, I'll ask her.'

'But that's all I want you to do,' he reminded her.

'Can I say something?'

'Of course,' Dexter replied, not expecting what came next.

'I miss you.'

Dexter didn't know what to say. He wanted to say that he missed her too, but did he? It took a few seconds to decipher the dilemma. 'Miss you too,' he stated.

After putting the phone down, he sat back. He felt good, a nice warm glow was in the belly. He was feeling connected to another human being, a woman, it felt liberating to speak his truth, regardless. He had thought of Perdi lately, there was something about her that he adhered to. Having to retain the professional mode, Dexter went to the balcony to practice some Qi Gong. He needed to focus and concentrate, the job was coming to an end, he could hardly afford to be distracted at this stage. It wasn't until the evening time that Dexter received a text from Perdi: *Hilton, Park Lane*, it read.

After the tai chi Dexter looked down onto the street. He noticed a black Audi parked a couple of streets away. After returning with some binoculars Dexter zoomed in on the car and in particular, the license plate: NO12 ONE. After changing into a tracksuit, he took the stairs to the ground floor. 'Evening Dexter,' Terence said.

'Evening Terry,' he replied.

'Jogging?'

'Why not, last of the summer, have to make the most of it,' Dexter joked, making his way towards the entrance.

The car was still there as Dexter went the back way. He opened the rear door and quickly sat in the back seat. 'Who are you?' Dexter demanded, as his right hand grabbed the throat from behind.

'Let….me………….'

Dexter closed the door and relaxed his grip. The hand was exchanged for a pistol which was pushed into the side of the head. 'I'm listening,' he said.

'I was sent by……' Dexter pulled back the trigger. 'Some fella from Holland.'

'To do what exactly?'

'To find out where you live, that's all, I promise.'

'And have you found out?'

'No, was told somewhere around here, to just park up and see if I see you.'

'Who told you about the karate club?'

'He did.'

'Who's he?'

'Look, I'm just a driver, that's all, haven't a clue what this is all about.'

Dexter believed him. He hadn't seen him before and could tell from his reaction that he wasn't in the game. 'ID?' he demanded. The man reached into his jacket pocket and passed his wallet to Dexter. 'You do it,' he added, to which he took out his driving licence. 'British?'

'From Pimlico,' came the answer.

'Work ID?' The man's hands shook as he passed over a registration contract with a chauffeur company. Dexter knew them, having met the owner once or twice. 'William Smith?'

'That's me.'

'William or Billy?'

'Either. Friends call me Billy.'

Dexter handed the documents back and put the pistol away. 'Billy, listen to me. The man from Holland, what's his name?'

'The boss didn't mention a name, just told me to go to a community centre and follow a Jag.' Billy looked around at Dexter. 'That's the truth.'

Dexter patted him on the shoulder. Billy was just another wheel in the cog - Dexter looked at his finger, there was a wedding ring – just someone earning a living to pay for his family. 'Tell your boss.... I don't know, tell him you waited and saw nothing.'

'Okay.'

Despite his sympathy, Dexter had to be assertive. He took out his pistol again. 'Don't let me see you again Billy.'

'You won't, promise.'

Dexter put the gun back into his waistband and opened the door. After getting out he bent and stuck his head into the car. 'Not bad driving,' he joked.

'Not as good as yours,' Billy gasped. 'Impressive, where did you learn to drive like that?'

'Long story Billy, maybe one day, I'll explain, until then, have a good evening.' Dexter slammed the door and waited until he drove off. Satisfied that Billy wouldn't return Dexter walked back the way he came.

'That was quick,' Terence commented.

'Forgot something,' Dexter said, before running up the stairs.

Putting the gun away, he contemplated about going for a run, *maybe a good thing, clear the head*, he thought.

The run did the job. Dexter felt better when he returned. After a shower, he retired to the bedroom. One thing had been bothering him though: how did Billy know where the karate club was?

The Hilton was one of London's finest, it always has been, and it always will be. This was where Dexter was asked by Jasper to do his first-ever job. He was a waiter, serving Jasper's table when they got into a conversation about one of Dexter's passions: photography. Jasper had just started an agency and was on the lookout for fresh talent. He had been given a job to follow a wife whom the husband suspected of cheating. Dexter was successful and Jasper offered another job, which he accepted. From living in a rented room in Victoria Dexter soon progressed and moved into the ranks of the professionals. The ones from Sandhurst, Oxford, Cambridge and the like. The money was good, and he enjoyed the work, a lot had changed since those days of the Hilton, he was looking forward to going back.

'Yes, he left something at the club last night,' Dexter said, speaking to the Head Concierge.

'Mr……..?'

'Sokolova, Sergei Sokolova.'

'Yes. What did you say it was?'

'It's personal, if you know what I mean.'

'Oh, I see sir. Would you like to leave it at the desk?'

'Sure, no problem, I'll drop it later. What time do you finish?'

'7 pm.'

It was 6:45 pm when Dexter went to the car park. The Jaguar started perfectly and purred its way over Vauxhall Bridge and towards Mayfair. Walking past the staff entrance brought back memories. They were good ones, Dexter enjoyed being a waiter, he excelled at silver service, and loved setting the tables with polished silver cutlery and wine glasses.

Dexter walked up to the concierge desk. The strange thing was that Dexter remembered the man from when he worked there. He used to see him in the staff canteen. A Concierge job is something you never give up, can be exciting, as well as lucrative. 'Tony?' he asked, hoping he didn't recognise him.

The man looked at his watch, slowly and deliberately. 'Tony isn't here I'm afraid sir, can I help with anything at all?'

'Spoke with him earlier, really needed to see him.' Dexter sighed as he held up the bag. 'A guest forgot something at a club last night, need to return it.'

'Tony will be back at 7 am.'

'Guest really needs it,' Dexter persisted.

'Name of the guest sir?'

'Sergei Sokolova.'

'One moment please,' the Concierge said, picking up the phone. Dexter noticed his name badge: Raul, it said. Underneath were the five languages he spoke: English, French, Italian, Portuguese and Spanish. Pride of place though were the "golden keys" badge on each lapel. This was important, signifying that like London cabbies have to do the knowledge, so must the concierge in their trade, it means they know London's history and landmarks as well as the best restaurants, bars and museums. A real source of information, that's for sure. Raul looked at Dexter as he was waiting for someone to pick up the phone. With no success he put the phone down and turned to Dexter. 'Mr Sokolova doesn't seem to be available. You can leave it with us, we'll make sure Mr Solokova will receive it,' Raul politely stated.

'That's fine.' Dexter took out a pen. 'What room?'

Raul tapped on the keyboard. '235,' he answered.

'235,' Dexter uttered to himself, as he wrote the numbers on the side of the bag. Dexter was just about to hand over the bag when he paused. 'On second thoughts, I'd better come back tomorrow.' He took a step closer to the desk. 'It's personal,' he whispered.

Raul more than understood, knowing that guest's discretion is of the utmost importance. 'I understand sir,' he said.

'Thanks for your help anyway,' Dexter said, before walking towards the hotel entrance.

'Excuse me?' Dexter turned around. 'Where do I know you from?' Raul asked, curiously.

'Was thinking the same thing,' Dexter said. 'Do you live around Earls Court?'

Raul smiled. 'Yes, yes, I do,' he said.

'There you go,' Dexter concluded, continuing walking to the door. Before the doorman got the chance to open the door, Dexter looked at the reflection, Raul was now busy talking to another guest. He turned around, passing through reception to the lift area. Knocking three times he waited for an answer. He tried again, this time saying Sergei's name through the crack of the door. After no response Dexter looked around – just to make sure there were no guests, porters or chambermaids lurking around – before taking out a square piece of plastic card, not to dissimilar to a credit card.

After a few swipes he opened the door. The room was neat and tidy, looking like it hadn't been touched. The only sign of occupancy was a suitcase by the window, some clothes on the bed and a briefcase under the table. Dexter walked to the window to look at the view. Even though it was only on the second floor the scene across Hyde Park was spectacular. He thought of Perdi as he made out the serpentine in the distance. After checking the drawers Dexter went to the briefcase. The lock was by numbers, three on each side. Holding the case up to his ear he gave it a subtle shake. *Definitely worth a look,* he thought, continuing to hold it against his ear, adjusting the numbers. The click as it opened sounded crisp and nice, but not as nice as what the contents were. Dexter went to the bathroom for some tissue before picking up the three diamonds. They say they are a girl's best friend, and Dexter could see why. They looked beautiful against the early evening blue-grey sky. There was a sound. Dexter heard the door being unlocked. He put the diamonds in his jacket pocket, closed the case and returned it to where it was. There were two men talking, one in broken English with a strong Russian accent, the other a soft cockney. Dexter wondered where he had heard the latter before as he stood behind the door, pistol in hand. One of them went into the bathroom and closed the door while the other walked into the room. It took one swipe of the pistol as he fell into Dexter's arms. Carrying him to the bed Dexter recognised the face. It was Billy. Dexter shook his head as he rushed to the door. 'Billy? What has happened?' came a voice from the bathroom. As he opened the bathroom door, Dexter closed the door to the room. Oh well, one door closes, another one opens, he said, as he composed. Not having the time to wait for the lift Dexter took the fire escape down to the mezzanine level. One of the benefits of having worked here was that he knew his way around. The rush to the Jaguar was swift. Starting up the engine Dexter put his foot down and tore into Park Lane.

Back at the apartment he called Perdi. 'Just thinking of you,' he said, as he rolled one of the diamonds around his forefinger and thumb.

'Really?'

'Yes, why not?'

Perdi laughed. 'You're funny Dexter,' she said.

'Really?'

'Yes, you are.'

'Tomorrow's the last day before Sergei's coming to the bank. Please take care.'

'Thanks, I will.'

'Goodnight.'

'Goodnight.'

Dexter put the phone down and continued to play with the diamonds. He lined them up, admiring them, before his thoughts turned to Sergei. Dexter smiled at the thought of him seeing Billy slumped on the bed before running down the corridor, erratically pressing the lift buttons, in shock of not knowing what had happened or – more importantly - who was responsible. And Billy? *He'll learn*, Dexter thought, deciding on a swift gin and tonic and some Miles Davis.

'Billy Price? Another one,' Jasper said, as he sat back in his favoured brown leather swivel chair. 'What's he up to nowadays?'

Jasper had called him in to say that the evidence had been handed over. Dexter could now ask him about the man who had tailed him the other night. 'Another what?' Dexter asked, hoping for some clarification.

'Worked for the government that they had to *let go*, shall we say.'

'Reason?'

'Apart from being useless? Wasn't up to it. You should know by now who cuts it and – just as importantly – who doesn't.'

Jasper was right, Dexter did. He'd met them, some were blatantly from the *who you know* school, clueless. Ohers fell into the some of the many temptations the job offers: Women, money, clubs, and – as with Mike – gambling. The one levelled at Dexter - which he had to really be on top of - was entrapment. It had been tried a few times. Beautiful women were his weak point, and he had met a few of them as well. There was one a few months ago in Morocco, Nadia. He was in the foyer of the La Mamounia when she came and sat next to him. The signs were there, but sometimes he couldn't resist. After a chat he arranged to meet her later in the evening. After a walk in the market, they went for a mint tea in a café overlooking The Jemaa el-Fna. A trip to a nightclub was on the cards when Dexter became aware of the conversations being recorded. He then politely declined, saying it wasn't possible. Nadia followed him from the café to the hotel, asking what was wrong? Dexter said nothing, he just needed to go and rest as he was sightseeing tomorrow. He promised to call her when he returned, which of course, he never did. All it takes is one incriminating thing to be recorded and a case will be difficult. The defence will say the witness is unreliable and have proof. It happens. Dexter shuddered even thinking about it. That was a close one to say the least. The suspects are now in jail awaiting sentencing. The wrong thing said could be taken out of context and they would be free. 'I've never heard of him before,' Dexter said.

'Was a friend of Michael Goman.'

'So that was how he knew the karate club…….'

'What's that?'

'Nothing Dexter replied. 'So, evidence supplied. Anything else you want me to do?'

'That's it really. Just make sure you stay safe. They won't be apprehended until a warrant is issued, could be today, tomorrow, next week, who knows? They will be desperate and the more I delve into it they are dangerous.'

*You don't know half of it,* Dexter thought, before asking about the payment details.

'As usual, the rest of the fee will be paid when charged.'

'Definite holiday,' Dexter stated, with a steely determination, thumping the desk.

'You know this game Dexter, anything can happen.'

Dexter walked towards the door. 'One last thing?' he said.

Jasper sat forward, putting his elbows on the desk. 'Be quick Dexter, have an appointment at the Army and Navy Club.'

'The photos and the marked cash, did they say that's enough to secure a warrant and a charge?'

'Not definite, but a good chance. Would be great if we had some tangible, something that could show how their money's being laundered, but we don't. Heard someone saying diamonds are making a comeback, replacing the drugs, but….' Dexter was about to open the door when Jasper called him. 'Why?' he asked.

Dexter flashed a smile. 'Just wondering,' he said.

'Dexter....................?'

But it was too late, Dexter had left the office, so to speak.

Standing in the doorway Dexter had to make a phone call. After dialling the number, he waited for an answer. 'Executive cars.'

'I'd like to book a car please.'

'Address sir?'

'London Hilton.'

'No problem, what time please sir?'

Dexter looked at his watch. It was 12:30 pm. '1 pm?'

'No problem sir. 'To where please sir?'

'Battersea Power Station.'

'That's no problem sir, I'll have a driver collect you from the hotel. Name and room number?'

'Actually, I'll be waiting in Hertford Street, outside the Panama Embassy. I have a request, if that's okay?' The controller then asked what the request would be. I've been given a personal recommendation for a certain driver.'

'Of course, sir, we understand that customers have built up relationships with certain drivers, we're more than happy to provide, if we can that is. Name?'

'Billy Price.'

'Oh, Billy, seems to be popular, one moment, let me see where he is.' Dexter waited a few seconds as he heard the controller radio where Billy's location was, before giving him the new job. 'Hello sir, no problem, he'll see you at the Panama Embassy, Hertford Street, 1 pm. Anything else I can help you with?'

'That's all, thank you.' Dexter then made his way for a quick sandwich before the informal meeting with Billy Price.

The manoeuvre was more or less the same as the one the other evening in Vauxhall. The only difference was not being as rushed. By the time Billy looked into the rear-view mirror to see who his passenger was it was too late. 'Battersea Power Station please,' was the order as the barrel of the pistol was placed behind the driver's head. 'You can take it nice and slow, there's no rush.'

Billy followed the orders carefully, taking his time to complete the short ten-minute journey. 'Where shall I drop you?' he asked, as they approached the iconic building.

'Just park over there,' Dexter ordered, seeing a vacant space next to a builder's cabin. 'Now, Billy boy, what has been going on?'

Billy looked at Dexter through the rear-view mirror. 'Regarding?'

'Billy, please, I like you okay, but don't push it. Now, who are you driving for?'

'I told you, some Russian geezer.'

'And what do you know about this Russian geezer?'

'Nothing, it's just a job I was given, I don't ask questions.'

Dexter pressed on his neck, the part he chopped last night in the Hilton. Billy winced. 'What's wrong?'

'Aching.'

'Why?'

'Didn't sleep last night.'

Dexter pressed a little harder. 'Really?'

'Ouch. Stop.'

'What's the Russian's name?'

'Pavel.'

Dexter relaxed the pressure. 'Pavel, you sure?'

'Positive.'

Dexter didn't want to press him on this, if he did, it would show that he knew the name wasn't real, would give the game away. 'What do you know about Pavel?'

'You'll have to ask my boss. I just do my job.'

'When did you last work for him?'

'The other night when I was following you.'

Even though Dexter knew it wasn't the truth, he had to accept it. 'What did you do before becoming a chauffeur?'

'Many things.'

At this point Dexter had enough. 'Does the name Michael Goman mean anything to you Billy?'

Billy frowned and looked down. There was a pause before he answered. 'No, it doesn't,' he answered.

Billy wasn't cooperating, and he wasn't going to. He was the sort that would die before snitching. Thought he was doing the right thing by protecting his employers. He was old school and - unlike Mike - couldn't be bought. Dexter knew this so changed tactics. Before getting out of the car he attached a silencer to the pistol. Looking out the window he saw there was no one around. He leant forward and opened the door at the same time. 'If you change your mind regarding Pavel and Michael Goman, you will be doing the right thing, you will be helping others. There is not much time.' Dexter got out walked to the front of the Audi, looked around and took aim. As he was about to shoot the tyre a bullet ricocheted on the ground. Dexter jumped behind the Audi as a car drove up and skidded to an abrupt halt. There was another shot, as he opened the passenger door for cover. 'Get down!' he shouted, to Billy.

There was another shot this time hitting the windscreen. Billy crawled out and took refuge next to Dexter behind the door. Dexter took the silencer off and returned the fire. The car did a u-turn and sped out onto the main road. Dexter chased it; the driver was clearly identifiable: it was Leonid Andreyev. The passenger was Yulia.

'Shall I chase them?' Billy asked, getting to his feet and inspecting the shattered windscreen.

'No, not worth it,' Dexter replied. 'You can help me find the bullets quickly, before somebody raises the alarm though,' he added.

Billy called for a windscreen replacement before the search for the three pieces of spent ammunition. 'Brings back memories,' he sighed.

After finding the bullets and the arrival of the mechanic, Dexter called a cab. 'Think we better have a chat, don't you?' Dexter suggested.

Billy agreed. 'Think we do,' he said. He paid the mechanic, telling him he'd collect later and jumped in the taxi with Dexter.

'Saatchi Gallery please driver,' Dexter said, closing the door.

It was a pleasant afternoon, so they sat outside with a pot of tea. 'How did you know I knew Mike?' Billy asked.

'Figured it must have been someone from the karate club,' Dexter replied, taking a sip of the Earl Grey.

'Was shocked about that.'

'Me too.' Dexter turned to Billy. 'Do you believe he's actually dead?'

'Yes.'

'How do you know for sure?'

'Mike had no family. Only an ex-wife in Venezuela. I identified the body.'

The one grain of hope Dexter was hanging onto that Mike may still be alive was dashed, just like that, in one sentence. It felt like a punch to the gut. 'You were close?'

'Used to be. Done a couple of jobs with him, but we lost touch over the years, you know, both went our separate ways, just a phone call now and then.'

'Coming to think of it, I didn't really know that much about him except that he was married to Andrana.'

'It's a secretive game. In a way I'm glad I'm out of it, miss it sometimes, but overall, happy just to have a regular job, no looking over my shoulder.'

Dexter didn't say what Jasper said about him being fired, didn't want to offend him. Besides, he needed some information. 'Think my days will be coming to an end soon,' he admitted.

'Why did they try and shoot me?' Billy asked. 'What have I done? Who were they anyway?'

'They were your employers I'm afraid.'

'Pavel?'

'His name is not Pavel. It's Sergei, Sergei Sokolova. A diamond dealer from Amsterdam. That was his brother, an accountant embezzling money from a bank in Mayfair.'

Billy seemed a little taken aback. 'What?'

'That was his brother who took a pop at you. Nice employers huh?' Dexter took a sip of tea. 'And that won't be the last I can tell you. Do they know where you live? If they don't, they will soon find out. Now they have seen you talking with me they'll think you are a snitch, and they don't like that.'

Billy said he was worried if they found his address. 'What about my family?' he asked. 'What can I do now?'

Dexter got straight to the point. 'Help us lock them up,' he said. 'More tea?' he added.

'How do I do that?'

'Tell us where you have been driving Sergei, and what you have seen.'

Billy took a few seconds to digest before answering. 'You're on,' he said.

Dexter felt like he'd clinched some sort of major contract or something. He held up his cup. 'Cheers,' he said.

Dexter took his phone number, said he'd be in touch, before sharing a taxi ride back to Battersea Power Station. After Billy dropped him off at Battersea Park, Dexter went and sat by the Pagoda. There was a man practising tai chi under a tree. It was a different style but looked graceful and fluid. Amongst the tranquillity Dexter looked at the discharged bullets. They were the same as from the car park, fired from a Makarov. If only he could get his hand on Leonid's gun. Now that would really be game, set and match. Tempted to call Perdita, Dexter observed the tai chi. There was a gentle breeze to the late afternoon air, making the analogy he'd heard from a master in China who said when practising tai chi, *try to weave silk,* all the more relevant. The man finished and looked over. Dexter didn't do or say anything, he didn't need to, he knew the feeling.

## Chapter Twenty-nine

Dexter was making some coffee the following morning when the phone rang. 'My friend says that Nasser has booked a table for four tonight at the club,' Perdita said.

'The interviews, today, right?'

'In the afternoon, not too sure though.'

'They're probably going after, have something to eat then celebrate. How's Leonid, I mean his character, anything strange about his behaviour recently?'

'Not that I've noticed, seems the same, still serious, why?'

'Nothing,' Dexter replied. He then thanked her, saying he couldn't wait to see her again. Putting the phone down he caught the smell of the coffee, as he went to open the curtains. It smelt good, like it should. It was raining, quite heavy, he didn't mind, in fact he welcomed it. It had been a decent summer weatherwise so there were no complaints. After fixing some coffee he went back to the balcony, staring out onto the Thames. The rain gave it some life, as if simulating. He wished Perdi was with him, sharing this moment. The time had come to bring down the curtain on the bachelor life. For some reason he delved further, *what a move somewhere?* Always wanting to move to the coast, he visualised a town in Sussex, maybe a modern apartment overlooking the sea, himself with Perdi, and a baby. *No,* he thought, smiling going to the sofa and collapsing on it. He tried to fight the thoughts, tried to dismiss them, but couldn't. They continued. *What about abroad?* Dexter got excited. He loved the Caribbean. Then he thought about somewhere he would love to move: Brazil. *Why not?* he thought, anything is possible. Living in a small town by the beach. Perdi could find a job easy, he could do something different, maybe some manual work, gardening, or even teaching English. He put on some John Coltrane. Brazil has a strong connection with jazz, an important factor for Dexter. He could manage to leave London and start afresh with Perdi, but he couldn't live without his jazz. With a crack of lightning Dexter came back to reality, he finished the coffee and thought about the day ahead. It was going to be a throwback to the old days as he prepared for a long day of waiting to photograph the four suspects.

Perdi called him. 'Sergei's been announced as a new non-executive director for the company,' she said.

'Not for long,' Dexter promised, as he put his camera in his rucksack and headed for the door. 'Speak to you in a bit,' he added, getting into the lift.

'Looks like rain all day,' Terence announced, solemnly.

Dexter tried to be optimistic. 'We need it,' he said. 'Good for the trees,' he shouted, halfway out the door.

There wasn't much traffic on the roads, so Dexter reached Park Lane in good time. One of the benefits of being in the hotel trade was that you built up contacts. Dexter was still in touch with Paul, the head valet at the Hilton. There was no car park at the Hilton, so Paul went with him to the Qpark, an underground car park across the road. As they walked back to the hotel Perdi sent a text. *They have just left the bank,* it said. Dexter had to rush. He paid Paul and ran to find a vantage point to take the pictures. As he left the car park, he noticed Yulia. He pulled the hood of the rain mac over his face and looked the other way until she passed. Knowing he had to be ahead Dexter waited for her to walk down the east side of Park Lane while he ran down the west side, crossing at Curzon Gate. It proved a good move as Yulia waited on the corner of

Curzon Street. She was talking on a phone, looking around, a little agitated. A few minutes later Nasser, Sergei and Leonid joined her. They seemed to be listening attentively as she pointed towards the car park. This was a good opportunity for some evidence. Dexter took out the camera and snapped away. They were okay, passable, but some close-ups would be ideal. He ran down the centre reservation then navigated across the road avoiding the cars as they sounded their horns. On the corner of Grantham Place, he went for it, caution was thrown out the window as he prepared to get a final few shots in. As he was focusing, he noticed someone familiar in the background, it was Perdi. *What is she doing*, Dexter thought? He tried to call her, but she didn't answer the phone. As he was looking at Perdi he noticed only Nasser, Sergei and Yuliya went into the club. Leonid had slipped away down Brick Street. Dexter ran to Perdi. 'What are you doing here?' he asked, angrily.

'I can't do it,' she said.

Dexter told her to go home as he started to pace quickly towards the car park. 'This is dangerous now. Leonid's on the loose, it's not safe. Go home.'

Perdi was running behind him. 'I can't do it,' she repeated.

Dexter stopped. 'Can't do what?' he asked, as the rain began to pelt down.

'I can't let them do it. I'm coming with you.'

Dexter looked at the rain running down her face. Her hair was wet, and the mascara was beginning to run. He held her. 'Please, leave this to me, go home, please,' he begged.

The answer was resolute: 'No.'

Dexter grabbed her hand. 'Okay,' you win, he conceded. 'Now, let's go.' Perdi held on tight as Dexter ran a little faster down the ramp into the car park.

After opening the passenger's door for Perdi he quickly ran over to the driver's side. There was a bang, Dexter ducked and drew his pistol. He knew straight away what was happening. 'Get down,' he shouted. Dodging two more bullets it was time to return fire. Dexter knew where the gunman was so stood up and let a few shots go in that direction. After a few seconds silence a car spun around the back and came towards him. Dexter managed to jump up and roll over the bonnet as the car narrowly missed him. As he got into the driver's seat Perdi was crouched down, holding her hands over her ears. 'Hang on tight, let's see if you think it's still glamorous now,' Dexter shouted, starting the motor.

Perdi let out a sharp shriek as Dexter put his foot down as hard as he could. The car flew at breakneck speed from the car park and onto the ramp, which seemed to compliment the dynamics, especially as the vehicle actually left the ground before returning with a bump onto Park Lane. 'Where are we going?' Perdi asked, trying to compose herself as she held onto the dashboard for dear life.

'You see that blue car ahead?'

'The BMW with Dutch plates?'

'That's the one. Mr Andreyev should be in it.'

Dexter had to speed up a little to catch the amber light at Hyde Park Corner. 'Has he seen us?'

'Not yet.' Dexter looked into the rear-view mirror as he made an extra effort. 'He will do soon though,' he added, racing down Knightsbridge.

'Thought he lived in Hendon?' Perdi said to herself, as the BMW took a left into Sloane Street.

Leonid must have known he was being tailed. He tried the one-two-three technique going down Sloane Street. Dexter stuck with him, including going around Sloane Square twice. Lower Sloane Street was easy for Dexter, he knew it so well, he really pressed against the accelerator and even managed to draw level at one stage, which he shouldn't have done, because he knew what the next move was. The window came down and Dexter found himself looking into the infamous Makarov. Perdi screamed, as Dexter rammed the car sideways, forcing the shot to go up into the air. 'Such glamour,' he said in jest as he slowed down, letting Leonid go in front. As they moved onto the Chelsea Bridge Road, they played cat and mouse, Dexter drew close enough to let Leonid he was not going to abate. Leonid – on the other hand – wasn't playing ball. His demeanour emphasised this.

As Leonid was about to soar over Chelsea Bridge something strange happened. A black Audi came across and blocked his path, swerving to one side the BMW hit a lamppost and spun around a few times before nestling just to the side of the bridge. Dexter parked up on Grosvenor Road and ran over to the smoking car. Before he knew it, he caught one in the arm. The pain was excruciating, and blood began to run down the inside of his sleeve. Out of nowhere the BMW was smashed into by the Audi. Leonid went flying, the gun was forced into the air by the impact. Dexter ran up to Leonid, who was struggling to get to his feet. He crawled, his arm outstretched, trying in vain to reach the revolver. Dexter kicked the weapon away, before turning to Leonid. 'Why didn't you kill me?' he asked.

'I have served in wars, I don't like them,' came the answer.

Perdi came over and attended to Dexter's arm, wrapping her jumpers around the upper arm to stop the flow of blood. 'Are you okay?' she asked.

'I'm fine,' Dexter answered.

'Who's in the car?' Perdi asked, alluding to the Audi.

Dexter smiled. 'I have a good idea,' he said. 'I'll leave you two work colleagues for a second.' After picking up the Makarov, he went to the Audi and opened the door. 'How did you know?' he asked.

'Told Sergei I had something especially important for him. Said he would send someone. I had a good idea who it would be,' Billy answered.

'Which was?'

Billy pulled out a handkerchief. 'This,' he replied, holding up a diamond.

'You knew where to get him then?'

'My manor,' Billy stated, putting the diamond away.

The sirens of police cars could be heard as Dexter suggested that Billy should maybe leave. 'You don't need the hassle of giving statements and all that. Go home to your family, and thanks for everything,' Dexter said.

'No problem Dex,' Billy said, closing the door before driving off towards Churchill Gardens.

Dexter walked back over to Perdi and Leonid. Leonid was now sitting with his back against a wall. Dexter thought about why he didn't kill him, after all, he was a trained Russian marksman. Maybe he was just a younger brother doing as he was told by Michail. It happens.

The Police arrived and called an ambulance for Dexter, who explained everything. One of the senior detectives took him to one side. 'The other three have been arrested at the Playboy Club,' he said.

'How did you know they were there?' Dexter asked.

'Jasper contacted Scotland Yard, told us where they were.'

Dexter wondered who had told Jasper? He looked over at Perdi, who gave a knowing smile.

'You can come to the Yard tomorrow to give statements. Go and get that seen to,' the detective said, referring to the wound.

Dexter threw Perdi the keys. 'Hospital please,' he said, walking towards the Jag.

'Mr Spencer?' Dexter turned around. 'Would you like to press charges?'

Dexter looked over at Leonid. He watched as two uniformed Policemen lifted him to his feet, then escorted him into a waiting car. Dexter had to think for a few seconds. The fact that Leonid could have killed him three times shaped his decision. 'No, I don't think so,' he uttered.

'I understand Mr Spencer,' the detective said.

'Well done,' Perdita commented, as they sat in the car.

'He'll have enough to deal with,' Dexter said, sympathetically.

Perdi turned the key and ignited the engine. 'Ready?' she asked.

'Look at you.' Dexter said.

'Starting to enjoy this,' she said, taking control of the Jag, as they headed to the University College Hospital at Euston.

On the way Dexter had a little time to reflect. He mentioned Jasper telling Scotland Yard. 'How did he know where they were?'

'My uncle told him.'

'And who told your............' Dexter looked at Perdi. 'You?'

'When you saw me following them on Park Lane. Had to make sure they were actually going into the club. My friend had finished her shift. Could you imagine if they went somewhere else?'

Dexter laughed. It was a release. He needed it. It was part of the comedown that would now begin. This was the worst part of the job, when it is over, the euphoria can kick in. The mind and body have to acclimatise to normality. It can take some time. Perdita joined in. It can be infectious like that. They laughed at the insanity of the situation. Even the throbbing pain Dexter was experiencing couldn't help, in fact, it made it even more surreal and humorous.

## Chapter Thirty

'Debriefing dear boy,' came the order.
'Time?'
'Midday.'
Dexter turned over and looked at the clock. It was 8 am. Even with his arm in a sling he had slept well. The only problem it posed was taking twice as long to make a gin and tonic. The Doctor said that the bullet had entered the upper arm and wasn't as bad as it looked. There were no stitches required and after being cleaned and dressed, Dexter was allowed to go home. Perdi drove him back to his apartment. As he wondered where she was, he smelt some sausages being fried. Dexter tried to get up. 'Don't even try,' she said, walking into the bedroom with a cup of coffee.

'I'm okay,' he sighed. 'You look different?' Dexter commented, looking at Perdi bemused.

'Drove to my house after the house after the hospital, collected some clean clothes before driving you here. You don't remember.'

Dexter couldn't remember much after the hospital. The sleeping tablets saw to that. 'Where you going now?'

'After giving you some breakfast, going to work.'

Dexter liked that. He liked women who work. Perdi had got up, showered, and was ready for the day, this impressed him. 'Sure, you are okay. What will it be like with no Nasser and Leonid?'

'Will be a lot better,' she robustly replied, putting some scrambled egg and sausages on a plate. Dexter sat up. 'Here,' Perdi said, holding a tray for Dexter to take. She then went and got some coffee before a quick kiss and heading for the door. 'I'll call you later.'

On that note she was gone. There was silence as Dexter took a sip of coffee and picked up the fork. He could feel a woman's presence. It felt good, warm, and reassuring. After eating he managed to get up and put Quadrophenia on to accompany him whilst in the shower, which was a task to say the least.

'Gets worse,' Terence said.

'What does?' Dexter inquired.

'Was a shooting just over there,' he explained, pointing in the direction of Chelsea Bridge. 'Was on the radio this morning.'

Dexter had to play innocent. 'Really, anyone hurt?'

'Just said non-life-threatening injuries. Something about diamonds and money laundering.'

'Makes a change from drugs,' Dexter joked.

'Suppose it does.' Terence looked up. 'What happened to your arm?' he asked.

'A little mishap you could say,' Dexter responded, heading for the door.

The weather was changing, was getting colder. Dexter had to wear a jacket. It was a grey Hugo Boss, complimenting the grey cashmere pullover. He felt relaxed as he walked to Mayfair. Stopping on Vauxhall Bridge he observed neighbouring Westminster Bridge, thinking of Mike, understanding the loneliness he must have felt after losing Anandra. It had never occurred to Dexter before; it was something that a staunch bachelor doesn't experience. Loving a woman isn't part of the vocabulary. This was a singles game, not a couples or some marriage way of life. The two couldn't co-exist, it would be impossible: or would it?' Dexter looked down into the deep abyss of old Mother Thames. She doesn't have an answer, then again, who does? On this note Dexter continued to walk. The vibe was different form yesterday and the past few weeks, he felt free again.

Jasper congratulated him, said what a good job he had done, was proud of him. Sebastian was thrilled that his much-loved business was in good hands again. Said he had made his niece a director, promoted her. 'Sounds a good girl,' he said, before gushing about Billy. 'Came and made some statements yesterday,' he proudly announced, gently thumping the desk.

'Evidence will be watertight,' Dexter said.

Jasper wasn't even listening. The relationship had gone back to how it is when there's no job on the go, there's nothing to say, nothing to relate to. If another one comes in and Dexter takes it, it will be down Ronnie Scott's again with The Bullshot and talking about jazz. Until then, there's not much to say. This suited Dexter fine, ne needed some time for himself. He got up and made his way to the door. Looking over Jasper hadn't even noticed the movement. Closing the door behind him Dexter stepped out into Shepherd Market and decided that it was the time to indulge some art at the Royal Academy.

Three months had passed quickly. Dexter's arm had healed and was functioning again. He had to take some time off karate - and could just about manage the Tai Chi - but was going back in a couple of days, just before the verdict. The trial was in now in progress, but Dexter had no interest, nothing could be changed, he'd done what he could, so what's the point.

On a positive note he had done what he said he would do, take a holiday. A week on a beach in Turkey did the trick. It was a package holiday, everything was taken care of, all he did was sunbathe, swim eat and swim. He returned tanned and reinvigorated.

Since Jasper told him that Perdi had been promoted he hadn't seen her, which was a good thing in a way, but he couldn't help but think how odd it was to feel really close to someone one minute then feel differently the next. As much as he liked her, he didn't really miss her. The urge to take her to the Royal Opera House to see the Bolshoi perform had petered out. He went anyway, even standing at the stage door with a bunch of flowers for Natalia. She made a beeline when she saw him, laughing and apologising. Dexter said it wasn't a problem, there was nothing to be sorry for, and was just pleased she was working and looking fantastic. Nothing else was said, Pavel, the court case, nothing, it was sweet and simple, Dexter preferred it that way.

On the day of the karate lesson Sensei Tibbs announced that a visiting Sensei from overseas would be taking the lesson. 'Very highly regarded,' he said, welcoming them to the dojo. Dexter had to smile; it was Uba. Dexter enjoyed the lesson, it was hard work, but enjoyable. Though Dexter wasn't going to the verdict, they arranged to go for a meal after. 'Same place?' he asked.

'Same place,' Uba confirmed.

The jury's unanimous decision was guilty. The sentencing reflected the hierarchy. Sergei got fifteen years. Nasser, ten and Leonid five. The belief was that this was a dangerous group of individuals capable of anything. Their reach was global and had to be terminated. Later that evening Uba spoke of the enjoyment seeing their faces as the sentences were passed. It was all about justice for her. Dexter said he wanted to give her something. He showed her the three diamonds he got from Sergei's room at the Hilton. 'Take them,' he said.

'I will return them to Angola where they belong,' she said, in a serious tone.

After leaving the restaurant Uba said she had to go back to her rented apartment as she had to get up early.

'Where are you staying?' Dexter asked.

'Guess?' she smiled.

Dexter immediately hailed a taxi. He opened the door and Uba got in, Dexter quickly followed. 'Vauxhall please driver,' he said, closing the door. Dexter asked the driver to specifically cross Westminster Bridge. As they approached, he noticed Uba getting a bit fidgety. She looked at him and smiled, it looked forced. 'Anything you want to tell me?' he asked.

+ THE END +